***"There's no need to ask me to dance,"
Belle told her reluctant escort.***

"Oh, yes, there is," Boone snapped, grasping her by the wrist, "if only to get away from these two." He glared at his matchmaking mother and daughter, then pulled Belle onto the dance floor.

Drawing her into his arms, he grumbled, "Maybe if we dance, *that* will satisfy them."

Belle stiffened. "What is it about me that you find so unattractive?"

Boone gave her a startled look. "Why...nothing, ma'am."

"Don't *ma'am* me, Boone O'Malley. You make me sound like your grandmother."

His blue, blue eyes met hers and he actually smiled. "All right then, *Arabella*...I don't find you unattractive. On the contrary..." He didn't finish the sentence. Instead he pulled her close. Close to his body and the rhythm of the music.

"Maybe," he suggested, his voice husky in her ear, "just maybe, we'd get off to a better start if neither one of us talks."

Dear Reader,

Weddings, wives, fathers—and, of course, Moms—are in store this May from Silhouette Special Edition!

As popular author Susan Mallery demonstrates, Jill Bradford may be a *Part-Time Wife*, but she's also May's THAT SPECIAL WOMAN! She has quite a job ahead of her trying to tame a HOMETOWN HEARTBREAKER.

Also this month Leanne Banks tells a wonderful tale of an *Expectant Father*. In fact, this hero's instant fatherhood is anything but expected—as is finding his true love! Two new miniseries get under way this month. First up is the new series by Andrea Edwards, GREAT EXPECTATIONS. Three sisters and three promises of love—and it begins this month with *On Mother's Day*. Sweet Hope is the name of the town, and bells are ringing for some SWEET HOPE WEDDINGS in this new series by Amy Frazier. Don't miss book one, *New Bride in Town*. Rounding out the month is *Rainsinger* by Ruth Wind and Allison Hayes's debut book for Special Edition, *Marry Me, Now!*

I know you won't want to miss a minute of the month of May from Silhouette Special Edition. It's sure to put a spring in your step this springtime!

Sincerely,

Tara Gavin
Senior Editor

Please address questions and book requests to:
Silhouette Reader Service
U.S.: 3010 Walden Ave., P.O. Box 1325, Buffalo, NY 14269
Canadian: P.O. Box 609, Fort Erie, Ont. L2A 5X3

# AMY FRAZIER

## NEW BRIDE IN TOWN

Published by Silhouette Books
America's Publisher of Contemporary Romance

To the memory of Jean Powers.
I can hear her laughter and encouragement still.

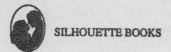 SILHOUETTE BOOKS

ISBN 0-373-24030-9

NEW BRIDE IN TOWN

Copyright © 1996 by Amy Lanz

**Printed in U.S.A.**

**Books by Amy Frazier**

Silhouette Special Edition

*The Secret Baby* #954
*\*New Bride in Town* #1030

\*Sweet Hope Weddings

## AMY FRAZIER

has loved to listen, to read and to tell stories from the time she was a very young child. With the support of a loving family, she grew up believing she could accomplish anything she set her mind to. It was with this attitude that she tackled various careers as teacher, librarian, free-lance artist, professional storyteller, wife and mother. Above all else, the stories always beckoned. It is with a contented sigh that she settles into the romance field, where she can weave stories in which love conquers all.

Amy now lives with her husband, son and daughter in northwest Georgia, where the kudzu grows high as an elephant's eye. When not writing, she loves reading, music, painting, gardening, bird watching and the Atlanta Braves.

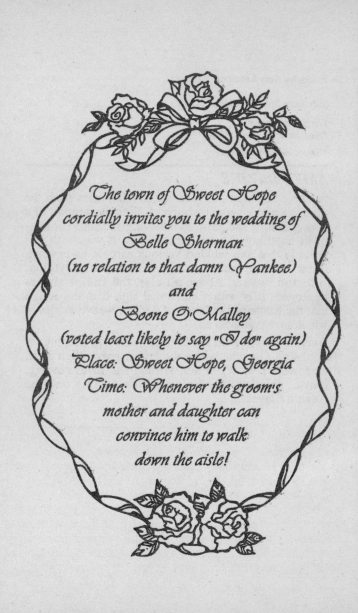

The town of Sweet Hope
cordially invites you to the wedding of
Belle Sherman
(no relation to that damn Yankee)
and
Boone O'Malley
(voted least likely to say "I do" again)
Place: Sweet Hope, Georgia
Time: Whenever the groom's
mother and daughter can
convince him to walk
down the aisle!

## Prologue

"You're lucky to be alive, Ms. Sherman, that's all I can say. Lucky to be alive." The nurse bustled around the hospital bed, clucking sympathetically. "Focus on that, honey, instead of on that no-account fiancé. Seems to me any man who'd abandon a woman on her deathbed isn't worth having in the first place. No, sirree. Now, you just lie back and rest and decide what you're going to do with the rest of your life. Think no more of your past, sugah. You've been given a future. A second chance."

With a comforting pat on the pillow, a whoosh of white and a lingering antiseptic smell, the nurse was gone.

Arabella Sherman lay immobile amid the cool, stiff sheets and tried to process the full import of the nurse's words.

Yes, she'd almost died in that car wreck. A multicar pile-up on the interstate during a blinding rainstorm. Yes, she was lucky to be alive. She'd realized that the minute she'd opened her eyes and looked into the worried face of her erstwhile fiancé, Porter. She'd been touched by his look of concern. She needn't have been.

He hadn't been concerned for her so much as he'd been sitting on pins and needles, waiting for her to regain consciousness so he could dump her. While it had taken him three years of engagement to commit to a wedding date, it had taken him barely three minutes to end it all. Well, what do you know? He *could* make a quick decision. Arabella shook her head on the pillow and felt the pounding in her temples resume. Perhaps he was the kind of guy who'd never thought he'd be called upon to deal with the worst in "for better or for worse" or the sickness in "in sickness and in health." Nothing like a little car wreck, a little brush with death, to bring out the truth about people.

Funny, but it didn't bother her the way she thought it should. The old Arabella would have been distraught. Would have thought more about the severed relationship than about her recovery. Would have eventually taught her kindergarten class with red-rimmed eyes until she'd figured out a way to make it up to Porter. To return her life to the safe, predictable equilibrium she'd always experienced.

But, having crossed a divide of sorts, this was the new Arabella, and even as bedridden as she now was, she felt... *free.* Nothing like a little crack-up on the highway and a little peek into the great beyond to give that old bumper sticker new meaning: Don't Sweat The Small Stuff. The nurse had been right. That no-account fiancé had turned out to be the small stuff. Her own safe and predictable past, as the new Arabella reviewed it, had been nothing but the small stuff. She herself, with her demure kindergarten-teacher attire and her attention to every niggling detail and her belief in the civilizing qualities of seemliness, had been the small stuff. Underappreciated. Barely noticed. Small stuff.

But now... now she'd been given this incredible second chance, and, by golly, she sure wasn't about to waste a second of it on the small stuff.

Wiggling her fingers and toes tentatively under the scratchy sheets, Arabella Sherman vowed that when she was at last rid of this hospital bed she was going to make some changes. She was going to make a noticeable, positive difference in the world. She was going to live life to the fullest and appearances be damned.

And she was going to get herself a whole new look.

## Chapter One

He stared at the ladder and at the eye-level, bright-red-painted toenails and at the tiny rose ankle tattoo and thought, *A barefoot floozy. Alice Rose O'Malley, you sent me to help a floozy.* Taking a silent step backward on the sidewalk, Boone O'Malley planted his hands on his hips and assumed a wide-legged stance. Just what had his mother gotten him into this time?

The woman on the ladder still hadn't noticed him, so intent was she on unhooking an old sign from the storefront. It wasn't in Boone's well-bred Southern genes to stare, but darned if he could help it. In all his thirty-eight years, he'd never seen a woman quite like the one before him.

It wasn't so much the way she was dressed, although the gauzy, pale purple outfit she wore defied description. Neither dress nor pants, it was so layered and billowy and insubstantial looking that Boone felt if he pinched her, he'd find nothing but air. And it wasn't just the bare feet, although this *was* Main Street, and the woman appeared old enough to know better than to parade around on the hot

April pavement with no foot protection. And it wasn't just her scent, which was more like the subtle hint of vanilla than perfume. Maybe it was the sight of that pink Little Mermaid watch on the wrist of a grown woman. Or the faint but unmistakable tinkle of bells he heard every time she moved.

More than likely, however, it was the way people passing stared at her. And smiled. Smiled as if they were enjoying a free show. If there was one thing Boone O'Malley couldn't endure it was being the center of attention. And he couldn't for the life of him understand why anyone else would behave in such a way as to draw attention to him or herself. One thing was for certain: this woman was an attention getter whether she intended to be or not.

With undisguised irritation, Boone coughed. "Ms. Sherman?"

The woman gave a tiny squeak of surprise. Letting go of the sign that now hung by one corner, she promptly lost her balance on the rickety old stepladder and fell in a gauzy lavender cloud.

Instinctively, Boone stepped forward and extended his arms. To his surprise, he caught not an armful of airy fabric but a very warm and very soft and very real woman. *Very* real. And before he could say jackrabbit, he found himself staring into the deepest, softest pair of brown eyes he'd ever had the confusion of getting lost in. Found himself staring and unable to catch his breath.

Unable, that is, until he heard the raspy voice of Homer Martin at his elbow. "I know you caught her, son," cackled Homer, "but she's over the legal limit, and I'm afraid you're gonna hafta throw her back. Hee, hee, heee!"

A chorus of snickers and titters followed Homer's teasing, jolting Boone back into the here and now. The sidewalk sure was crowded for a weekday morning. He felt his cheeks grow hot at his neighbors' obvious amusement. It didn't take much in Sweet Hope to be the talk of the town, and Boone O'Malley intended never to hold that specious honor.

He quickly let go of the woman in his arms. She, however, was not so quick to release him. Moving languidly, questions playing in her doe-soft eyes, she trailed her fingers over his shoulders, then down his arms to the very tips of his hands, leaving a disconcerting wake of pure sensation. She stepped back and smiled at him, an angelic smile that beckoned him to join in the merriment.

Boone would have none of it. Taking the woman firmly by the elbow, squiring her through the overly interested group of Sweet Hope residents to the open storefront door, he insisted, "Ms. Sherman, I would speak with you *in private.*" He glowered at the still-smirking Homer Martin. *"Business,"* he added emphatically.

"Your loss," quipped Homer as Boone propelled the lavender lady through the doorway.

Once inside the cool dimness of the old Main Street storefront, Boone released the woman's elbow and let out a long breath.

Smiling that angelic smile, she fanned herself with one graceful hand to the faint but distinct accompaniment of tinkling bells. "I take it, suh, your sense of humor has wilted in our early spring heat."

Boone was unprepared for the honeyed Southern cadences twining through her speech. Why had he assumed she wasn't from the area? That name of hers? *Sherman?* When his mother, Alice Rose, had sent him to help a Ms. Sherman, a new friend of hers, Boone had fully expected a transplanted Yankee, clipped, machine-gun-rapid speech and all. But this woman had spoken words soft and slow and sweet enough to talk the moon out of the sky. Soft enough to send a shiver down his spine. Slow enough to wrap around his pulse. And sweet enough to make Boone O'Malley forget he still had a schedule full of appointments today.

"I'm afraid you have me at a definite disadvantage," she continued. "You know my name, but I don't believe I know yours. Are you Sweet Hope's superhero?" She smiled a slow, heartbreaking smile. "A homegrown gallant who dashes about town, saving damsels from toppling ladders?''

Ignoring the banter in her voice and the mischief in her eyes, Boone pulled himself together and extended his hand. ''Boone O'Malley,'' he said simply. ''Alice Rose is my mother.''

She put her hand in his. He tried not to think about her tender touch. ''Arabella Sherman,'' she said, her voice pure silk. ''My friends call me Belle.''

''Well, *Ms. Sherman...*'' Better let her know right from the start that this was definitely not a social call. ''I hear you and my mother have worked out a barter. Looks like I'm her end of it.''

Ms. Arabella Sherman laughed softly but thoroughly enough so that her glossy brown curls danced about her face. ''This town and its system of barter! Who would think that for a little fancy embroidery work I could acquire—''

''Ms. Sherman,'' Boone cut in, not liking one bit the twinkle in her eyes, ''I'm here to give you an estimate on the work you need on your storefront.'' He glanced abruptly at his watch. ''I have a full day.''

''Of course. How thoughtless of me.'' The twinkle disappeared from her eyes, but a wisp of smile lingered at the corners of her pretty mouth. It seemed to tell Boone that he was off the hook. For now. ''Look around, Mr. O'Malley.'' She swept her hand dramatically about the cavernous room that had long ago housed Sweet Hope's largest mercantile. ''The work I expect to do is mostly cosmetic. I want to retain the original flavor of the building—a place where all Sweet Hope met—except that in the back I wish to soundproof what was the office-storage area. That will be where I tutor.''

Boone looked around the room in which they stood. Examined with nostalgic fondness the worn counter where he'd often waited as a child with his mother as she'd selected fabric. Took in the floor-to-ceiling shelving that had housed every imaginable gadget known to man. Or so he'd thought as a boy. Scuffed a toe over the worn wooden flooring that had felt the weight of every single resident for miles around. If he squinted hard enough he could almost see that old ice-water-filled cooler in the corner where, as a teenager, he'd bought his future wife their first shared Coca-Cola. He felt the familiar, unbidden and very painful twinge deep within him and tried to concentrate on the public history of the room, not the personal memories.

A place where all Sweet Hope had met, this Ms. Sherman had said. Well, she was right there. The meeting place for the commerce of daily life. Commerce and sociability. That's what this old mercantile had been. Almost the heart of Sweet Hope. As much as he'd like to see it used again, he'd hate to see it changed too radically. Boone O'Malley disliked radical change.

"What are you planning to do with the main room?" he asked softly, still half a step in the past.

Arabella glided to the old counter and ran a hand lovingly over it. "This will be the coffee bar. The shelves will house the used books. The center area will hold the café tables and a few overstuffed sofas." Her voice became eager, filled with a joyous anticipation. She turned her warm gaze on Boone and caught him once again in its depth. "I feel a tremendous energy in this room. I do hope I can bring it to life. I want it to buzz. With conversation. With ideas. That's why the back room must be soundproof. So as not to disturb the tutoring."

Boone actually shook his head to break the spell her brown eyes held him in. "Coffee bar? Used books? Tutoring? Ms. Sherman, what the devil are you planning to do with this old building?"

"Alice Rose didn't tell you?"

No, Alice Rose hadn't told him what Arabella Sherman had planned for the mercantile. She'd been too busy telling him how her new quilting-group friend had—how had his mother put it?—cut a swath through Sweet Hope. Actually, Alice Rose had said that in the short month Arabella Sherman had been in town she'd cut a swath through daily stuffiness as large as the one her Union namesake had cut through Georgia more than a hundred years ago.

To Boone, that was no recommendation.

"No," he answered gruffly, "I'm afraid she didn't."

Arabella's face lit up. Her hands began to tell the story even before she began to speak. Graceful hands. Fingers that caressed the air the way they'd caressed Boone's arms not too long ago. Despite his best intentions to remain detached, Boone felt an involuntary sensation of Arabella Sherman's long, graceful fingers on other parts of his body.

Why had he ever agreed to give this particular estimate?

"Providing your estimate is not too high," Arabella said, "I soon hope to have Sweet Hope's first coffeehouse, used bookstore and literacy center up and running."

Boone groaned.

"Are you ill, Mr. O'Malley?" She stepped forward and laid a hand on his chest.

"Not yet," he muttered, feeling the heat of her hand sear like a brand above his heart.

"Then what?"

Stepping away, Boone replied, "Ms. Sherman, I'm in the construction business. If something needs to be built or restored or renovated, I do it. But I can't in good conscience recommend a customer throw his or her money away."

"What are you saying, exactly?"

"Sweet Hope is a little town. A traditional little town. It's not chic. It's not cutting edge. Never was. Never hoped to be. What you're proposing is...is...big city." He glowered at her for emphasis. "I suggest you sell this building to the historical society and find yourself a storefront in Atlanta. Your idea sounds perfect for Atlanta."

"Atlanta! I'll have you know I just escaped Atlanta. I *picked* Sweet Hope specifically for my plan, and I have no intentions of leaving. Atlanta! Atlanta, indeed!"

Boone almost smiled at the tiny bundle of purple indignation before him. He sure had pressed her button, and the result was a sight to see. Ms. Arabella Sherman was all aflutter.

"This is a good idea, Mr. O'Malley. Neither you nor anyone else can tell me otherwise. Why, your own mother thought it a splendid idea."

Boone did smile. Ruefully. "I think you ought to know that Alice Rose has always delighted in seeing the establishment tweaked."

"I'm not tweaking anyone! I intend to help. I intend to make a positive difference."

"How? By bringing some big-city culture to the boondocks?"

Arabella's gauzy outfit ruffled like the plumage of an exotic purple bird. An agitated exotic bird. "Don't use sarcasm on me, Mr. O'Malley. The coffee shop and used bookstore are intended to be fun. My real work will be with the literacy center. Did you know Georgia ranks tenth in all the states for its rate of illiteracy? Not a very distinguished honor. I intend to try to help. You know the old saying—if you're not part of the solution, you're part of the problem."

Boone quirked an eyebrow at the diminutive Ms. Sherman. "A social worker?"

"A former kindergarten teacher. What difference does that make?"

"Lots. I'm afraid you'll find the residents of Sweet Hope less biddable than five-year-olds."

"And what is that supposed to mean?"

By the tone of her voice, Boone felt sure he'd pressed another button. This time a significant one. But he persevered. Better to give this perky bundle of do-goodism the straight story than have her get in way over her head.

"Illiteracy is certainly a problem," he ventured. "I can't argue with you there. And your desire to help is noble. But things aren't always as easy as they appear. As bad as illiteracy is, worse for some is the stigma of admitting they need help. If folks around here need help, they go about getting it quietly. Not right out in the open in a storefront on Main Street. From a stranger. It's like airing their dirty laundry in public."

Arabella pushed out her lower lip and exhaled sharply, setting the curls on her forehead bobbing. "It's attitudes like yours, Mr. O'Malley, that compound the problem. Because an issue is sensitive, I should hide it? Because something is difficult, I shouldn't tackle it?"

"No, not at all," Boone replied, trying not to smile at the woman's righteous indignation. She was so worked up. Such a scrapper. And so pretty. "I'm just warning you not to get your hopes up. You need to get to know the people of Sweet Hope. Let them get to know you. Change comes slowly in this part of Georgia. People are concerned as much with appearances as with the issues. They're not fond of public displays."

He beetled his brows at her and hoped she caught his message.

"I do not intend to make a public *display* out of either my person or my cause, Mr. O'Malley. And my ideas will work. I will make them work."

Arabella folded her arms across the front of her lavender gauze, pulled herself up to her full height and skewered Boone with a defiant look. Despite the fact that her full height barely grazed his chin, she did present an indomitable figure. If she said she'd make it work, he believed her. And heaven help the established folk of Sweet Hope.

Boone held up his hands and shook his head. "It's your money," he said in surrender. "Now, what did you want that estimate for? Exactly."

Arabella brightened instantly. The woman was nothing if not mercurial. But he had to admit he admired a woman who didn't hold a grudge.

"Exactly," she purred, her honeyed voice sending another shiver of unwanted sensation down Boone's spine. She began to move—to float—around the large room. "I think we can get away with a good coat of paint in this room. And some additional electrical outlets. Miraculously, there's already a sink behind the counter."

"Thank heavens for small miracles," Boone muttered as he followed the tinkling lavender vision around the room. Tinkling? "Do I hear bells?" he asked irritably.

"Of course you hear bells," she replied as if to a child. "Now, as for the soundproofing..."

The bells were the last straw. He had to get out of here. He was trapped in an old building with a woman who looked like the heroine of an animated Disney movie. In no time at all he was sure she'd burst into song. And then all those cute fuzzy little animals would come out of hiding. Good Lord, he was losing it. He was a builder, for heaven's sake. A pragmatic man. A strong, quiet, dignified man who, because of a mother with a penchant for mischief, had dropped down a rabbit hole into... "What?" He started at the touch of a hand on his arm.

"Mr. O'Malley, I really am concerned about you. You seem overheated. Can I get you something cold to drink? Would you like to sit down a minute? I'm sure I can find an old crate around somewhere."

"No. No." He waved her away. "We need to do this estimate." This was the last time he'd let his mother tempt him into a barter. He didn't care if he *was* to get a month of her Sunday fried chicken dinners. It wasn't worth it. Not at all.

"I think I have a clear idea of what you want," he managed to get out. "Paint. A dozen new outlets.... By the way, do you even know if the wiring in this building can support any changes?"

"I'm aware of what you may think of my mental abilities, Mr. O'Malley," Arabella said with a patient smile and a quirk of one eyebrow, "but, believe me, appearances can be deceiving. I did my homework before I bought this building. The structure and the utilities are sound. I've made an apartment upstairs. My home. As... unconventional as I may appear, I do admire the conventions of safety in the home."

For some reason Boone felt as if he'd been rebuked. But so gently—she was still smiling—that he couldn't be certain. Or offended.

"Yes," he said, rubbing his chin thoughtfully. "Well, Ms. Sherman, it seems pretty cut-and-dried. I could have a crew get to this no sooner than the middle of next month. They'd be done in a week, tops. It would cost you five thousand dollars."

Arabella looked as if all the air had been let out of her gauzy purple outfit. Her fingers fluttered to her throat, and her mouth opened in a little round O. "Five thousand dollars," she repeated softly. "And not until the middle of next month. Oh, dear." Clearly, this didn't meet her needs.

Boone saw the light at the end of the tunnel. His offer was unacceptable. Ms. Sherman would look elsewhere. He had fulfilled his end of the bargain with his mother. He had indeed given a fair and honest estimate. It was not part of the bargain that Ms. Sherman must accept his estimate. He need never see this disconcerting woman again. And his Sunday fried chicken dinners were safe.

Forget that just a twinge of guilt passed over his heart. He had nothing—absolutely nothing—to feel guilty about. Except the fact that he had caused this lovely, enigmatic woman to look distressed. In a moment he just knew he would regret, he softened and asked, "Do you feel the estimate is unfair?"

"Oh, no." She looked at him, and he found himself noticing that the edges of her dark brown eyes were flecked with gold. For a moment he forgot where he was until she spoke again. "It's just that I'd hoped we could do it sooner. And cheaper."

"I'm sorry," he said. And, unaccountably, for an instant he was. "Spring building's in full swing. I have a huge Victorian replica out on Flat Shoals Road. And three cottages at the lake. And the renovation of the Little Theater. I just can't spare a crew for a small job like this till then."

He expected her to thank him and to show him to the door. She didn't do either. Instead she tented her long, slender fingers as if in prayer and raised those deep, dark eyes to look him square in the face. "Mr. O'Malley," she implored, "we must think of an alternative solution."

*"We?"* Boone took a step backward. He could say no to her words, but those eyes ... What was wrong with him today? For the past six years, ever since his wife's death, Boone O'Malley had been able to resist the imploring eyes and gentle smiles of every woman Alice Rose had thrown in his path. Now, his daughter could wrap him around her little finger with a single look, but that was another story. Women—women who presented the possibility of a romantic relationship—had left him unmoved.

Until now.

Until Ms. Arabella Sherman in all her quirky, floaty purpleness had fallen into his arms. Ms. Sherman with her too-red nail polish and her free-spirit bare feet and her silly kiddie watch and her provocative ankle tattoo and her seeming lack of care about what other people might think. Ms. Sherman who was nothing like Boone's demure, refined, circumspect ideal of womanhood.

Totally inappropriate Ms. Sherman had jump-started something so deep and hidden within him that if he didn't get out of this storefront *right now* and away from those woodland-brown-and-gold-speckled eyes, he was going to promise something he would definitely regret.

Without another word he turned and started for the door, almost knocking over his mother in the process.

So intent was she on the obvious but rather mystifying distress of the scowling Mr. Boone O'Malley, Arabella hadn't noticed Alice Rose come in.

"Gracious, Boone!" Alice Rose exclaimed as she tried to get out of her son's way. "You act as though you're running from the law!"

Not the law, thought Arabella, but something. Our prickly Mr. O'Malley is definitely running from something.

"Sorry, Mama, but I just finished giving Ms. Sherman that estimate. I'm on my way to my next appointment."

"Hold your horses, son. Tell your next appointment you were held up paying respects to your mama. They'll understand. Now ... what did you and Belle decide?"

Arabella couldn't believe it, but this big, muscular man managed to look the tiniest bit sheepish before the diminutive and elderly Alice Rose. A faintly trapped look passed over his handsome features. Darn. Arabella had always been a sucker for that backed-into-a-corner, stray-animal look, whether on man or beast. She might not understand why Boone O'Malley felt trapped, and it might not be her place to find out why—yet. But, recognizing a creature in distress when she saw one, she felt compelled to ease his discomfort by speaking in his behalf.

"Alice Rose, your son gave me his best estimate—a very fair estimate. But I'm afraid even that's more than I'm prepared to pay or wait for. I'll have to look elsewhere." Real disappointment washed over her at the thought of the delay.

"Now just a minute, you two," Alice Rose piped up. "If money's a problem, we can surely work out a barter."

Arabella brightened at the idea that something could be worked out. She had a small inheritance from her father and also from a favorite aunt as backing for the store, but not so much that she didn't have to watch expenses.

"Why, I'm sure, if the work's not too difficult, Belle could do part of it," Alice Rose continued. "To get a discount."

"I could," Arabella agreed eagerly. "I'm very handy."

Boone shot her a look that conveyed serious doubt. Serious doubt and extreme reluctance. But this time Arabella's empathies were swayed not toward Boone's unexplained discomfort but toward the prospect that Alice Rose could finesse some kind of deal here. If she could, Arabella would be that much closer to her dream. She found herself rooting for Alice Rose.

"You don't need a crew for this job, Boone," Alice Rose persisted. "You could come over after work a few hours a week to help with the more difficult aspects. Gracious, as for cleaning and painting, I can help a little during the day. Of course, we'd want you to buy all the supplies so that Belle can take advantage of your contractor's discount—"

"Mama!" Boone interrupted none too gently. "Are you suggesting I come over here after a hard day's work and *volunteer* my time and energy on this cockamamie idea for a business?"

Arabella bristled. How dare he think her ideas *cockamamie!*

"Volunteer? Certainly not," Alice Rose replied. "We can barter. I'm prepared to help Belle out a little bit in that department, too."

Boone rolled his eyes. "A free and honest estimate alone cost you a month of fried chicken dinners."

Looking from mother to son, Arabella wondered just what had put Mr. O'Malley out of sorts. Gracious, it was still early morning, and he had the six-p.m. grumpies. Now, she herself always liked to start the day fresh. Eager. Optimistic. No point in starting out prickly. Where could you go from there?

But the dickering wasn't over. Alice Rose tapped her index finger on her chin in thought, then pulled her trump. "Pies! That's it! You do realize, Boone O'Malley, that dessert was not included in the original barter?"

"Mama!"

"If you want dessert, you're going to have to work it out in this storefront. I'm sure Belle can come up with something in addition."

Boone inhaled sharply and looked at Arabella. "Begging your pardon, *ma'am,* but I doubt you have anything I need."

Oh, yes, I do, thought Arabella. You, *sir,* need an attitude adjustment. And I'm just the woman who could give you some pointers.

"Don't be too hasty, son." Alice Rose's words cut into Arabella's thoughts. "Cassie has been bugging you to redo her room for weeks now. Belle would be the perfect consultant. I happen to know from quilting circle that she has a strong eye for color and composition."

"I don't know...." The still unexplained trapped look returned to Boone's eyes.

"Cassie?" Arabella was curious. Could this be Mr. O'Malley's wife? Alice Rose had never mentioned a wife.

"My daughter," Boone muttered. "She thinks she's outgrown her bedroom."

"Just the Holly Hobbie decor, dear," Alice Rose added. Arabella pictured a cute little-button of a girl, maybe nine or ten, wanting to be all grown up. "Well?"

Boone threw up his hands. "This is crazy! I can't make that decision for Cassie. She and Ms. Sherman might not even see eye-to-eye."

"Well, let them decide for themselves on Saturday."

"Saturday?" both Boone and Arabella asked in unison.

"Yes," chirped Alice Rose. "We'll all be at the Pioneer Days celebration. What a delightful way to get together."

"I hadn't really thought of going," Arabella protested. "I have so much to do here."

"That settles it," Boone declared. "Ms. Sherman never really thought of going."

"Nonsense!" Alice Rose showed no intention of dropping the matter. "Pioneer Days is always held on the town green—right in front of your storefront, Belle, dear. You'd be too distracted to work. Of course you're going. Boone can drop by and pick you up."

"Absolutely not!" Boone snapped.

Arabella was startled by the ferocity of his words. It was becoming clear that Mr. Boone O'Malley wanted nothing to do with her. Neither at her storefront nor in a public social setting. Was it she? Or was it he? Was it personal? Or was this man just not a people person in general, as she was? From what she'd seen of the out-of-sorts Mr. O'Malley this morning, she couldn't tell for certain. But her curiosity had been piqued. As prickly as he was, there was an ill-defined look of need in his eyes that drew her to the man.

Boone gazed at her with chagrin and said, more softly, "I have to be on the green early in the morning to tend the barbecue pits. I'll be busy. I'm sorry."

"That's quite all right," Arabella assured him with her sweetest smile. "I think I can manage to cross Main Street onto the green without undue catastrophe. Falling from the ladder has been the only accident I've had in the entire month since I've been in Sweet Hope.''

At the mention of his rescue earlier, Arabella thought she detected a hint of added color in Boone's tanned cheeks. She wouldn't forget his help for quite some time. The feel of his strong arms around her. The reassuring bulk of his body pressed up against her own. Oh, no, she wouldn't forget that easily. And she'd wager Mr. O'Malley, despite his prickly, protesting exterior, wouldn't, either. The color in his cheeks confirmed it.

"You fell, dear?" Alice Rose asked with concern.

"Yes, but Mr. O'Malley was there to catch me," Arabella replied, unable to control the huskiness in her voice.

Alice Rose looked sharply from Arabella to Boone then back again. "May I make a suggestion?"

"Can we stop you, Mama?"

"Watch that mouth, Boone O'Malley." Alice Rose's eyes sparkled. "I think, since we're all on the brink of a major barter, we could dispense with the *mizzes* and the *misters*. I think we're all adult enough to be on a first-name basis. What do you say?"

Arabella couldn't help the grin that spread across her face. Couldn't help but think that Alice Rose was some strong lady. She looked at the big, blond man standing apart from Alice Rose and herself. His blue eyes had gone almost gray, hinting at a storm of barely controlled emotion. Watching him struggle with something—she wished she knew what—she added to her former assessment of him. He needed an attitude adjustment, yes. But a man wound that tightly—over what?—needed a hug. On second thought, Mr. Boone O'Malley could probably use one a day for the rest of his life. In lieu of a hug, she held out her hand to him for the second time that day.

"It's fine with me," she said. "How about you . . . Boone?"

Slowly Boone held out his hand and grasped hers. "Arabella."

She was struck by the sense of pure masculine strength and security his grip imparted. Struck, for a moment, speechless. But silently she wondered if he would ever feel comfortable enough with her to call her Belle.

The white lace curtains streamed into the room on the April evening breeze, beckoning Belle to leave her embroidery and sit by the window. She couldn't resist. Picking up her glass of iced tea, she dragged a footstool to the window, then sat, her arms resting on the sill.

What a wonderful, wonderful new home she'd chosen.

From her loft apartment above the storefront, she could look out over Main Street and the entire town green. It was as if all of Sweet Hope was her front yard.

Evening was her favorite time of day. By now the stores along Main Street had mostly closed, leaving only a couple of restaurants, the movie house and the Little Theater open for business. The large green, often empty during the day, came to life with families in the evening. Children played on the two old Civil War cannons or danced impromptu jigs in the bandstand. Parents organized pickup games of softball. Teenagers hung out, parading their plumage for the opposite sex. After a month in Sweet Hope, Belle could tell the names of almost every person on the green this evening. They felt like family.

Sighing, she lowered her chin onto her arms. This was why, given her second chance, she'd left Atlanta. She'd left with the sweet hope of finding a place where she'd know her neighbors' first names, walk instead of drive, feel more acutely the changing of the seasons and be more than just a cog in a wheel. Where she'd be someone special. Make a difference.

Sweet Hope. She sure had found it. A new life with a new circle of friends. Belle chuckled at the thought of Alice Rose trying to strike a deal this morning. That woman. As determined as she was generous, she had the exterior of an elderly Southern lady and the inner strength of a steamroller.

The sudden appearance on the town green of a father holding the hand of his little girl made Belle sit up and take notice. Where were Mr. Boone O'Malley and his daughter, Cassie, tonight? Was there a Mrs. O'Malley to tame the mister's prickly nature? If so, why couldn't *she* redo Cassie's Holly Hobbie decor? Whoever got to do it, it was perfectly clear that Boone didn't want Belle to do it.

He didn't want to do her storefront, either. No matter that Alice Rose would withhold his desserts.

But why not?

They'd made no final deal this morning. The only thing they'd agreed upon was the use of their first names, and that at Alice Rose's behest. Boone had acted as if that alone was a major concession. Strange man. In need of a hug. If there was a Mrs. O'Malley, she sure was derelict in that department.

And if there wasn't a Mrs. O'Malley? Despite the emotional pull toward the man Belle had felt at times during the morning, Boone O'Malley's marital status really didn't matter, except to satisfy Belle's curiosity. As difficult as it was to get the problematic Boone out of her mind, she would. She'd had enough of reluctant men, thank you very much. She was just curious. She was free to be curious, wasn't she? Heck, she was free to be anything. That was just the point of second chances. She didn't have to add Boone to her list of causes. But, being a student of human nature, she could follow his story, couldn't she?

Belle lowered her cheek to her arm and gazed sideways out the window. Oh, well, the story would surely unfold rapidly in a town this size. Perhaps even on Saturday at Pioneer Days. One could always hope.

Smiling, Arabella Sherman watched the golds of twilight slowly change to the purples of night. She had plenty of time. In fact, she had her whole new life.

## Chapter Two

Belle squinted against the noonday brightness at the crowd of celebrants gathered on the green for Pioneer Days. She didn't quite know what made this occasion qualify as *pioneer*. As far as she could see, any prairie ambience had been supplanted by a Deep South country-fair atmosphere. In the dappled shade of newly leaved trees, craft booths dotted the perimeter of the green. A bluegrass band tuned up on the bandstand highlighted by bunches of colorful balloons. Children tugged at their elders, impatient to get to the games of chance, the refreshments, the fun. Brightly striped tents had been set up within the ring of booths. Underneath, people settled at trestle tables, waiting to be served the plentiful country cooking. The aroma from the barbecue pits alone was ambrosia to Belle's senses.

Boone O'Malley had said he'd be tending the barbecue pits.

Smiling at the thought of seeing the prickly Mr. O'Malley again, Belle adjusted the drop waist of her cream-colored antique dress and the brim of her gaily beribboned straw hat.

and decided to postpone the pleasure of matching wits with the man. Until she knew his marital status, she wouldn't be able to choose between friendship or a simple business relationship. Those were the only two choices she allowed herself.

"Belle! Belle! Arabella Sherman!" A woman's voice rang out, but, looking around, Belle couldn't seem to locate the source. "Dear..." Belle now recognized Alice Rose's voice at her side as she felt the older woman's arm twine with hers.

"Alice Rose, how good to see you." And it was. Belle always found herself caught up with the older woman's enthusiasm and energy. "Where's the rest of your family?" She knew for a fact that Alice Rose was a widow living alone on her farm, so "the rest of your family" meant Boone and his family. She hoped, however, that the question appeared innocent enough.

"Oh, Boone's supervising the barbecue pits. And Cassie's...somewhere. That girl needs no encouragement to get into mischief." Alice Rose smiled with grandmotherly pride.

"And Mrs. O'Malley?" Belle prodded gently.

Alice Rose raised one eyebrow. "Mrs. O'Malley? Do you mean Boone's wife?"

"Yes." Belle swallowed her sudden discomfort. Just her luck to appear to be chasing after a married man when that wasn't her intent at all. Not at all.

Patting Belle's arm, Alice Rose murmured, "Why, don't you know, dear? My Boone's been a widower now these six years. It's just him and Cassie in that little bungalow on Oak Street." She squeezed Belle's hand and chuckled. "Although the unattached women in this town have sure been trying to change that."

"I see," Belle replied softly. Remembering Alice Rose's quick willingness to suggest her contractor son for an estimate on the storefront, she wondered how much of that willingness was just helping out a newcomer, or how much of it was motherly matchmaking. "Alice Rose," she asked, "you wouldn't be throwing me at your son, would you?"

With a display of ruffled indignation, Alice Rose retorted, "Why, not at all, Belle Sherman. Not at all. Whatever gave you that idea?" She softened the retort with a warm smile. "Now, run along and enjoy yourself with the young folks. You look a little peaked. Look like you could use something to eat. I hear the barbecue's mighty tasty this year."

"Alice Rose...."

"That's what I hear." The older woman shrugged and grinned. "Oh, there's Simon Mayfield. He's rich as Croesus. I'm going to run over and see if I can get him to buy a roll of chances on our quilt. Now, go have fun, dear. I'm sure to see you again before the afternoon's over."

Alice Rose bustled in the direction of a dapper elderly gentleman with a walking stick. Halfway in her pursuit of the hoped-for donor, she turned and called to Belle, "Oh, yes. You look especially lovely today. *Especially* lovely." With a wink she turned once more toward the unsuspecting Simon.

Now, what was that supposed to mean?

Belle smiled in the wake of Alice Rose and her revelations. Ever since the two women had met in quilting circle a month ago, a warm and natural bond had grown between them. Belle, scarcely remembering her own mother, had been drawn to the loving and outgoing Mrs. O'Malley. Her community involvement, her generosity, her zest for life were qualities the new Belle wished to emulate.

Funny how, just now, the new Belle had experienced a little blip of interest when she'd found out there was only one *Mrs.* O'Malley, and that was Boone's mother. Funny, because she, Arabella Sherman, was not necessarily looking for a romantic entanglement. Having just recovered her life, she was looking to spread her wings. To fly. Free.

But knowing that Boone O'Malley was also free... well, what could that knowledge hurt?

With a little happy skip Belle began to wander through the crowd, not looking at anything in particular, just pleased to be alive on this glorious April afternoon. A particularly

large family in front of her veered to the right, leaving her
with an unobstructed view of the barbecue pits.

There, supervising the workers as they basted and turned
the large slabs of ribs, stood Boone O'Malley, tall and lean,
dressed in a polo shirt, jeans and moccasins, his blond hair
shining in the sun, his head and shoulders wreathed in
smoke. His expression oh, so serious.

Serious, that is, until a beautiful young woman holding
two cans of soda approached him. She gave Boone one can,
then settled comfortably at his side. It was then that he
broke into a smile the likes of which Belle had rarely seen.
She certainly hadn't seen one like it from Boone O'Malley
the morning the two of them had met. But now here he
stood, a gorgeous, leggy blonde at his side, and the man
didn't seem to be able to stop grinning.

Just then he bent and planted a kiss on the young woman's cheek, then tipped his head back and took a long draft
of soda.

And what did Belle care? Boone O'Malley was no concern of hers. Although it did surprise her that he was at least
twice the age of the woman at his side. No wonder he'd
shown no interest in Sweet Hope's unattached women.

While Belle watched, the woman reached up to massage
Boone's shoulders. He offered no resistance until she
touched her soda can to his neck. And then he reacted
swiftly by swatting her on her backside and laughingly
pushing her beyond the barbecue area. She gave him a wink,
then sashayed off in the direction of a group of young adults
more her own age.

With a grin Boone turned back to his work, but in turning, he caught Belle's eye. She caught her breath. How
handsome he looked when he wasn't scowling.

He didn't look away. Instead he skewered her with an almost questioning gaze, and Belle felt the heat rise to her
cheeks. He couldn't know she'd been watching the little
scene earlier, could he? Well, there was no turning around
now without looking vaguely guilty, so why not be neighborly and say "Hey"?

At that moment the band began to play a lively bluegrass number. A little musical prompt. Casually, Belle made her way to the barbecue pits.

His grin having faded away, Boone's expression was now unreadable. "Ms. Sherman . . . Arabella," he said.

"Boone." Suddenly she felt shy.

"Has my mother put you to selling raffle tickets?"

"No."

"She will."

The conversation faltered and died.

Belle desperately searched for a new topic. "Your date seems to be having a good time," she ventured without thinking. "She's very beautiful."

Boone stood absolutely still. Looking straight at Belle, he began to smile. The smile widened to the broad grin she'd seen him lavish on the young woman earlier. Then, to Belle's surprise, the grin developed into a deep, rolling laugh. What a wonderful laugh this man was capable of. So infectious was it, Belle began to chuckle, not even knowing the point.

Caught up in the unexplained merriment, she started when Boone came out of the barbecue area, put his hand under her elbow and guided her in the direction of the bandstand where Belle could see the beautiful blond woman who'd been at Boone's side earlier, engaged in animated conversation with several other young people. Boone propelled Belle right in that direction.

When the woman spotted Boone, her face literally glowed. She stopped talking to the others and turned, waiting for him. Clearly, she adored the man. Inexplicably, Belle's heart sank.

Stopping before the young woman, Boone said, "Arabella Sherman, I'd like to introduce you to . . . Cassie, my daughter."

His daughter. Belle smiled and breathed the tiniest—and most unexpected—sigh of relief at the mistaken identity. So this was the little girl with the Holly Hobbie decor that she'd outgrown. I guess she has, thought Belle. I wonder why she's kept it this long. Maybe, just maybe, it's daddy who doesn't want the change. Doesn't want to admit that his child has grown up. And has she grown up.

The young woman gave Belle a brilliant smile, extended her hand and said, "I'm pleased to meet you." Then ever so subtly she gave her father a questioning look.

Boone nuzzled his daughter playfully. "Ms. Sherman thought you and I were an item."

Cassie shook her blond mane, and laughter bubbled up from deep within her. "That's a hoot!" she exclaimed.

Hands on his hips, Boone rocked back on his heels. "I thought so. If Ms. Sherman—"

"Arabella," Belle prompted.

"If *Arabella* can imagine I've captured the interest of an eighteen-year-old, I guess there's hope for this old fossil yet."

Cassie rolled her eyes. "Daddy! Thirty-eight is no old fossil. Now, if you'd just start thinking and acting like a thirty-eight-year-old instead of a—"

"Watch your mouth, girl," Boone growled in mock warning.

Belle was fascinated. Here was a whole new side to Boone O'Malley. A warm and loving, faintly mischievous father.

Cassie turned to Belle. "Arabella... May I call you Arabella?"

Boone scowled.

"Of course. But my friends call me Belle."

Boone's scowl deepened.

"I'd like to call you Belle." Cassie put her hand on her father's chest and gently pushed. "Although Daddy would prefer I call you Miss Belle or Ms. Sherman. Southern manners and all, you know."

"Well, *you* should know," Boone interjected stiffly. "You were raised right."

Cassie slipped her arm around his waist. "You did raise me right," she reassured him softly. "But in case you haven't noticed, I'm not a little girl anymore. I'm all grown up."

The look in Boone's eyes said how he knew it. And regretted it.

Feeling that she'd stumbled over an oft-repeated, very private bone of contention, Belle almost turned away. Cassie, however, called out to her for support.

"Belle," she asked, "you consider me a peer, don't you? You can't be that much older than me. And you mistook me for Daddy's girlfriend, after all."

Belle smiled. The young woman standing before her had the body of a mature woman and the doubts and hesitation of a little girl. How desperately she seemed to want to be viewed as an adult. Belle's heart went out to her.

"Although I'm quite a bit older than you—fifteen years, to be exact," Belle said carefully, "I think that after a certain point age becomes a state of mind. Almost irrelevant. Why, just look at the friendship between your grandmother and me. We've never once mentioned the difference in our ages."

"Exactly!" Cassie gave her father a squeeze. "So you see, Daddy, I'm not going to offend Belle by using her first name, and I'm not going to embarrass my upbringing, and I'm not going to bring shame on your ever-present sense of propriety."

With obvious fondness and a hint of exasperation, Boone looked at his daughter. "Is this what they teach you at college? Specious reasoning? Overblown drama? Manipulation?"

Cassie chuckled. "No, I picked that up from Grammy. How it skipped a generation in you, I'll never know."

"Speaking of your grandmother," Belle ventured, noting the clouds gathering in Boone's eyes, "she and I were working out a barter with your father...."

Boone's nostrils flared. His body tensed. His gaze became darker still, and Belle detected a distinct hint of warning, as if he didn't want her to broach the subject of the proposed barter involving his daughter.

Well, he hadn't intimidated Cassie, and he wasn't going to intimidate her. Belle forged ahead. "I need some renovation work done. In trade for your father's expertise, I would be willing to help you redo your bedroom. Alice Rose seemed to think that would be fair trade."

Cassie's eyes widened. "And Daddy agreed?"

Boone's black look said he most definitely hadn't agreed.

"I think we left it," Belle said diplomatically, "that you and I should talk."

"I'd love it!" Cassie exclaimed with all the joy of a little girl. "You don't know how long I've been at Daddy to let me change old Holly Hobbie." She winked at Belle. "In case you hadn't noticed, Daddy is allergic to change."

"Not allergic," Boone muttered. "Just cautious."

Cassie hugged him. "If you're too cautious," she warned playfully, "that's going to be your epitaph. Here Lies Boone O'Malley, A Man So Cautious He—"

"That's enough, young lady." Boone's tone of voice was anything but playful now.

"Perhaps we should discuss this later," Belle suggested.

"Yes," Cassie agreed, "later. Right now there's food to be eaten, bargains to be had . . . and dances to be danced." She looked pointedly at Boone.

Belle couldn't believe that his look could have gotten any more ominous. But it had.

Cassie persisted. "Since we're *not* an item, Daddy, and the band's playing a waltz, you're free to ask Belle to dance." She looked at Belle. "Daddy dances like a dream."

Silence. Boone examined his moccasins. Belle examined her hands and felt an unwanted blush creep into her cheeks. She knew enough already about this man to realize Cassie had just backed him into a corner. He was too *well raised* to leave a lady high and dry. But she also knew, with certainty, that Boone O'Malley did *not* want to dance with her.

Finally, however, Boone asked softly, "Arabella, would you care to dance?"

Belle looked up into eyes now the color of stone-washed denim. How could she say no? "Yes, I think I'd like that," she murmured.

Boone took a deep breath. First his mother. Now his daughter. What had the O'Malley women gotten him into?

He looked at the woman before him. She was smiling that angelic smile. All soft expectation in a dress that looked as if it had come out of his great-grandmother's trunk. Pretty, yes, on Arabella Sherman. But totally inappropriate for the afternoon's events. And that wide-brimmed, fluttery hat... How did Cassie expect him to waltz with this woman when her hat would take up a quarter of the dance floor?

Boone sighed, a deep, long-suffering sigh. "Arabella, that hat has got to go."

Taking no obvious offense, Belle gracefully swept her hand up to the brim of the hat. Removing it in a motion that set her dark curls bobbing, she handed it to Cassie. "Would you do the honors?"

"I'd be delighted." Taking the hat, then putting a hand each on Boone and Belle, Cassie winked and said, "I guess there's nothing now but to dance."

Boone guessed not.

For the second time today he placed his hand under Belle's elbow and guided her through the crowd. This time to the temporary dance floor set up below the bandstand.

How long had it been since he'd been on a dance floor? Ages.

As Belle now glided sweetly into his arms, he realized with a jolt that it had been too long. He'd almost forgotten how good a woman could feel. And Arabella Sherman sure felt good. Contrary to her appearance, she was no wisp that disappeared in his arms. Surprisingly, she had substance. He could feel a definite strength. Yet she was soft in all the right places. And she smelled so good. Not of perfume, no. But of baking and sun-drenched days. Rather than a provocative scent, a happy scent. Nothing faintly upsetting, he assured himself. Barely noticing the change in his own mood, Boone relaxed. Not even the vague tinkling of bells provoked him.

He was thus unprepared for her question, uttered softly, close to his ear. "Are you angry that Cassie's all grown up?"

The sweet cadence of her voice wrapped itself around his senses like a pesky kudzu vine. And the root of her canny observation burrowed straight to his heart.

Boone tensed, uncomfortable that this stranger had seen too much, and then had not seen fit to keep silent about it. Coming to a complete standstill in the middle of the dance floor, he pulled back enough so that he could look Belle in the face. He'd quickly learned one very frustrating thing about Ms. Arabella Sherman: she could wear the most outrageous outfit, propose the most cockamamie project, or ask the most personal question without ever looking as if she meant to provoke or offend. If she'd just look as if she meant to cause a squabble, Boone would better know how to deal with her.

But here she stood, still in his arms, gazing up at him as if she *cared* about how he felt. As if her question about Cassie wasn't snooping. As if somehow his answer was important to her. It was that quality of disingenuous openness that irked the bejeebers out of him.

He didn't mean to snap at her, but his question came out snappish. "Why would you ask that?"

Belle smiled and tilted her face to him. "Cassie seems so desperately to want to be seen as an adult. And you seem to…resist. With the redoing of her room, for instance. Why is that?"

That damned room. How could he tell this near stranger that the Holly Hobbie bedroom was one of the last things his wife had done for their daughter before she'd died? Erase it and you erased one of the few remaining vestiges of that time when Cassie was a little girl and the future held limitless possibilities. Erase it and you erased something physical—more than just a memory—of a woman who would be alive today if not for his, Boone's, lack of caution. The old pain welled up inside him. No, he wasn't about to make his pain public by discussing that room, or his failure, or his admittedly unrealistic desire to keep Cassie his little girl for just a while longer.

"Do you have children, Arabella?" The question sounded brusque even to his own ears.

"No," she answered softly. "Not yet."

"If you don't have children, I can't expect you to understand."

For a moment Belle's expression crumpled. In trying to protect his own emotions, he'd hurt her. And he felt an instant of regret. She seemed like a nice woman despite her quirkiness. A sweet woman, even. Why did she have to be endowed with the uncanny ability to plumb his emotional depths? For six years, by not ruffling the surface, he'd not disturbed those depths. And now...now, with just a question and a gentle look, this woman troubled the waters *and* the man who'd tried desperately to stay afloat these past years.

"Boone?" That honeyed voice. "The music's over."

He looked around and realized that they were the last couple on the dance floor as the band broke for cold drinks. Still in his arms, Belle looked up at him with concern. How long had he been standing locked in the past?

Abruptly, he released her and took a step back. "Thank you for the dance, Ms. Sherman. I need to get back to the barbecue."

He turned and left the dance floor, trying to ignore the curious glances of his Sweet Hope neighbors.

Well, now, that was a less than satisfying turn about the floor, thought Belle as she watched Boone's stiff, retreating form.

Just what was wrong with her question? One little inquiry into a father-daughter relationship, and the man froze up. What was it about Boone O'Malley? One minute he seemed relaxed, the next he was a scowling bundle of reluctance. He was certainly a case study. And with her track record of interest in challenging cases, if she was not careful she might just find herself too interested in him.

With a sigh she looked around for Cassie and her straw hat. At almost the same instant Belle saw Alice Rose step in front of Boone, preventing him from returning to the barbecue pits, Cassie, wearing the hat, materialized at Belle's side.

"It didn't look as if you two were having fun out there," the young woman observed, the miniscowl on her face reminding Belle of Boone.

"No," Belle answered softly, "I don't think you could call it fun."

"A lovers' spat?"

Belle was jolted by the young woman's assumption. "No. Of course not. Nothing like that. Goodness, what a thought. I just met your father this week, Cassie. He doesn't, however, seem comfortable with me."

Cassie twirled a ribbon on Belle's hat and smiled. "Daddy's not comfortable with free spirits. As you can tell by the talk about changing my room, he's a cautious, buttoned-down kind of guy. Not that Grammy and I don't work ceaselessly to change all that."

Belle looked over at Alice Rose and the now-cornered Boone. His mother sure was bending his ear about something. Perhaps she was trying to unbutton him just a little. He looked unmoved.

"Well, with his attitude I don't see him accepting the barter your grandmother proposed," Belle replied. "And if he doesn't, the work on my storefront will take a setback while I scout up another honest contractor—who works cheap."

Cassie's eyes lit up. "I didn't put two and two together. Are you the one who's redoing the old mercantile?"

"That's me—the one who's *planning* to redo the old mercantile."

"Oh, that's funny." Cassie chuckled. "The other day Daddy was frothing at the mouth about some big-city do-gooder who was planning to open a coffeehouse, used bookstore and literacy center in, of all places, little ole Sweet Hope's historic mercantile. Planning to turn us all into coffee-drinking, poetry-reading hippies, he just bet. And that was *you?*"

"I plead guilty," Belle replied, cutting a glance at Boone where he stood in animated conversation with Alice Rose. So, he thought she was an off-the-wall do-gooder, did he? The chances of her clinching a barter with Boone O'Malley just seemed to get slimmer and slimmer.

"Well, I think it's a terrific idea," Cassie declared, "especially the literacy center."

"You do?"

"Yes, I do. And so does Grammy." Cassie looked thoughtful. "And you might just have fulfilled my community-service requirement."

"I don't understand." Belle didn't understand more than just Cassie's community-service requirement. She didn't understand how two members of one family could have outlooks on life so darned different from that of a third member. She glanced over at the odd man out, only to see Alice Rose jabbing him in the chest with her index finger.

"I go to Byron College, a small day college halfway between here and Atlanta," Cassie explained. "It's very community oriented. Every summer students have to fulfill forty hours of service work. As part of the credits necessary to advance. Thinking ahead, I was dreading shelving books all summer in the library. If you need help, I'd rather do something really useful like working with you in your center."

Belle brightened considerably. "That would be wonderful, Cassie. You'd have to take an orientation at the literacy center in Atlanta, but that could count toward your hours."

"You really want me to help?"

"Do I?" Belle laughed. "You don't understand that in the last few minutes I've doubled my center staff without spending a penny! You bet I want you to help. Now we just have to convince your father to agree to Alice Rose's barter. That's going to be tough, seeing that the man doesn't seem to want anything to do with me."

Again she looked over at Boone and decided he didn't seem to want to have much to do with the unrelenting Alice

Rose, either. What could have the older woman so worked up?

"Oh, I think things can be worked out," Cassie said, patting Belle's arm in a grandmotherly fashion and smiling a Cheshire-cat grin. "You two just need to get to know each other. You got off to a rocky start, is all. What you need is a second chance."

At that moment Boone began to back in their direction, seemingly in retreat from a very adamant Alice Rose. Cassie held out her hands to keep her father from backing right over them.

"And if you're smart, you'll pay heed to your old mother, Boone O'Malley," Alice Rose scolded, then looked up innocently as if seeing Belle and Cassie for the first time. "Why, look who's here. Belle, dear. And the band's just started up again." Alice Rose pulled a face. "You two had so little time that first waltz."

Boone looked at Belle and groaned.

Belle, herself a bit nonplussed by the machinations of the O'Malley women—for she didn't put it past Cassie to be in on this little maneuver also—quickly said, "Boone, there's no need to ask me to dance again."

"Oh, yes, there is," he snapped, grasping Belle by the wrist, "if only to get away from these two." He glared at his mother and his daughter, then pulled Belle none too gently onto the dance floor.

Drawing her into his arms, he grumbled, "Maybe if we dance one whole dance from beginning to end, *that* will satisfy them."

Belle stiffened. "Mr. O'Malley. What is it about me that you find so unattractive? Exactly."

Boone gave her a startled look. "Why... nothing, ma'am."

"Don't *ma'am* me, Boone O'Malley. I'm only five years younger than you. You *ma'am* me, and I sound like your grandmother."

He actually smiled. "All right, then, *Arabella*... I don't find you unattractive. On the contrary..." His blue, blue eyes caught and held hers. Almost mesmerizing. And the soft, rumbling way he'd said her name made a little frisson of pleasure race through her body. "On the contrary..."

He didn't finish the sentence. Instead he pulled her close. Close to his body and the rhythm of the music.

"Maybe," he suggested, his voice husky in her ear, "just maybe, we'd get off to a better start if neither one of us talks."

That was all right with Belle. She couldn't have talked if her life had depended upon it. For some reason the sensation of being in this big, powerful, cranky man's arms did strange things to her body. Like misplacing her tongue, for one. She sighed and let him lead her through the steps of the waltz.

Cassie had been right. He did dance like a dream.

Belle suddenly felt as if the world moved in slow motion. Every sensation heightened. Boone's hand, splayed across her back, pinning her to his chest, created a tingling heat that rose up her spine and spread throughout her limbs. As he held her right hand lightly, she could feel the calluses on his strong, work-hardened palm. Her left hand, resting on his shoulder, felt the warm, well-defined muscles underneath his lightweight shirt. The top of her head only grazed his chin, and so closely did he hold her that Belle was forced to turn her face to his neck, to lean the side of her head against his shoulder. Held thus—cocooned—she let herself rest against this powerful man. Let herself rest and felt serenely happy.

Inhaling the scent of him—a masculine combination of hickory smoke and sunshine—she heard him sigh. Felt him lower the side of his chin ever so gently to her hair. Realized he'd clasped her hand just a little more firmly. She smiled to herself. So Mr. Boone O'Malley wasn't made entirely of prickles. What an interesting fact to know.

As far as Belle was concerned, the waltz was far too short.

As the music ended, Boone drew away. But this time not abruptly. Belle almost felt as if he'd thought the dance too short, as well.

Glancing down at his moccasins, he appeared to be weighing his next words. Finally, looking at her from under half-lowered eyelids, he said slowly, "If you still need my help, I'll bring the materials by your place this Monday evening. Around seven. You can work out the details with Alice Rose and Cassie."

Not waiting for her response, he turned and threaded his way through the crowd, leaving Belle openmouthed but overjoyed.

The only cloud on her horizon was that she had no one with whom to share her joy. No one, that is, until she spotted Alice Rose and Cassie, arm in arm, standing on the edge of the dance floor, watching her. Each woman sported a megawatt grin that could, in and of itself, power the entire town.

Boone plunked the last of the barbecue utensils into the cauldron of hot, soapy water. The only bad thing about supervising this gustatory extravaganza every year was that he never got to go home until the last ember was dead, the last leftover rib wrapped for refrigeration and the last utensil washed. The only two people he could count on, every year, to stay with him till the very end were Alice Rose and Cassie. He looked out over the green and watched them now in the twilight, chasing down odd scraps of litter.

How he loved those two meddlesome women.

He chucked aloud to think of how they'd pushed Arabella Sherman and him together. Well, they'd won the battle. He'd danced one whole dance, uninterrupted, with the woman, and he'd agreed to help her with the materials and the more tricky aspects of her renovation. But the war was not over. He had no intention of being cajoled, bullied or tempted into a romantic relationship.

Especially not with a woman who breezed through life as if she didn't give a fig for what people might think of her dress or her words or her actions. Get involved with a very public, very outgoing, very unpredictable woman like Arabella and you'd have the whole town watching to see what would happen next. No, thank you. Boone O'Malley liked his relationships *very* private. Especially now that he had an almost adult Cassie to think of.

Cassie. On the cusp of womanhood. Looking lovelier every day and aching to test the power of that loveliness.

Boone knew he couldn't run his daughter's life. He'd raised her as well as he knew how. Now he had to step back and trust that upbringing. One thing he could still do, however, was to set a good example. And for Boone, setting a good example meant behaving in a dignified, circumspect manner. He wanted his daughter to see him as a strong individual, a successful businessman, a respected member of the community, a person who went about performing any good works quietly. Modestly.

She didn't need to see him as a love-struck fool. That's why, despite his mother's and his daughter's best efforts, he would not be pulled into a romantic relationship. Especially not with one highly visible Arabella Sherman.

An hour later, in near darkness, Boone, Alice Rose and Cassie made their way out the wrought-iron entrance to the town green. There on the low brick wall sat Belle, her big straw hat overturned in her lap, a circle of children seated at her feet.

Now what was the woman up to?

"Come see," she called to them. "Someone left a litter of kittens at the edge of the green. How thoughtless. The little things could have wandered out in traffic. Or been trampled by the crowd."

Or been picked up and taken in by you, thought Boone ruefully.

Alice Rose and Cassie knelt to ooh and aah over the kittens in Belle's hat.

"Why don't you take them to the animal shelter tomorrow?" Boone asked. Seemed logical to him.

"Oh, I couldn't. They've suffered enough trauma already. I've found homes for three of them. I only have two left."

"And what do you intend to do? Sit out here until you find takers for these two?" Irritation rose in Boone. It was dark, for Pete's sake. And this wasn't her problem.

Belle tilted her chin at him. Defiantly. "I do."

Alice Rose cuddled one kitten. "Well, I'll take this one. I think fifty acres is big enough to hold another cat."

"And I'll take this one." Cassie held up what looked to be the runt of the litter.

Boone groaned.

"Daddy!" Cassie rolled her eyes at him. "What fuss you make over an itty-bitty kitty. We can name her Holly Hobbie in honor of my soon-to-be dearly departed bedroom. What do you say?"

What did he say? He'd say Ms. Arabella Sherman was becoming too entangled with his family and his everyday life. And he didn't like it. Not one bit.

## Chapter Three

As promised, Boone arrived at Belle's storefront Monday evening at seven o'clock. With barely a how-do-you-do, he began to unload supplies from the back of a shiny black pickup truck parked at the edge of the sidewalk. He'd obviously come to work and was already practicing his laconic, strictly business mode.

Belle smiled as she began to help him unload the gallon paint cans. He might have come with business in mind, but somewhere between his regular workday and now, he'd taken the time to shower and change into clean clothes. Oh, the faded chambray shirt and jeans had seen use in their day, but they were freshly laundered and pressed. And Belle detected just a *hint* of after-shave. The idea that Boone O'Malley might care how he looked in front of her pleased her.

"Arabella! Watch where you're swinging those paint cans." Boone's voice came across loudly and urgently. "If you're not careful, your storefront's going to need new plate glass."

Feeling the heat rise to her cheeks, Belle promised she
would daydream no more about how Mr. O'Malley's well-
washed apparel snugged up against his lean, well-muscled
body. Or how silently—quite gracefully—he moved on
moccasined feet from truck to store interior. Or how sinu-
ously the long, lean fingers of his work-hardened hands
wrapped themselves about his tool belt as he strapped it
around his waist. In abstracted irritation, however, she
swiped away the curls of her hair that bounced in her eyes
and obstructed her view.

When her efforts to control her hair—and her view—
proved in vain, she pulled a hot pink bandanna from the
pocket of her shorts and fashioned a kerchief around her
head. There, maybe that would hold in her curls and her
heat-affected brain at the same time. She looked up to discover Boone staring at her. Lucky the kerchief covered her
ears. She could feel them turn as pink as the bandanna.

"Well, wh-what's first?" she managed to stammer. As
eager as she'd been to start this project, somehow she hadn't
quite foreseen the overheated eagerness Boone's presence
would engender. She needed to adopt a little of his cool, no-
nonsense approach.

"I thought I'd try to get one wall of outlets installed tonight," he replied, a glimmer of bemusement sparking in his
eyes as he gave her kerchief the once-over. "That way you
can start painting tomorrow."

"Is there something I can help you with tonight?"

"No." His expression became closed. All business again.
The instant of bemusement gone. "In fact, if you have
anything to do upstairs in your apartment, I'll be fine down
here alone."

Belle laughed. "I have something to do everywhere.
But..." She spread her hands to indicate the dozen or more
large boxes on the floor in the center of the room. "I have
hundreds of donated books to sort and tag. I'll just work
quietly here if you don't mind."

Boone glanced uncomfortably at the harsh overhead lighting, then at the floor-to-ceiling storefront windows on either side of the entrance door.

"Don't you want to put some tarps or some sheets over the windows?" he asked. "Working here at night, we'll stand out like prize guppies in a lighted aquarium."

"Oh, won't that be lovely!" Belle exclaimed, opening the first of the book boxes. "Get everybody that passes interested in our progress. Pique their curiosity. Maybe I need to make a Coming Soon sign to put in the window with a countdown till opening day."

"Please, Arabella, don't draw any more attention to this project than is absolutely necessary."

Hearing a soft, sincere plea in his voice, Belle looked up. "Why, Boone O'Malley, I do believe you don't want the whole town to see you working with me."

Boone's apparent discomfort increased. "It's not that. It's just that I'm not a goldfish-bowl kind of guy. I like to do my job quietly. As behind the scenes as I can make it. No fuss. No muss. No spectators."

"I can respect that. But can you understand that for my project here to work, I need people in town to be curious? Interested. Excited, even. What better way than for passersby to see our progress each evening? If they stop in to ask questions or chat, so much the better." Belle tapped her chin in thought. "Maybe I should even set up a coffee-maker in the corner. Just in case."

Boone groaned. "Ms. Sherman," he muttered between clenched teeth, "you are making a simple job difficult."

"Difficult for whom?" Quite frankly, in the past two or three minutes he'd brought up a couple of possibilities—quite promising possibilities—that she hadn't even considered. She'd have to tell Alice Rose that she was certainly getting her money's worth from her son.

Shaking his head, his lips a straight, hard slash in his face, Boone glanced at his watch. "I'd better get to work if I expect to accomplish anything in this fishbowl tonight." Taking out a tape measure, he knelt next to the baseboard.

"Oh, Boone?" Belle didn't know quite what mischief came over her. Maybe the devil made her do it.

"Yes?" With a tremendous sigh he stopped measuring and turned to her.

"Do you know what you're doing? Electricity wise, I mean. I know you're a contractor and all. But doesn't this job call for a master electrician?"

Boone settled back on his haunches and narrowed his eyes. "You're pulling my leg, aren't you?"

"Sort of," Belle had to admit. "But a part of me is concerned. You can't die from a bad plumbing job...but botched electrical work, now, there's a real worry."

Unexpectedly, he smiled. A rueful smile, but a smile nonetheless. "Isn't this a little late in the game to be asking about my credentials? You know, insulting me is one thing, but I think you just insulted my mama's judgment."

Golly, but his teasing grin was attractive.

Belle straightened, put her hands on her hips and matched his suddenly open gaze. "I apologize if I'm out of line. I'd just like to know if a burned-out mercantile is going to make Sweet Hope headlines any time in the near future."

"No, ma'am." Still smiling, Boone returned to his measuring. "That's how I got my start. Trade school. Electrical engineering. Right out of high school. That's how I made my first real dollar." His voice suddenly became harder. "It was only later that I tried to become a big wheel. Went back to school to learn it all." Abruptly, he changed the subject. "How about you? You always set out to fix the world? To make people sit up and take notice?"

Belle was stunned. If she didn't miss her mark, they were having a conversation. Unable to contain her smile, she bent and began removing used books from the closest box.

"As a matter of fact, no. For most of my life I've been as quiet as a mouse. And about as colorful."

Boone turned quickly to look at her. She could see the disbelief in his eyes. But, bless Alice Rose's heart, she'd raised a son with manners. He didn't say a word. For that alone he deserved an explanation.

"A year ago I had an auto accident," she began, noticing a wince of pain pass across Boone's face. "A terrible wreck. I almost didn't make it. But when I finally pulled through, I decided to do all those things I'd only ever dreamed of."

"Without a thought as to what people might think?" His voice was raspy, edged with an unexplained sorrow.

"As long as I don't break the law, or go against my conscience, or hurt anyone, I don't see where what other people might think matters. The way I see it, appearances really don't matter."

"That attitude's a luxury I can't afford," Boone declared brusquely. "I have to think of Cassie."

Belle was about to ask him what he thought his eighteen-year-old daughter needed protection from when the front door opened and in walked Amanda Best, the editor of *The Sweet Hope Gazette*.

"Belle. Boone. I was just passing and couldn't help but notice the work you two are doing."

Casting Belle a doleful look, Boone replied, "No, I suppose you couldn't help but notice."

Belle ignored his remark. "You know, Amanda, we were just talking about setting up a coffeepot. In case folks dropped in."

"Another time, dear. I was working late, and I need to get home to my family. I just wanted to speak to Boone a minute."

Boone stopped work. "What can I do for you?" After that earlier instant of sadness-tinged vulnerability, he was again all business.

"I'd like your permission to run a feature on the work you did for the tornado victims over in Cartersville."

As Boone froze, Belle cocked her head with interest.

"I don't think you've got much of a story there," Boone protested. "Stick to the plots and subplots over at the town hall."

"Boone O'Malley." Amanda crossed her arms over her chest and skewered Boone with a perplexed look. "If ever a man hid his light under a bushel, it's you. People want to read *good* news in their newspapers for a change. And what you did was good. Plain and simple."

"What did he do?" Belle asked, extremely curious now.

"Nothing," Boone snapped.

"Oh, fiddledeedee." Amanda waved a hand dismissively at the glowering Boone. "After that tornado ripped through Cartersville last month, Boone here sent a crew of roofers. He paid their wages, and offered tornado victims their services. Free. And materials at cost."

Turning his back on the women, Boone returned to work. "It was the least anyone would do," he muttered.

"It was a tremendous gift, Boone O'Malley, and you know it. But it seems as if you and I might be the only ones in Sweet Hope who know anything about it. And I think that's a shame. Even if you're modest, I think a feature story might motivate others to go out of their way to help next time, no matter what the disaster or cause."

"She's right, Boone," Belle urged. "You have an opportunity here to set a wonderful example."

Still not looking around, Boone said flatly, "I have no intention of being anyone's public example."

"Boone!" both women exclaimed.

"What's he done now?" Cassie's laughing voice rang through the storefront.

"It's what he won't do," Amanda huffed.

"Oh, maybe Grammy and I can work on him," Cassie replied. "Only don't count on it. And don't count on any progress tonight. By the set of his shoulders, I can tell you Daddy's not going to budge."

"Cassie!" The warning tone of Boone's voice was unmistakable. "What are you doing here?"

"Now that's a fine how-do-you-do for your only daughter. I'm here to bring Belle some books. A ton. In the trunk of my car."

"And I'm going home. I'll walk out with you," Amanda said. In a soft aside to Cassie, she added, "See what you can do about getting your father to let us do a feature on some of his charitable works.''

Cassie rolled her eyes. ''Come on, Belle. It'll take the two of us to unload.''

The three women walked out the door to Cassie's car parked next to the black pickup, leaving Boone inside the storefront. He was, by now, so out of sorts that he could barely focus on the wires he held in his hands. If he didn't calm down, Belle would be reading about a burned-out mercantile in *The Sweet Hope Gazette*.

Whatever she read, it wasn't going to be a feature about his *charitable works*. Lord, how he hated folks who tooted their own horns. He took a deep breath and concentrated on the work in front of him.

He didn't even look up as Cassie and Belle made numerous trips from Cassie's car to the growing stack of books in the center of the floor. Damn. He'd known Belle's goldfish-bowl approach to renovating the storefront was going to bring nothing but unwanted attention. He hated attention. And he hated getting railroaded into doing things against his will. Like that newspaper feature. Just let Alice Rose get wind of it and he'd never hear the end.

Working in Belle's storefront for an evening was going to be just swell. He was going to be on display. Why, he wouldn't put it past Buster McCabe to see him and drop by to try to convince him to build that topless bar out on Route 41. The work he'd already turned down a dozen times before.

Arabella Sherman might not care about what people thought of her or her actions, but at the same time she should give a little thought to the consequences of those actions. Damned fishbowl project.

''Daddy!''

Startled, Boone looked up to see Cassie, a stack of books in her arms, standing over him. He stood and looked around the storefront. Belle was busy unloading boxes.

''Yes?''

"I've come to tell you good-night. I'm spending the night with a friend who has an apartment near campus. We're going to study together for tomorrow's sociology exam."

Boone clenched his teeth and felt the muscles in his jaw tighten. Cassie knew how he hated her driving on the inter-state after dark. She knew how he hated these sleep-overs at friends' apartments. She knew it, and she did it anyway. He opened his mouth to object, then thought better of it. Cassie was of age and a great kid. She needed to know that he trusted her good judgment.

"This is the last load of books," she said, indicating the pile in her arms. "I need to get going or we'll have to pull an all-nighter."

"Drive safely, honey," Boone said. It was the only thing he could find to say in light of his reluctance to let her go.

As Cassie stood on tiptoe to kiss him, the pile of books tipped and slid to the floor, pulling the strap of her purse. Books, purse and the contents thereof slid across the old hardwood floor. Before Cassie could retrieve her belongings, Boone saw several familiar square foil packets amid the tissues, change and cosmetics.

The blood began to pound in his temples as he stooped to pick up a packet.

Cassie quickly retrieved the packet before he could grasp it, then said softly, "Now, don't have a cow, Daddy."

"Cassie O'Malley," he asked with rising dread, "what is the meaning of this?"

"It means I'm prepared," she answered defiantly.

"I think you ought to skip that friend's apartment to-night." He looked at Belle, who seemed overly intent on her books. "We have things to discuss. At home. In private."

Dear God, he'd hoped this day would never come. It wasn't as if he hadn't discussed the facts of life with his daughter. He had. Ever since she was small, he'd discussed life openly and had answered her questions as honestly as he knew how. It wasn't her knowledge of the facts that upset him. It was the idea that maybe his baby was putting those facts into practice. He wanted to stop the world for just a few minutes. He wanted the two of them to get off. He wanted to beg her to be cautious. To follow her head as well as her heart and hormones. He wanted to talk to her again about the pitfalls of sexual experimentation as well as the joys.

For God's sake, this was his little girl. He wanted nothing more than to protect her from harm.

"Daddy," Cassie said evenly, scooping the spilled contents back into her purse, "there is nothing more to discuss. I'm eighteen. You just have to trust me."

"Trust you!" Boone bellowed. Out of the corner of his eye he saw Belle's head snap up. He immediately lowered his voice. "Trust you when I find *these* in your purse?"

"You act as if I'm hiding something from you. I'm not. And the fact that I have *these,* as you so quaintly refer to them, in my purse is no indication that I'm using them. It's proof that I'm prepared. That I'm thinking. Would you rather I went through life unprepared?"

"I'd rather—"

"I know what you'd rather," Cassie shouted, tears welling in her eyes. "You'd rather I stayed your little girl forever. Under your protection. Never changing. Just the way you'd like to preserve everything and everyone in this town. In your life. That way you don't have to admit that life goes on. That way you don't have to *live.*"

"Cassie, that's enough!"

"Yes, that's enough. I'm out of here."

"Cassie!"

His daughter whirled about, then slammed out the front door in a storm of eighteen-year-old righteous indignation.

Dear God, she was driving on that interstate angry, and he hadn't even had the chance to tell her he loved her. Watch over her, he silently prayed, even if she doesn't want me to.

He inhaled sharply as he felt Belle's hand on his arm.

"I'm sorry you had to see that," he muttered, turning to resume his work.

"I don't think you're in any shape to finish up here tonight," Belle said softly. "Let me get us a couple cold drinks, and we can talk about it, if you like."

"No." He would not like.

He looked at the woman standing before him, her hair tied up in a hot pink kerchief, big, dangly, gold earrings bobbing at her neck, shorts too short for a thirty-three-year-old "businesswoman," and an oversize man's shirt that came from who knew where. No, there was nothing he wished to discuss with this woman about raising a daughter.

"I know I don't have children," Belle persisted, "but I know what I see."

"Which is?" He wished she'd remove her hand from where it burned a brand on his arm.

"I see a young woman struggling for her own identity. Apart from that of her very strong father." Instead of removing her hand, she applied pressure so that he turned slightly and faced her. Faced her and stared into those earth brown eyes that begged him to spill his guts to her.

Well, he wasn't about to spill his guts to Arabella Sherman. What went on between him and Cassie was *private*. No talk-show circuit for Boone O'Malley and his daughter.

"And just how is that observation supposed to help matters?" he asked, not attempting to disguise the sarcasm in his tone.

Belle shrugged and removed her hand from his arm. "Understanding what's going on is the first step in problem solving."

"Now, that's profound. That little bit of wisdom will certainly make me feel better about my daughter having sex with some big man on campus."

"You don't know that she is. But I'll tell you one thing— yelling at her, treating her like a child, will drive her to do just the opposite of what you want. Now, *that's* childish."

Boone threw his arms into the air. "Why am I even discussing this with you?" He wanted to ask, why am I discussing things childish with a woman who wears a Little Mermaid watch? But he bit his tongue and didn't.

Stepping in front of him, Belle reached up and touched his cheek with one hand. As much as her touch jolted him, her gaze disturbed him more. It was a burning look that said she could see right down to the bottom of his soul.

Her words only added fuel to the fire. "Because you're a loving father, and you're afraid."

This time Boone didn't wait for her to remove her hand. He reached up and removed it himself. And then he stepped away. Away from her intimate touch. Away from her too-knowing eyes. Away from words that left him vulnerable.

"You're crazy," he muttered as he began to gather his tools. "What am I afraid of?"

"Of losing your daughter," Belle replied softly.

"You can bet I'll do my damnedest not to."

"You won't lose her if you don't push her away."

That was it. He'd had enough. "Lady," he said, "we've just met. I agreed to do some work for you. But that does not entitle you to offer advice on the way I choose to run my life. You may like your business in a goldfish bowl, but I don't. So if you want this storefront up and running, I suggest we stick to discussing electrical fixtures and paint colors."

He glowered at Belle, who stood before him uncowed. In fact, her eyes seemed to flash with an even greater intensity. Somehow he didn't think that, as long as they breathed the same air, they would ever stick to the subject of electrical fixtures and paint colors.

He grabbed the last of his tools and stormed out to his pickup.

Boone ran around the corner onto Main Street. His own street, Oak, was only two blocks over. After leaving Belle's storefront earlier that evening, he'd had every intention of falling into bed. Into a deep and mind-deadening sleep. But now it was eleven-thirty, and rest eluded him. With Cassie gone for the night, the little bungalow seemed empty and huge. Even if Cassie were home, he doubted he'd be able to get any peace. Arabella Sherman and her all-too-public Ms. Fix-It attitude had his insides churning. Maybe a run would obliterate the memory of the well-intentioned Ms. Sherman. Would wear him out enough to sleep later. It sure couldn't hurt.

As he jogged past the wrought-iron entrance to the green, he heard voices raised in argument. One male. One female. The male sounded drunk. A touchy situation. It wouldn't hurt to jog across the green, just to make sure no one was in trouble. He saw a police cruiser parked at the far end of the green. He didn't have to be a hero. He'd just make sure everything was copacetic.

Under a lamp near the bandstand, right across from Belle's storefront, Boone could see a man and a woman apparently struggling over possession of a large, cowering dog. The man was obviously staggering drunk. And the woman was dressed in what looked like pajamas and bunny slippers.

Boone didn't need a closer look to know who the woman was.

Arabella Sherman.

He stopped dead in his tracks. "Sweet Lord," he intoned, "just tell me she's not standing out in the middle of the green in her nightclothes."

He watched as Belle gained control of the dog's collar. "Eban Smart," she said clear as day, "drunk or not, you have no right to abuse this dog."

"You ain't seen nothin'."

"I saw you from my bedroom window. Saw you strike and kick this poor creature."

"Ain't none of your business," Eban slurred as he lunged for the dog's collar. "'S my dog."

"Not anymore," Belle retorted, turning with the dog to walk toward her storefront. "You want him back, you see me in small claims court, Mr. Smart."

"Why, you meddlin' little bitch." Eban lunged again and this time caught Belle's pajama sleeve.

That was all it took to galvanize Boone. Sprinting the distance between them, he bellowed, "Smart! Get your hands off her!"

Eban whirled drunkenly around at the sound of Boone's voice. Obviously he wasn't the only one to respond to the shout. A pair of police officers jogged briskly across the green toward the odd threesome.

Boone groaned as he slowed and stepped between Eban and Belle. Just his cup of tea. A solitary nighttime run, interrupted by Arabella Sherman and another of her very public causes. And as if this confrontation weren't enough, the movie house began to let out the late-show crowd. A couple of dozen Sweet Hope residents slowed to a snail's pace outside the theater to see what the to-do on the green was all about.

Fortunately, the police officers didn't even need to ask what was going on. One of them wrapped an arm about Eban and pulled him toward the squad car. "Come on, Smart," he said. "You can sleep it off in the station. Again. You're in luck. We're having pancakes for breakfast."

Their departure left Boone with Belle, in pink satin pajamas and fuzzy bunny slippers, and a very forlorn, obviously flea-bitten mutt. Not to mention a ring of curious onlookers.

"Come on," Boone commanded none too gently. "Let's get you out of the lamplight." Limelight was closer to the truth, he thought regretfully.

"Why, thank you, sir," she replied with a sweet smile, taking his arm as if he were escorting her to a cotillion. "What do you think I should name my new dog?"

"I think you have more pressing matters to think about," Boone hissed under his breath as they walked across Main Street under the amused stares of their neighbors. "Like how to keep the news of this little caper from spreading through the county."

"Oh, nonsense," Belle hissed back. "Just pretend we're out for an evening stroll." And then to Boone's horror she began greeting people. "Ms. Jenkins, hello! Dr. Upshard.

Mrs. Upshard. Hello! Hello! Miss Echols, how did you enjoy that movie? Is that so? Well, I'll just have to see it for myself."

Damn. Was the woman stark raving mad? He felt as if he was in a retelling of *The Emperor's New Clothes*. When they reached the door, at the side of the storefront, that led to Belle's apartment, he was never so glad to touch a doorknob in his life. He nearly pulled it from its frame in his attempt to open it and thrust the unsuitably clad Belle and her moth-eaten hound into the tiny inner entryway.

In the cramped space, pressed against Belle much more closely than he could have wished for, Boone felt suddenly at a loss for words. He looked down at her, at the now gaping, V-shaped opening to her pajama top, and spotted a tiny rose tattoo just at the beginning swell of her left breast. Hadn't that thing been on her ankle just days ago? Or did she have a bouquet sprinkled all over her body? The thought made the corner of his mouth twitch involuntarily.

"Well, now," Belle said brightly, "that's what I call an eventful evening."

It wasn't exactly what Boone would call it. "What are you planning to do with the dog?" he finally managed to ask.

Wrinkling her nose, she answered, "I can't very well invite him upstairs until he's had a bath. And it's a little late for that. I suppose we could make him comfortable in the basement until tomorrow morning."

There was that *we* again. He'd had no intention of staying longer than was necessary to see Belle safely to her door. But he had a sinking feeling he was about to help make this sorry-looking animal comfortable for the night.

"Would you mind taking him down in the basement while I rummage around in the fridge for something to feed him? I think Eban Smart starved him as well as abused him."

She turned her face to him with such a look of outraged concern that he would have had to be a cad to decline her request. He reached down and grasped the dog's collar. "Where's the basement light switch?" he asked in resignation.

\* \* \*

Belle stopped at the head of the basement stairs to watch Boone with the dog below. She'd found some raw hamburger in her refrigerator and had mixed it with an egg and some Cheerios. Cholesterol city. But a dog that scrawny couldn't complain. It didn't seem to be complaining now as Boone gently settled it onto a pallet of clean rags. A man, even a prickly man, couldn't be all bad if he was kind to strays.

Clearing her throat to let him know she was coming, she descended the stairs.

She put the bowl with the meat mixture in front of the dog, gratified to see the creature tuck in to its supper with gusto.

"What a shame," she said, "that anyone would mistreat a dog."

"I agree," Boone replied, standing beside her. "But what you did runs against rural tradition."

"What are you talking about?" She stared at Boone in amazement.

"I'm not saying it's right or wrong, but messing with a Southern man's dog is akin to cattle rustling in the Old West."

"You can't be serious, Boone O'Malley." She couldn't read the closed expression on his face, and she couldn't understand why this man always *sort of* agreed with her while at the same time the general tone of his comments made her feel as if he thought she'd made a major blunder. "Eban Smart abused this animal. It's obvious," she said stiffly.

"Then you should have reported it through proper channels. Instead of playing vigilante . . . in pajamas and bunny slippers."

Belle bristled. "So that's it. It's not what I did but how I was dressed when I did it that bothers you. I was preparing for bed when I noticed the problem. Would you have preferred this poor thing sustained further injuries while I took the time to dress for the occasion?"

A lopsided grin emerging across his features, Boone held up his hands in mock surrender. "Ms. Sherman, I've had an eventful day. I don't plan to end it with an argument with you. I'm just telling you that you'd better be prepared to meet Smart in small claims court."

Stooping to pick up the now-empty bowl, Belle petted the tail-wagging dog until it settled once again on the pallet of rags. "I'm prepared," she said quietly, more to the dog than to Boone. "Don't you worry. I'm prepared."

"Well, then, I'd better get along. He'll be fine down here till you can bathe him tomorrow."

Belle stood and followed Boone up the stairs.

At the top of the stairs in the tiny entryway, she held out her hand and touched his arm. There was something she had to know.

"You don't like me much, do you?" she asked without preamble. The new Belle had discovered the direct approach was often the most illuminating.

"Arabella," he admonished, the sound of her name on his lips sending little shivers through her body, "you are a kindhearted woman. And that's a compliment. But the way you go about things is not the way I go about things."

"The way I go about things upsets you?"

He had that backed-into-a-corner look on his face that Belle had seen before. "It drives me crazy," he admitted, pinching his eyebrows together in a pained expression.

"But that doesn't mean you dislike me, does it?" She told herself the question came of curiosity and nothing more.

A look that was definitely not pain flitted across his features. "No. That doesn't mean I dislike you," he said softly, almost reluctantly.

Belle smiled. "Good. Because I like you, Boone O'Malley, even if you are the prickliest man I've ever run across. I'm grateful that you accepted Alice Rose's barter on my storefront. And grateful for your help tonight."

Quickly, before he could protest, she stood on tiptoe and kissed his cheek. "Thank you," she murmured against his skin.

With a motion that startled her, he turned his head.

Suddenly she felt his lips upon hers. Suddenly she felt his arms around her. Felt herself pulled up hard against him. Suddenly her pulse pounded wildly and her blood thrummed red-hot. Suddenly she felt more than like for Boone O'Malley. Felt, instead, raw physical desire. Suddenly. Far too suddenly.

He groaned as his tongue swept her mouth. Opening for him, she felt awash in primal sensations. She felt alive. Her body throbbed with the rhythm of drums. His tongue, mating with hers, set her soul to singing. Sakes alive, if this man's kiss could do this to her...

She couldn't think. She could barely breathe. She could only feel.

He ran his hands down her back and over her bottom. The feel of his touch through the satin of her pajamas set her skin afire. She felt her limbs begin to melt. She half closed her eyes.

As quickly as he'd pulled her to him, he pulled away, holding her shoulders with his strong, long-fingered hands.

"Arabella." His voice husky and almost angry, he shook her gently. "I'm sorry. That was a mistake. This is crazy. And I can't afford to be crazy. Maybe you can, but I can't."

A spark of anger flared in Belle. For him, she felt certain, it wasn't a matter of *can't,* but *won't.* It didn't matter, however. She was not going to struggle against a man's reluctance. She'd done that once before and had almost lost her self-esteem. She was no schoolgirl, for whom a passionate kiss meant forever-after. She would survive. Without Mr. O'Malley.

"I don't recall asking you to go crazy," she said evenly, looking him right in the eye.

"Fine." He dropped his hands from her shoulders. "Just as long as we each understand."

"Understand?"

"That we're oil and water, Arabella Sherman. That's a fact and there's no changing it."

Belle jutted out her chin defiantly, willing the still-shimmering shadow of his touch to disappear. "You make us sound like salad ingredients, Boone O'Malley. Not a very flattering image, I must say."

Shaking his head, Boone actually chuckled. "What can I say? My mama raised a silver-tongued devil."

As he turned to go, Belle asked, "Will you still work on my storefront?"

"Why wouldn't I? I gave you my word." Boone looked a little surprised. "I'll see you tomorrow evening."

With that he walked out the door, leaving Belle in deep thought. Pity, she mused. Your word is about the only thing you're willing to give. And—just for curiosity's sake, mind you—I'd like to find out why that's so.

## Chapter Four

Thinking about last night's kiss, Boone sat in brooding silence in his usual booth in the Hole-in-the-Wall Café, and toyed with the eggs and grits on his plate. Actually, after last night's show on the green, he'd toyed with the idea of not showing up for breakfast. But he was a regular at the Hole-in-the-Wall, and his absence would have been more noticeable than his presence. He'd come in this morning, however, dreading the side glances and remarks that were sure to come his way.

Funny, though. For the past half hour he hadn't even noticed if he was being noticed. His mind was all on that kiss. Ridiculous, that's what it was. Putting so much thought and energy into something that had been a natural reaction. What red-blooded male wouldn't have kissed a woman who'd kissed him first? In the past six years he'd kissed his share of women without lasting ado. The thing that galled him right now was how the memory of last night's kiss stayed with him. Maybe the memory was so strong because he found it a total surprise that he'd had that natural reaction to Arabella Sherman, of all people. Maybe it was because he'd never kissed a woman who sported rose tattoos and satin pajamas in public and who still managed to appear angelic. Innocent, even. Maybe it was those damned bunny slippers. And that was the crux of the matter: that he could be so moved by a woman who was so obviously wrong for him.

"Coffee, sugah?" Edna, the café's veteran waitress stood over him, coffeepot poised for action. "You sure do look as if you could use it. A working man like you, Boone O'Malley, should know better than to keep those late hours." Pouring Boone's second cup, Edna grinned broadly and winked in an exaggerated manner.

"Don't mess with me, Edna." Boone narrowed his eyes. It was going to be a long day.

"Pooh. What fun are you when I can't even get a rise out of you?" Edna turned to attend to her other customers just as Sam Shaw came up to Boone's booth.

"Mornin', Boone."

"Mornin', Sam," Boone mumbled.

Sam didn't make a move to sit or leave.

Boone squinted up at him. "Anything I can do for you, Sam?" He hoped it was nothing complicated. He couldn't handle complicated right now.

"Could you find the time to come out and talk to Old Zach? He's giving me a hard time about our boundary line again."

Boone breathed a sigh of relief. He could handle this. Old Zach had grown a little senile. During his worst times, he would accuse his neighbors of stealing his land. Boone didn't know why, but he seemed to be the only one in town who could reassure Old Zach that wasn't the case. Yeah, he could handle this with his eyes closed. Later, after a transfusion's worth of coffee.

"Sure," he agreed. "Get the deeds in order, and I'll be by sometime late this afternoon."

Sam grinned as he turned to go. "It'd save me and my neighbors a heap of trouble if you'd let us in on your secret to handling the cantankerous sort." He chuckled. "Maybe you could bottle it. Save you a lot of time."

Harrumphing, Boone returned to his sour examination of the dregs in his coffee cup. Sure, bottle it, and he could use some on himself. Lord, did he feel cantankerous.

His longtime friend Ray Clark slid into the booth opposite Boone. "Don't try to talk to him, Ray," Edna admonished as she plunked a cup of coffee before her newest customer. "He's as snappy as a cornered opossum."

Ray grinned. "It wouldn't have anything to do with the talk going around town, now, would it?"

Boone rolled his eyes. "Some day I'm going to fold my tent and head out for some nice, big anonymous city. Some place where the only thing people talk about is my reputation as an honest, hardworking contractor."

"How dull." Ray's grin widened. "Those of us who know you would much rather talk about you maneuvering that great fair catch when Belle Sherman dove off the ladder...."

Boone groaned. "People are still talking about *that?*"

"That and the pajama party with Eban Smart."

"Did anyone stop to mention that neither Smart nor I was wearing pajamas? That *we* were fully clothed?"

"Nope. Must have slipped their attention. But rumor has it that one of you was three sheets to the wind. Now, that wouldn't have been you, would it?"

"Right." Boone grimaced. "Smart was sober for a change."

Ray chuckled. "Lighten up, good buddy. Folks are saying that you're finally coming round to rejoining the human race."

Amplifying his grimace with a scowl, Boone retorted, "I never left it. If you hadn't noticed, I'm a productive member of this community. Have been and probably will be till I die."

Ray's expression suddenly became serious. "That's not what I'm talking about, and you know it. When was the last time you kicked up your heels? When was the last time you thought about getting back into circulation? About jump-starting your life?''

"I have a life. I also have a lot of responsibilities. I can't afford to sit around and focus on me."

"What responsibilities? Cassie's grown. Alice Rose is doing just fine on her own. And Peg..." Ray's voice softened. "Boone, Peg's been gone six years now. Six years."

If Ray Clark hadn't been his best friend *and* his wife's brother, Boone might have hit him. At least told him to mind his damn business. The pain was that bad. Even after six years, the sound of his wife's name brought back the pain. And the guilt. He looked across the table at Ray. It always surprised him to see the absence of blame in his friend's face. Instead, he saw concern.

He took a deep breath in order to control his response. "What are you asking me to do, Ray? Make a fool of myself in public just so folks can see I'm fine? Because I am. I'm just fine."

"Then there's nothing holding you back from asking Belle Sherman out, now, is there?"

Nothing, except for the fact that Boone didn't want to hook up with anyone, let alone the town's most visible newcomer.

He forced a grin. "Ray, just because, after eighteen years of marriage, you're still acting like a newlywed doesn't mean the whole world needs to pair off. Some of us are happy just as we are. Single working stiffs. Enjoying our families. Occasionally seeing friends. Helping out in the community."

"Which leads me to the school board meeting tonight," Ray interrupted. "You planning to go?"

"Not really." He'd promised Belle he'd meet her at her storefront to continue the electrical work. "What's going on?"

Ray shook his head. "Aw, the kids are agitating for open campus again. Seems the upperclassmen think they should come and go as they please. Lord, most of them have licenses and cars. Can you imagine whereall they'll be instead of school? Boggles the mind."

"You going?" Boone asked, knowing Ray would. His friend·had a seventeen-year-old junior.

"Oh, yeah. You couldn't keep me away. Why don't you come, too? If things get hot, we might need the voice of reason."

"Not a chance. When Cassie graduated, my days at the high school were over. It's a matter for the kids and parents directly involved. I have other things to worry about." He thought about Cassie spending more and more nights at friends' apartments. About her liberated attitude toward sexual preparedness. Let other parents handle their kids. He had his hands full with his own.

Rising from the table, Boone said, "I have to get going. Have to check with my site managers, but first I have to pick up Manuel Navarro at the hardware store."

"Manuel? He working for you now?"

"No. Just helping out. More and more, the day laborers we get speak only Spanish. None of my managers are bilingual. Looks like I might be heading back to night school to pick up a second language. Otherwise, Manuel will get behind running his own business, acting as translator for me."

"I can't convince you to come with me to the school board meeting?"

"Not a chance. Actually, I'm working tonight, so I couldn't if I wanted to."

"At Belle's storefront?"

Boone groaned. "Does *everyone* know I'm helping out there?"

"'Bout now, everyone," Ray replied, smiling broadly. He cocked one eyebrow. "Well, I can't say as I blame you for skipping an old school board meeting to work with Belle Sherman." He chuckled. "She's some woman, Boone. Why, a woman like that could keep a man on his toes for a long, long time. Having fun. Enjoying life. Trying new things...."

Ignoring the bait, Boone shook his head. "Goodbye, Ray. If you can see your way to keeping that mouth of yours shut, maybe we can take a day off soon for some bass fishing.''

Boone tossed a tip on the table, paid at the cash register, then stepped outside into the early-morning sunshine. A funny thought hit him as he slid behind the wheel of his truck: despite his protestations inside, he was actually looking forward to working on Belle's storefront tonight. He sure hoped that surprising attitude had nothing to do with last night's kiss.

With Manuel in the passenger's seat, Boone pulled off Flat Shoals Road onto the site of the huge Victorian replica under construction. He didn't see his manager's truck. And instead of the usual activity of journeymen and day laborers, he saw only a knot of day laborers engaged in animated conversation around a vintage VW convertible.

He pulled his truck next to the group. When he cut the engine, he could hear the babble of Spanish punctuated by the tinkling of bells.

Dear God, tell him it wasn't so. Not here. Not at work, too.

Jumping out of the truck, he saw his worst fears materialize. From the back seat of the open convertible Belle dispensed coffee and doughnuts and brightly colored leaflets, which the workers examined with interest.

Boone groaned. What was she up to now?

"Manuel," he said, trying to keep his temper under control, "please tell the men the coffee break's over. I'll try to get to the bottom of this with Ms. Sherman."

As Manuel plowed into the knot of workers, Belle looked up and caught Boone's eye. She actually had the good grace to look faintly guilty.

Belle took a deep breath. Boone sure didn't look happy to see her. She'd suspected he wouldn't want anyone other than the construction crew or prospective buyers on any of his sites. That's why she'd planned to be out here early and gone before he came to make his inspections. And she'd have been all right if she hadn't gone out of her way to the wrong house. She'd remembered him saying he was working on a big Victorian replica on something-Shoals Road. She hadn't remembered the road name, but she'd remembered passing a huge Victorian on Earnest Shoals. She'd gone there, only to find that house—a mausoleum if there ever was one—finished and occupied. And now she found herself behind schedule and pinned under the disapproving gaze of the boss man.

"Morning," she offered hopefully.

As Manuel Navarro moved the workers back to their jobs, Boone approached the VW, either not hearing or ignoring her greeting.

"What are you doing?" he asked, his words clipped, the tone faintly threatening.

Belle swallowed. Where was the man who'd kissed her last night? She didn't see a shred of him in the deadly serious man who now approached her.

"I had an idea," she began. "Last night after you left." She wasn't about to tell him his kiss had kept her awake and up half the night. Had kept her thumbing through a week's worth of previously unread newspapers, trying to relax enough to fall asleep.

Boone now stood before her, his legs spread, his hands planted on his hips, his body language all impatience. "What does this idea have to do with my workers?"

The sooner she spit it out, the sooner he'd understand and maybe stop scowling. She plunged ahead. "Plenty. I was reading where thirty percent of Americans now speak Spanish. And that the metro Atlanta area has become a magnet for Hispanics, many of whom speak little English."

"And you plan to rectify that." His words were a statement. Flat and cold.

"Why, yes, I do." She was disappointed his impatient expression didn't relax with her explanation. "I'm planning to run a literacy center. I think, up till now, I've entertained a very narrow definition of literacy. Why couldn't it include the concept of English as a second language? I know contractors in the area have begun to hire more and more Hispanic day laborers. Why not start with them?''

"It's an excellent idea." If it was so excellent, why did he look exasperated? Why did he sound as if he were keeping his temper in check? "But, as usual, your execution's misguided. If you're going to recruit, don't disrupt my work sites to do it. If you have something to pass out, give it to me. And I'll give it to my site managers to distribute. There's a right way and a wrong way of doing things, Arabella. And the wrong way could be downright disruptive and dangerous." Handsome and virile as he was, he sounded like a cranky old schoolmarm. "I see you don't have a hard hat," he continued. "This is a hard hat site."

"I'm sorry." She really was. She'd never intended to be a pest, even if she didn't agree there was only one way of doing things. "It won't happen again. It wouldn't have happened today except that I got behind schedule when I went out to that Victorian on Earnest Shoals Road. You know the one? Did you build that one, too?" Maybe interest in his work would smooth his ruffled feathers.

Instead of relaxing, suddenly Boone tightened all over. His fingertips clenched, pressing hard into the hip fabric of his jeans. The blue of his eyes turned to a flat and steely gray as if an opaque curtain had been drawn over the window to his soul. The muscles in his jaw tensed, and his words came out taut and pained.

"No," he answered, "that house isn't one of mine. I don't build on Earnest Shoals Road."

And why not? Belle wondered, but his that's-the-end-of-that tone of voice kept her from asking aloud. Instead, she reached for the sheaf of papers she'd printed up on her computer in the wee hours of the morning.

"Here," she said, her tone of voice more brusque than she intended. "This is the information—in Spanish—about the literacy center. I would hope you'd make it available to your workers."

"Of course. I'm not Simon Legree." He took the papers, his fingers brushing hers for a fleeting second, reminding her that there was indeed warmth in this man.

"I never implied you were," Belle insisted softly. She was beginning to suspect that Boone O'Malley was not so much hard on others as he was terribly hard on himself. But why? What events had molded him into this obstinate man?

It was interesting to see how different people responded to the twists and turns of life. Some people—like herself—met adversity and, because of it, determined to open up. Others shut down. She suspected something or someone had caused Boone to shut down. A pity. Because she found herself more and more drawn to this man who showed occasional and quickly retracted glimpses of tenderness. But more than that, she'd never been able to stand by and do nothing while another living creature experienced pain. And her instincts told her Boone O'Malley was in pain.

Belle took a deep breath. As much as she wanted to help, she knew from experience that pushing would only make matters worse. The best thing to do under the circumstances was to make as graceful a retreat as possible. And wait for a future opportunity to get the reluctant Mr. O'Malley to open up.

"Well," she said finally, "I'd better leave you to your work. I want to paint the wall you finished last night. No use promoting a center that won't be operational in the near future."

Boone didn't speak or alter his stance. Silently he glared at her as she started the old VW. Pulling off the site, she could see him in her rearview mirror, hands on hips, scowling after her as if he wanted to make certain she did indeed leave. For good.

Instead of feeling put out by this man's perennial prickliness, Belle's parting thought was that no human being should be so tied up in knots. She felt herself drawn to discover the source of Boone O'Malley's pain. Perhaps, just perhaps, from her own experience she could show him how to ease it.

* * *

Gathering the paint brushes for cleaning, Belle cast a satisfied glance over the storefront wall she'd just finished painting. Gracious, how a coat of paint brightened this old mercantile. A little shiver of anticipation ran through her. Her dream—a little oasis of culture and literacy right here in Sweet Hope—was unfolding before her very eyes. She couldn't wait for Boone to add to the progress tonight.

The sound of the front door opening jolted her out of her thoughts. She looked up to see Cassie standing in a butterscotch puddle of late-afternoon sunshine. The young woman seemed hesitant to step farther into the room.

"Hey, Cassie! How'd the exam go? Sociology, wasn't it?"

A dazzling smile spread across Cassie's face. "You remembered." She seemed pleased at that little fact. "It went okay. I'm glad we put in the study time. Are you busy, or could we talk?"

"Come on in. I was just about to quit and get something cold to drink. In fact, while I wash up these brushes, you could run upstairs and get us a couple Cokes out of the fridge. You can bring Sebastian down with you. I know he's lonely, but it took me all morning to get him cleaned up. I didn't want him galumphing around down here with open paint cans. I should have everything put away in a sec, though."

"Who's Sebastian?"

"My new dog. Your dad helped me rescue him last night around midnight."

Cassie raised a speculative eyebrow. "Daddy?"

"I'm not sure he was a willing participant, but the end result's the same. I'll tell you all about it when you get back...oh, yes, you have to go outside and up the apartment entrance. Maybe someday I'll have your dad build an inside stairway. When I can think of something to barter in return."

Shaking her head, Cassie left Belle, who silently amended her promise. She didn't think she'd tell Cassie *all*. She probably should keep quiet about that kiss.

In no time, Belle had washed the brushes at the sink behind the counter. She'd just finished putting the last lid on the last paint can when a giant ball of furry exuberance hurled itself at her, toppling her smack on her fanny in the middle of the floor. She heard the skitter of bells across the hardwood.

"Sebastian! Get off me, you big oaf!" Belle laughed as she warded off the dog's happy kisses. "Gracious! There's nothing worse than canine halitosis." Clambering to her feet, she warned him, "If you don't learn some manners, I can unsave you just as readily as I saved you." She softened her words with an affectionate scratch behind his ears.

Laughing, Cassie scurried about, picking up several tiny silver bells that had come loose in the reunion. She stood and held them out to Belle. "What are these?" she asked.

"Oh, those. I sew them on all my undies. They keep me company." She chuckled. "But now I have Sebastian for company. Maybe I should hang the bells that came loose on the front door so I'm not surprised when people—or dogs—come in." Sebastian flopped down at her feet and looked up at her with adoring eyes. "Oh, dear. I've never owned a dog. What am I going to do with you?"

"Ask Daddy," Cassie offered. "We always have several. Beagles. Very well behaved." She smiled. "Of course, they would be if Daddy raised them. Grammy keeps them out at her place. I'm sure Daddy could give you some pointers on training ole Sebbie here."

"I'm not so sure. As far as your father's concerned, I rustled this dog, and he won't stay mine when Eban Smart takes me to court."

Pulling up a couple of crates and the cans of Coke forgotten in the scuffle, Cassie said, "This I gotta hear."

Belle launched into the story of last night's incident on the green, delighted to find someone from the O'Malley family who found it amusing rather than embarrassing. When she'd finished, she looked at Cassie and asked, "So, do you think my reputation's besmirched?"

Cassie flashed her a brilliant smile. "I think this town has needed someone like you, Belle Sherman. To shake it up and air out the stuffiness. Lord, how I hate the sanctimonious stuffiness. And I hate watching Daddy, year after year, become more a part of it."

Belle saw an opening, and she didn't hesitate to use it. "Are you saying that your father wasn't always so... cautious?"

"Cautious! Now, that's a mannerly way of putting it. You can say it, Belle. He's an old fuddy-duddy. At thirty-eight. And, no, he wasn't always so closed off."

Belle held her breath and waited in silence for Cassie to continue.

The young woman cast her a glance that was filled with pain. "I remember him before Mama died. He was so full of fun and new ideas. But all that changed after the wreck. After she died. I truly think Daddy blames himself for her death."

"The wreck?" Belle didn't understand.

"Six years ago Mama and Daddy were in a car wreck one rainy night as they were heading out to inspect the house Daddy was building for us. Daddy made it...." Cassie paused and took a deep breath, her eyes welling with tears. "Mama didn't." She finished so softly her words were almost inaudible.

Belle's heart flooded with a painful sympathy. Remembering how Boone had winced when she'd told him of her own auto accident, she reached out her hand and laid it over Cassie's. "I'm sorry," she said simply. "I'm truly sorry." She wished she had more to say, but more would only ring hollow.

Cassie turned her hand over and twined her fingers through Belle's. "The pain's bad enough when you lose your mother," she said, "but it only increases when you helplessly watch your father torture himself."

"I know," Belle agreed.

"You do? How could you know?"

"My mother died when I was seven. I barely remember anything about her except some old photos. What I do remember is how my father struggled to be a good father to my brother Rhune and me. Struggled because he really did love us. Really did want the best for us. But the light had gone out of his life. Extinguished. And he never—not even before he, too, died just a few years ago—found the flame to rekindle it. I always prayed that he would find it. Would find someone to help him relight it. But he didn't. What a waste."

"Yes," Cassie whispered, squeezing Belle's hand, "that's it. That's exactly how I feel. Daddy would give me the world if I asked. I just wish he could show me he's happy deep down inside."

Belle sighed, fearing she had presented too gloomy a picture. Squeezing Cassie's hand in return, she replied, "Something tells me your father will not waste his life."

"Do you really think that's true?"

"Yes, I do. I see a spark in your father. He may try to stamp it out when it springs to life, but it comes again and again. When he least expects it." She smiled. Dead men didn't kiss the way Boone O'Malley had kissed her last night. Oh, no. His spirit was not totally buried. Only healing. And Belle would love to be there when it sprang to life again.

"I hope you're right." Cassie dabbed at a tear that had spilled down her cheek. "Well, one thing's for certain. Grammy and I are glad Daddy's working with you on your storefront. You seem so full of life. So happy. We're hoping some of your happiness will rub off on him. It'll do him good."

"Or drive him crazy," Belle added.

Cassie chuckled. "That'll be good for him, too." She reached down to pet Sebastian, who slept restlessly at Belle's feet. "You know, I didn't come in here with the intention of baring my soul to you. I came in to see if you wanted to go to the school board meeting with me tonight."

"The school board meeting? Why do you want to go?"

"Call it a pet concern of mine—Daddy would surely call it meddling. The kids at high school have finally gotten the board to listen to them tonight. The upperclassmen want an open campus. I say go for it. I wish I'd had such a program. How can high schoolers become adults if they're always treated as children? Given no independence. Allowed to make no decisions for themselves." Cassie's look begged Belle's understanding. "I'm not sure they'll make any progress tonight, but the fact that the board's agreed to listen is a big step. I'm only one year removed from those kids. Some of them are my friends. They deserve my support."

"You're a strong woman, Cassie O'Malley, to stand up for what you believe in, even if it's not a popular belief."

Cassie grinned sheepishly. "Don't make me out to be too altruistic. The truth is, I'm a freshman in college, and people—my father included—still want to treat me like a child. I thought maybe if I attended tonight's meeting as a concerned citizen, I might show these people that I'm serious about being treated as an adult. You know, involved in the democratic process and all. Speaking my mind through the proper channels."

"And what about your father?"

"I didn't even ask Daddy to go. His opinion and mine would surely cancel each other. And Grammy won't leave her cat that's about to have kittens." She took a deep breath. "So I naturally thought of you."

"Naturally?" Belle didn't know what to think of Cassie's sudden openness with her. She was sure of one thing—Boone O'Malley hadn't seemed crazy about her friendship with his mother. He sure as heck wasn't going to be thrilled about her befriending his daughter, as well.

"Yes. You seem like such a strong, free spirit. Like the kind of person who would think kids can handle more independence."

"I do." Her own had been so hard won.

"And you seem to be a person who's not afraid to speak her mind."

"I'm not. Although your father will say I have no kids of my own, and therefore have no business appearing at a board meeting concerned with high school kids."

"We both know what Daddy will say," Cassie replied ruefully. "What do *you* say?"

"I say the health and welfare of the kids in the community is everybody's business."

And Belle truly believed that. She wasn't always going to be childless, she hoped. And if Sweet Hope was truly to become her home, she needed to prepare for the future by voicing her concerns now. Besides, the kids' request—to be given a buffer of independence between adolescence and adulthood, to be treated as thinking individuals—needed to be addressed. For them. Now. It might cause a ruckus with folks like Boone, but some issues just couldn't be quietly swept under the rug. Out of sight. Out of mind. People needed to work their differences out. Come to a consensus. As a community.

"I'd be glad to attend," Belle declared.

"Good!" Cassie leaned over and hugged her. "I'll come by about six. We can walk to the town hall together."

Belle returned the hug. She was beginning to like Cassie as much as she liked Alice Rose. Any qualms she'd had fell before hope. No one could make too much fuss over one meeting, or her budding friendship with a young woman who begged to be taken seriously.

Boone read the note taped to the unlocked storefront door.

Having been tied up with masonry problems at one of his sites, he'd hurried to get here in time to get in some work, at least, for Belle tonight. He'd been met by this note explaining that she'd had to attend a meeting.

And an unlocked, lights-ablazing storefront.

The note didn't say which meeting or when she'd left. The door could have been unlocked for hours. And the storefront all lit up for the world to gawk at. Lord, didn't the woman have sense enough to secure her own property? Sure, this was little ole Sweet Hope, but folks could get into all kinds of mischief here just as well as in the big city. The woman had already made one enemy in Eban Smart. She needed to be more cautious. Less trusting. He sure as heck hoped there wasn't an interior stairway that led from the storefront into the upstairs apartment.

With rising irritation Boone pushed through the doorway into the old mercantile, to the accompanying tinkle of bells. He started. This time he wasn't imagining things. A string of tiny silver bells hung inside the door. Did she expect bells to repel intruders? He snorted. Belle Sherman was a grown woman. He didn't need to be worrying himself about her lack of judgment. She'd learn. One thing was for certain tonight: he might get some work done in peace and quiet. Without the exasperating and all-too-lovely Ms. Sherman working her distractions on him.

He set to work with a vengeance. But even though Belle wasn't in the room, the thought of her and the way she could fray a man's nerves yipped at the corners of his mind like beagle pups after a bone. It had been that way all day long. Starting with the moment he opened his eyes this morning and thought about that kiss and the feel of her soft lips on his own. It hadn't helped when his best friend Ray had actually suggested he ask Belle out. And then ... to find her recruiting on his construction site, disrupting the workers' day with her coffee and doughnuts and leaflets, and his own peace of mind with her doe-soft eyes and her high hopes for the future.

To discover her on his territory, so to speak, had been painful enough. He'd seen in her eyes that she'd realized as much. But she couldn't have known the pain she'd brought him when she'd mentioned that Victorian on Earnest Shoals Road. The pain had been no less sharp because of her ignorance.

That house. That damned house.

He'd told Belle he didn't build on Earnest Shoals Road. Well, it was the truth. He hadn't even been on that road since the night six years ago. And he'd told her that the big, showy, Victorian monstrosity wasn't one of his projects. Technically, he'd told the truth. Technically.

Boone shivered at the thought of that house and his broken dreams. Tried to steel himself against the wave of pain and guilt that would inevitably wash over him with thoughts of that house. And that night. And Peg.

Would he ever reach a point in his life when he could think of his wife, his high school sweetheart, and not feel the pain?

Trying to pull himself back into the here and now, he stood and stretched his tension-filled limbs. Despite his dark thoughts, he'd finished two walls of outlets. Only one more to go. He glanced at his watch. Ten-thirty. What kind of meeting would keep Belle out this late?

Hearing laughter and the tinkle of bells, he glanced at the front door to see Belle and Cassie stroll into the room, arm in arm. Now, what the devil was this all about?

Belle's heart did a little flip when she saw Boone standing in the middle of her storefront. Except for his scowl, he looked as if he belonged right here. Big and blond, his tool belt slung low on those narrow hips, feet planted firmly on the hardwood floor, Boone O'Malley was a sight to come home to. Yes, indeed. For the tiniest instant she almost wanted to forget how the whole point of this second chance she'd been given was to be free. To spread her wings. To live unencumbered.

The sight of him now and the memory of his passionate kiss almost made her forget those lofty aims. Almost. But then she remembered how he also appeared to shun encumbrances. How he was reluctant, to a fault. About everything. But mostly about her, despite the kiss. That kiss. An aberration, she was sure. On both their parts.

She wasn't about to fall for a reluctant man again. A cautious man. Her Mr. Right, if he existed, would know her the minute he met her, and would sweep her off her feet. Until that uncertain moment Belle would let the joy of living do the sweeping.

"Hey, there," he said, his voice a low, sensuous rumble. "You both go to this meeting?" His scowl said he was prepared to dislike the answer.

"Yes," Belle replied cautiously. "We both went to the school board meeting."

He narrowed his eyes. "Whatever for?"

Cassie looked from Boone to Belle then back again. Abruptly she said, "Thanks, Belle, for coming with me. I have a ton of studying left to do." She stood on tiptoe to give Boone a swift peck on the cheek. "See you at home, Daddy."

Belle widened her eyes in a look that she hoped conveyed the message, *Stand your ground, Cassie O'Malley. Don't leave me here alone.* But either Cassie was not proficient in body language or she, childlike, chose to ignore the brewing storm. In any event, she turned, then swung through the front doorway with a breezy wave over her shoulder, leaving Belle with a simmering Boone.

"Maybe you'd like to explain," he suggested grimly, "why you dragged my daughter to the school board meeting tonight."

"Boone O'Malley! Why would I *drag* Cassie to the school board meeting tonight?"

"Because the topic was going to be open campus and increased independence for the kids. How they want to be treated like adults. And because you witnessed Cassie's and my disagreement last night about that very thing. You know she'd just love to speak up on her favorite topic."

Belle threw up her hands in exasperation. "Number one—Cassie asked me. Number two—how well the teenagers of Sweet Hope progress into adulthood is the concern of every citizen." Taking a step toward Boone, she shook a finger under his nose. "The place was packed. You should have been there."

"Me? Why me?"

"To hear those kids stand up and beg to be treated as thinking human beings. With needs. The chief among them being the need for honest communication. And trust."

He didn't flinch. "That's something that should be left between parent and child. It's not a matter for the schools."

"I disagree."

"*You* disagree!" His blue eyes were clouded in smoke. "*You* don't even have kids!"

So he kept reminding her.

Breathing deeply, Belle looked him straight in the eye. "Boone O'Malley, I feel that we're all responsible for each other. For the community. For the future of the community—our children. As the saying goes, it takes an entire village to raise a child. Regardless of what you think, I'm not trying to cram my beliefs down anyone's throat. I'm just trying for the same thing those kids tonight so desperately want—honest communication. An exchange of ideas in an atmosphere of mutual respect."

Boone stood before her, obviously unmoved. His words came out a warning growl. "I just want to know why," he countered as if issuing a challenge, "you picked my hometown of Sweet Hope to turn on its ear. And why you picked my family."

## Chapter Five

Belle felt as if she'd taken a blow to the solar plexus.

What did Boone mean to imply by his questions? Did he actually think she'd come to disrupt life in Sweet Hope? To disrupt his family? Was he so self-centered that he took her life-style, her beliefs, her words and her actions as a personal affront? As a threat to his—*his?*—hometown? If so, the man needed straightening out. And quickly.

"Mr. O'Malley," she began, her tone icy, "Sweet Hope may be your hometown, but it's now my home. Alice Rose and Cassie may be your family, but they are my friends. I have no intention of turning any of them on their ears, as you so quaintly put it."

"Then what are you doing all this for?" He looked genuinely perplexed.

"All what?"

"All this stirring up of folks. All this public display."

It was Belle's turn to be perplexed. "What are you talking about? Give me an example."

Boone slapped his hands on his thighs. "You really don't know the effect you have, do you?"

"No more questions until you've answered mine. How do I *stir folks up?* Give me an example."

"Just one?" Boone shook his head, his eyebrows squinched painfully. "Well, for starters, how about the first time you attended the ladies' quilting circle."

"Yes?"

"And as your share of refreshments, you brought wine and cheese."

Belle felt color rise to her cheeks. "I'll have you know I formerly worked in a very conservative and proper private school, and we always had wine and cheese at special-projects meetings."

"Hell, Arabella! I bet the faculty wasn't made up of little old Baptist ladies."

"It was not my fault that I didn't know the quilting circle was the church quilting circle. The extremely *dry* church quilting circle. And anyway, your mother was most gracious. That's why we became such good friends from the start, I think. Because she made light of it. Because she didn't act as if my social faux pas was an assault on her or her hometown."

One side of Boone's mouth twitched.

"So you can't use that as an example," Belle declared. "It was an innocent mistake. I may have stirred folks up, but not intentionally. And I most certainly did not create a public display."

Crossing her arms in front of her, she waited for him to give her a more striking example.

He'd said it earlier, but now he thought it again: she really didn't know the effect she had on people.

Looking at her standing there, arms crossed, seriously waiting for him to catalog her faults, Boone began to feel his irritation melt. Alice Rose had recognized it: you couldn't stay angry with a woman who wouldn't, in the first place, intentionally hurt a fly. A woman who wanted to listen to why she'd upset you.

Any faults he could have accused her of would have crumbled to dust when he exposed them to the air of reason. The wine and cheese. Her public rescue of the litter of kittens, then Eban Smart's dog. Even her support of the high school kids tonight. All these things had been done in a spirit of concern and generosity. He could see that in a New York minute.

And what was really eating him? Could he tell her that? Could he tell her that her filmy, floaty clothes and her sensuous way of moving and her angelic smile and her scent and her laughter and her optimism and her sheer womanliness drove him to distraction? Could he tell her that *that* was how she stirred folks up? Maybe not folks, but one man in particular. Him. And that it didn't so much bother him that she was so open in her charms. What really bothered him was the fear that if he succumbed to those charms, even the smallest bit, he'd be the one to make the public display.

He was an adult, for Pete's sake. A role model for his still-too-impressionable daughter. He could not afford to let his head be overruled by his body's traitorous yearnings.

He sighed. He couldn't tell her all that. Instead, he said, "You realize, don't you, that after speaking your mind at the school board meeting . . . I assume you did speak your mind?"

She tilted her chin proudly. "I most certainly did."

"Well, then, you do understand that every person with a cause will be knocking at your door. Wanting you to join forces with them. Speak your mind on who knows what. Speed bumps in the supermarket parking lot. Saving the spring peepers on builders' sites. Making men wear ties to work."

She pulled a face as if his exaggerations left her unmoved. "I hardly think, on the basis of my tiny involvement tonight, people will see me as a *voice.*"

"Especially with your involvement tonight—considering you have no children of your own, no stock in tonight's outcome—you've stamped *do-gooder* in block letters right across your forehead."

Belle bristled. Her floaty outfit actually shimmied. "For goodness' sake, Boone O'Malley, quit acting as if it's a communicable disease. Were you never in your life a do-gooder? A go-getter? A public figure?"

He had been. And it had cost him.

"Yes," he conceded tightly. "I've been all of those. A fat lot of good it did anyone."

Belle looked at him. Really looked at him. With that unnerving way she had of probing right down to the bottom of his soul. One of the things he found most disconcerting about this woman was the fact that she would leave him no secrets.

Her look of confrontation had disappeared. In its place was question. And tenderness. He could stand the question. The tenderness undid him. And then she reached out her hand and gently touched his arm. An act innocent and at the same time unsettlingly sensuous.

Inhaling sharply, Boone started at her touch.

"Why do you say that?" she asked softly. "That your actions did no one any good?"

At first he couldn't answer. His eyes were riveted on the way her face tipped toward his. Her face with its soft curves and its Georgia peaches complexion. A lovely, trusting face framed with a tumble of dark curls. A face that wordlessly begged for the right to ease his burden. How good that would feel. For after he'd told her of the great weight on his heart, surely she would take him in her arms. Soothe him with those long, cool fingers. Kiss away the hurt.

That was just the kind of woman she was. A woman who would want to ease another's burden. But he'd be damned if it were pity he wanted from Arabella Sherman.

"Boone?"

He guessed he should give her some kind of answer. Otherwise she'd probe till she got one that satisfied her. When he finally spoke, his words were flat. "I got married right out of high school. Starting my construction business without a degree, I guess I had a chip on my shoulder. Had to prove I could run with the big boys. I threw myself into

every civic organization I thought might help me climb the
ladder to success. Eventually, I did go back to school. I
wanted to be a man my wife and daughter could be proud
of. A man the entire town admired. A big man. A highly
visible, successful man. A go-getter.''

"And was your wife proud of you?"

Boone grimaced. "Peg always told me she'd be proud of
me if I were a day laborer. She hated the limelight. She was
so shy. So quiet. So reserved. All she really wanted was for
me to put in an honest day's work and come home to her
and Cassie.''

"And is that what you did?"

At that moment the bells jingled on the storefront's door
and Maxine Clayton, the wife of one of Boone's site managers, entered, a worried look on her face.

Thank God for the interruption. He hadn't wanted to
answer Belle's last question.

"I'm sorry to interrupt," Maxine apologized, strain
showing in every feature. "I know it's late. But, Boone, I
can't find Nat.''

Nat, Maxine's husband, was one of his best site managers—when he wasn't in the depths of depression. When the
black moods hit, which was more and more often these
days, Nat would disappear, and Maxine would fear the
worst. Always in the past Boone and Maxine had been able
to find him, to make him take his medicine, to bring him
home safely. Boone worried that some day that wouldn't be
the case.

Boone didn't need Maxine to say another word. "Arabella," he said, unbuckling his tool belt, "I have to go."

"Of course," Belle replied, sensing that this was not the
first time Maxine had come to Boone for help. She seemed
to do it so naturally. He'd responded without question.

Watching the two get into Boone's truck parked in front,
Belle wondered why it was he took on responsibility, why
he—strong and silent—reached out a helping hand to others while he seemed exasperated when she attempted to do
the same.

What a strange and complex man. A prickly, standoffish man one minute, a man willing to help the next. He set off in her both a flight mechanism and a compulsion to draw even closer to him. Over the past few days she'd come to think of his heart as a briar patch. Right now, standing in the middle of the old mercantile, she chuckled aloud. She felt a little like Uncle Remus's rabbit. "Don't throw me in that briar patch," he'd protested. The rabbit doth protest too much. As did Belle herself. Just recently freed, she told herself over and over that she didn't want to be thrown into the midst of Boone's briar-patch heart. With each encounter she had with him, however, with each new revelation, an inner voice told her that's just where she might be needed most.

She sighed, thinking of his revelations tonight. If Maxine hadn't intervened, how much more would he have revealed? She'd never know. The only thing to do now was to wait for another opportunity to get him talking. She'd see him again. They were bound together by the work on her storefront. And by Cassie's room.

Cassie had invited Belle to lunch tomorrow. To see the Holly Hobbie room. To make plans for the redecorating. Even if Boone was not present, there was much a woman could discover about a man just by his home alone.

Suddenly, without apparent reason, Belle felt light as a soap bubble. She gathered the ends of her lavender, crinkle-gauze tunic and pirouetted on the hardwood floor. Who knew if she had a late-night audience out there on the town green? The inky blackness of the plate-glass windows showed only her whirling reflection. She took great joy in its spritelike exuberance. Life, with its twists and turns, with its unexpected revelations, with its ups and downs, was wonderful. Simply wonderful.

She thought of Sebastian waiting patiently upstairs for her. She thought of the Rocky Road ice cream that beckoned in her freezer. She thought of Boone and how he could use a series of daily hugs, and how she wouldn't mind being the one to administer them. Laughing, she leapt through the air, then took her final curtsy before the plate-glass reflection. On her way down she reached out and flipped the switch to extinguish the overhead lights.

In her mind, the ovation was stupendous.


Wednesday morning, cowering under the bed as the tornado warning siren blasted, Sebastian would not be coaxed out into the open.

"Come on, you big lunk," Belle insisted, grabbing him by the scruff of the neck. "This is no time for negotiations. We only have a couple minutes to get to the basement. It'll all be over soon."

For better or for worse, she mused bleakly as she hauled the shaking dog out from his hiding place. April in northwest Georgia. Azaleas. Flocks of migrating birds. And tornadoes.

Tornado Alley. That's what this neck of the woods was called.

The warning sirens and the descent to the basement had become second nature to residents. A mere blip in the day's activities if, luckily, the storm passed over without touching down.

Sebastian, locked firmly in Belle's arms, set up a keening that nearly broke her heart. She may have gotten used to the drill, but it looked as if her new companion never would.

"Hush," she murmured in his ear as she tried to safely navigate the stairs. "Hopefully, this one won't even touch down. Hopefully, all we'll get is a little wind. A little hail."

As if on cue, she heard hail pummeling the exterior of the storefront. Sebastian howled and shook so badly Belle almost lost her grip.

Uneasily managing the last few steps into the basement, Belle breathed a sigh of relief, then plopped, dog on top, into the ragged, overstuffed armchair under the stairs. Her tornado chair. Holding Sebastian tightly with one hand, she reached out to turn on the battery-powered radio on the floor next to the chair.

The storm had passed to the north of them. That quickly.

"You see," she scolded the dog. "These things only last but a few minutes. We were lucky this time. But next time...well, we're going to need those few minutes to get our bodies into the basement." Sebastian moaned in obvious agreement. "It would help," she added, "if I didn't have to carry you."

Sebastian turned in Belle's lap and slurped an enormous kiss across her face.

"Oh, Lord!" It was Belle's turn to moan. "I'm already late for lunch with Cassie. Now I'm late *and* I smell like dog!"

The all-clear siren sounded.

She'd have to take the time to freshen up. Then check the exterior of her storefront for damage. Cassie, having just gone through a similar routine herself, would understand any delay.

Belle, however, was impatient to get to the house on Oak Street.

Belle reached the sidewalk in front of Boone's house just as Alice Rose pulled in to his driveway. Belle didn't see Boone's truck anywhere, but Cassie was clearing fallen branches off a little subcompact parked in front of the detached garage.

"This is such a typical Wednesday," Cassie moaned as Belle and Alice Rose approached. "I have an eight-o'clock class and a four-o'clock class with nothing in between. Nothing except disaster, that is. Didn't the last tornado warning come on a Wednesday?"

"Warning is the optimum word, dear," Alice Rose soothed. "Be thankful it wasn't a touch-down. You do remember how we didn't see your father for weeks after the damage in Cartersville."

There it was again. Mention of Boone's *do-goodism,* as he so dismissively put it. A devilish urge pinched Belle into speaking up. "Have you made any progress in convincing Boone to do that feature for the *Gazette?* The one Amanda Best's so keen on doing. About his silent volunteer work."

Cassie rolled her eyes. "Oh, Daddy'll let Ms. Best do a feature on him when you-know-what freezes over."

"Maybe not even then." Alice Rose chuckled, turning to Belle. "Did your building sustain any damage, dear?"

"No. Luckily. It seems the only damage to any of the stores on Main Street was hail holes in the awnings. I haven't put up an awning yet. I've been too busy with the interior."

Alice Rose smiled a very contented smile. "And how are you and Boone getting on?"

Belle suspected Alice Rose didn't mean with the mercantile's renovation. She sighed. "Your son thinks I came to Sweet Hope just to disrupt his hometown and his family. He thinks I singled y'all out specifically. To torture. He says I stir folks up. And create a public display."

"I take it," Cassie said, amusement dancing on her face, "he wasn't too pleased I took you to the school board meeting last night."

"The way he sees it, I dragged you. The implication being that I'm somehow corrupting you."

Alice Rose moved to thread her arms through Belle's and Cassie's. "Now, never you mind about Boone's objections. He'll come around. Just you wait and see. Let's go inside. I'm parched. Cassie, you did make plenty of sweet tea, didn't you?"

"Yes, ma'am," Cassie replied. "Your recipe. And your chicken salad, too. This time I didn't forget the lemon."

The three women walked arm in arm up the broad front steps that led to the bungalow's wraparound porch. Belle sure hoped Boone's objections could be ironed out. She didn't wish to back off from her friendship with Alice Rose and Cassie. Not even in her own family had she ever felt so at ease and accepted as with the two O'Malley women.

Cassie moved to open the front door and to usher Belle into Boone's home.

Somehow, she'd suspected he'd live in such a place.

Clean lines and warm wood tones met her eye. Spare and natural. No clutter. Nothing avant-garde. Just an inviting simplicity. Belle caught herself wishing Boone's heart was so invitingly simple.

"Well," Cassie chirped, "shall we eat first or scrutinize old Holly Hobbie?"

"I think, dear," replied Alice Rose, "that Belle should see your room, and then we can all discuss the redecorating over lunch."

Belle followed the two women as they made their way upstairs.

When she entered Cassie's bedroom she got the feeling not so much that here was a room its occupant had outgrown, but that here was a room designed with infinite love. A hand-painted wall mural of Holly on an old-fashioned tricycle formed the focal point. The blues and pinks and creams of the painting were carried out in the bed's quilt, the curtains and the wallpaper border. A dozen obviously handmade ceramics, created to tickle the fancy of a little girl, graced a knickknack shelf hung over the bed's headboard. Belle sighed. How she had wanted a room like this when she was growing up.

Cassie seemed to catch Belle's thought and said softly, "My Mama did this for me. Just before she died."

"No wonder your father hates for you to part with it," Belle breathed.

"So do I, in a way," Cassie replied. "But I've taken pictures of the mural, and I'll box and save the knickknacks and the curtains . . . for my little girl, someday. And I'd actually like to keep the quilt. Work around it as a centerpiece for the redecorating. Mama and Grammy and the quilting circle made it."

Belle moved to the bed and ran her fingers over the familiar wedding ring pattern and the exquisite quilting stitches. Love. That's what she felt emanate from this work of art. Love from mother to child. And Boone didn't have to worry. The way that Cassie had planned what she would keep and what she would store and what she would remember was testimony to the young woman's abiding love for her mother. No amount of redecorating could ever erase that. Belle envied Cassie that she had this much of her mother.

"I think," Belle said thoughtfully, "that, using this quilt, we can do your room so that even your father will approve."

Alice Rose sat down on the bed in front of Belle and took her two hands in her own. "Don't worry about hurting Boone, dear. Whatever we do in this room is going to hurt him. But it's hurt he needs to work through. My son needs to ford a river of hurt. Just to assure himself he can indeed get safely to the other side."

A dark sensation passed over Belle's heart. "Whatever do you mean?"

"This room was perhaps the last tug-of-war between Boone and Peg." Alice Rose patted Belle's hands but looked gently at Cassie. "Boone had been holding out the promise of a new and even better bedroom for Cassie in the house he was building for the family. I think Peg redecorated when she did to win Cassie over to the notion that the three of them were better off staying right here in this bungalow."

"New house?" Belle still didn't understand. "What new house?"

Alice Rose's voice was tinged with sadness. "Boone was determined to shout his success to the whole town. By building a showcase of a home. Proof positive that he could provide in grand style for his family. Peg, bless her heart, was a simple country girl. Hated show or affectation of any kind. She had it in her mind that she would never move in to that flashy Victorian Boone was building for them out on Earnest Shoals Road." Tears welled in Alice Rose's eyes. "She never did, poor love. She never did."

Belle's insides did a nasty flip-flop. The Victorian on Earnest Shoals Road. That big old mausoleum she'd visited by mistake yesterday morning. The one Boone had declared he'd had no part in building. The inner workings of this man were becoming more complex and more fascinating to her by the minute.

She glanced from Alice Rose, who had regained her composure, to Cassie, whose expression was unreadable. Any questions that Belle might have asked were postponed by a shout from downstairs.

"Cassie! Mama! I'm home!"

Cassie and Alice Rose looked quickly at each other.

"Does Boone always come home for lunch?" Belle asked.

Cassie colored. "Only when I make Grammy's chicken salad," she offered weakly.

"Does he know I'm having lunch with you today?"

"Somehow I never did get around to mentioning it," Cassie replied as she and Alice Rose again exchanged glances.

Belle thought she could detect the faint odor of conspiracy in the room.

"Well," Alice Rose said, rising briskly from the bed, her former emotions tucked away with the past, "I suppose Boone doesn't have much time. We should get lunch on the table. Belle, dear, you entertain him while Cassie and I get out the food."

Entertain him? *Entertain him?* Belle thought as she reluctantly trailed downstairs. These two drop a little bombshell of revelation about Boone and then expect her to nonchalantly walk into the room and entertain him? She had a million and one questions that she didn't feel comfortable asking either the two women or an unsuspecting Boone.

She almost felt sorry for him. She was certain he didn't want his wife or his past or his hurt discussed with a stranger. And this new knowledge... what did Alice Rose and Cassie expect her to do with it?

Entering the living room, she saw Boone leaning against the fireplace mantel. He looked at her sheepishly as if he realized the gentle ruse used to bring them together. The two of them had been had. By his mother and his daughter, no less.

With his big, blond good looks and his little-boy discomfort, he was heart-stoppingly attractive. But more than that, now with the tale Alice Rose had begun to unfold, now beneath the surface, Belle could sense hurt and self-imposed guilt. And that spelled danger. For Belle could resist a merely physically attractive man. But a man who'd been hurt and who needed the redemption love could bring presented a dangerous challenge she couldn't resist.

"Hey," she said softly. "I didn't know you'd be here."

"I didn't know you'd be here."

She shrugged self-consciously. "Cassie invited me. To start my end of the barter."

"Ah, yes. The room."

"The room," she repeated. What more could be said?


Boone felt a little sorry for her. She looked so uncomfortable. Now, what had his mother and his daughter been up to? If he knew them, they'd probably started by showing her that old baby photo of him naked on the bearskin rug. He shivered at the thought.

Searching for a safe topic, he asked, "Was your storefront damaged by any of the wind and hail?"

"No. Any of your projects?"

"No."

"Did you find Nat Clayton last night?"

"Yes." He knew he sounded too brusque, but he really didn't want to discuss his site manager's problems, and he really didn't want to make small talk about the weather. Surprisingly, he just wanted to look at Belle.

She wore a sleeveless, pale yellow dress. Yellow like spring daffodils. With a very long, gauzy green scarf tied about her waist. Funny, but this was the first time he'd seen her wear anything that accented her figure. She should. More often. He amended that as he felt his pulse skip. Perhaps it would be safer if she didn't.

"Boone? Is something wrong?"

He realized he'd been staring. Staring with a lopsided grin tacked on his face. Damn. Arabella Sherman did have some kind of power to knock him off kilter.

"I'm fine," he said, straightening. He struggled to get back to a safe topic. "Spring tornadoes," he said. "No matter how long I live here, I guess I'll never get used to them." And here stood a woman the mere thought of whom spun him up and around and down with greater confusion and intensity than any twister he'd ever experienced. He guessed he'd never get used to her, either.

Belle grinned. "When I was growing up in Atlanta, the house we lived in didn't have a basement. When the tornado alert sounded, my father would herd us all into the bathroom. My brother Rhune and I would huddle in the bathtub while my father would sit on the commode and recite Edward Lear limericks."

"Was he a naturally fun-loving man?"

"Not at all." Belle sighed, an unexpected sadness crossing her face. "In fact, that was the lightest I ever saw him. I almost looked forward to the tornado siren."

Her wistful words reached out and plucked at Boone's heartstrings. Just as he grew accustomed to seeing her in one light—upbeat or energetic or quirky—she showed him another facet of her personality. One thing was for sure: he was a goner if she showed him any more of this vulnerability.

"Don't say that," he replied brusquely. "The weather forecast's showing a band of tornadoes all the way back to Texas and the Gulf. For the next couple days, keep a radio on. And keep your fingers crossed we're luckier than Cartersville."

Belle sat on the floor of her storefront, sorting books, and began to wish, as Boone had, that the plate-glass windows had curtains. After a very subdued lunch with Cassie, Alice Rose and Boone, this afternoon had been one steady stream of interruptions. People with causes, stopping in to press her into service. People who disagreed with her stance, stopping in to convert her. She hated to admit it, but Boone had been right: the few sentences she'd spoken into the microphone last night in support of the high school students at the board meeting had branded her as someone not afraid to speak her mind. Boone O'Malley had been too polite to say *a big mouth*. But that's what he'd meant most surely. Someone who wasn't shy. Who wasn't afraid of the spotlight.

Someone who was as unlike Peg O'Malley as night was from day.

The more Belle heard about Boone's wife, the more she saw the unexplained hurt Boone still carried around, the more she realized she mustn't get involved with a man like Boone O'Malley. He wasn't just reluctant. He wasn't just cautious. He was tied to the past with knots so strong and intricate they required a patience and a concentration Belle was unwilling to give. Unwilling, because if she attempted to loosen them, she herself might become tangled, might become earthbound, might lose her newly won freedom to soar.

"Oh, no," she muttered, shaking her head and scooping up a stack of paperback romances. "We wouldn't want that. Oh, no, no, no, no, no."

"We wouldn't want what?" The sound of Boone's deep voice right behind her startled her into uttering a most unreserved squeak and pitching the books into the air.

She whirled around to see him watching her in obvious fascination, one eyebrow quirked, a real grin on his face. She made a mental note that she'd be willing to try that maneuver all over again in a heartbeat if it would mean he'd continue to grin like that. In a way that showered her from head to toe with a sunshiny, tingling sensation. He ought to smile like that more often. A smile like that could chase the gray out of November.

"Boone," she said, recovering, "I didn't expect you till later this evening." Actually, after the strained and hasty way he'd eaten lunch earlier, she was surprised to see him at all.

"That's just it. I can't make it this evening. I have another commitment."

"Oh." For the most fleeting second Belle wondered if he had a date. And then she wondered why it would matter to her. "Well, I have plenty to do to catch up with what you've already done. Can you come tomorrow night?"

"Sure."

His eyes a lazy blue she'd never seen before, he said "sure" in a low, rumbling way that suggested he might actually want to return. Surprise of surprises. Belle felt herself grow warm at the possibility.

"Here." He held out a flyer. "This was stuck in your door. Take my advice. I wouldn't get tied up with the tree people if I were you."

"The tree people?"

Taking the handmade flyer, she saw it was a call for a meeting tomorrow on the town green to discuss the problem of billboards and the related topping of trees. She knew that had been a problem in Atlanta, but she hadn't seen evidence of it in Sweet Hope. Maybe these people were just planning ahead, making sure it didn't become a problem here. It sounded like a sane approach to her.

She looked up at Boone and saw the faintest twinkle in his eye. Was he goading her?

"Why shouldn't I get involved with these people?"

"Because there are so few of them, their chief means of getting attention is by causing a public disturbance and getting themselves jailed."

"Oh, Boone O'Malley, you exaggerate. This flyer is calling for a discussion on billboards and tree topping. How incendiary could that become?"

Boone sighed. The lines etched in the tanned skin around his eyes deepened. "You don't understand the political dynamics at work here."

"Then enlighten me."

"Nigel Medford, who owns the shoe store here on Main Street, is a member of the town council. He also has part ownership in a billboard firm."

"And?"

"So far there's been no problem with topping trees in front of his billboards here in Sweet Hope. If you hadn't noticed, we don't have many big signs. But Medford's firm makes a practice of it near his signs in the city. I think the tree huggers planned this meeting tomorrow as a warning to old Nigel."

"And well they should warn him."

Boone leveled a gaze at Belle that looked like one he might bestow on a recalcitrant child. "The way I see it, these folks are making trouble where there is none yet."

"*Yet.*" Belle stared back at him in what she hoped was an equally determined manner. "The way *I* see it, these folks might just be trying to head off trouble. You know, an ounce of foresight is worth a pound of hindsight, or something to that effect."

"If you're thinking of hooking up with these people, you're playing with fire, Arabella Sherman."

Belle tilted her chin defiantly. How dare this man tell her with whom to associate or not? "How so?"

"Don't get me wrong. The tree people—a few Sweet Hope residents, a few outsiders—are decent folk. Just misguided. They operate on a shoestring. Chances are they won't have applied for a public demonstration permit for tomorrow. Chances are they'll set up on the green right in front of Medford's business."

"That would be the logical thing to do."

Boone harrumphed. "Well, the logical thing for Medford to do would be to use his town council influence to have the police cart these folks away. As a public nuisance."

"That is so petty!"

"Maybe. But Nigel Medford always did like to play hardball."

Belle crossed her arms over her chest. If Boone O'Malley was trying to scare her away from attending tomorrow's meeting, his words were having just the opposite effect. She hated bullies. And Boone's proposed scenario smacked of bullying on Mr. Medford's part.

"I don't like the look in your eye," he warned.

"Mr. O'Malley," she asked, "do I look like a child to you?"

The corner of his mouth twitched as his blue eyes clouded to gray. "I just thought you might appreciate a bit of neighborly advice. You being new to town and all."

Sure. Neighborly advice. And he accused her of meddling.

Instead of telling him what she really thought, she smiled sweetly and said in her most honeyed voice, "Why, aren't you sweet to be so neighborly? I will surely give your words some thought." She actually batted her eyelashes for emphasis.

To his credit, he looked a little nonplussed at the seeming ease of his persuasive powers. "Well," he said, "I've got to get along." He began to turn, seemed to ponder whether he should say something or not, then added, "When I came in just now, I noticed Eban Smart hanging out in your alley. I sent him on his way. But as long as you have his dog, he's going to figure he's got a score to settle."

Belle bristled. "He has the courts."

"'Fraid not." Boone shook his head. "Smart doesn't have two nickels to rub together, let alone money to hire anyone to help him in court. In fact, Smart doesn't have anything. You'd best watch out for a man who's got nothing to lose."

With that parting shot Boone turned and left the storefront. And Belle, with an uneasy feeling in the pit of her stomach.

## Chapter Six

Boone glanced at his watch. Noon. He glanced at the police chief huddled in conference over lunch with Nigel Medford.

Normally, Boone didn't come into the Hole-in-the-Wall for lunch. Normally, he ate a sandwich in his truck at one of his sites. But today the thought of that one-o'clock "meeting" of the tree people, and the suspicion that Arabella Sherman wouldn't heed his advice to stay away, had drawn him back to town. To check things out.

Yes, Belle had assured him she was an adult capable of making her own decisions. The problem, as he saw it, was that her decisions were impulsive. And impulsive decisions could be dangerous. Like a decision to hook up with these tree people. The way old Nigel and the police chief were going at it, a little detour to jail for the protesters looked inevitable.

And Boone did not want Belle thrown in jail. No matter if it would be just an in-and-out kind of procedure to put the fear of God—or Nigel Medford—into the demonstrators.

It would be a most unfitting Sweet Hope welcome to any newcomer, let alone Arabella Sherman.

Boone tried to tell himself he didn't really much care about the fate of the headstrong Ms. Sherman. But his mother and his daughter genuinely liked the woman. And they would be devastated by any mistreatment she might endure. He was doing it for them. The O'Malley women. Yes, that was it, plain and simple.

Not to mention the fact that Arabella could use someone to watch over her. Someone to preserve her dignity for her even if she wouldn't do it for herself. She really was a nice woman. He hated to see her get in with the wrong crowd.

Boone stirred his coffee thoughtfully.

It wasn't anything more than that. Really. Hadn't Alice Rose drilled it into him that a Southern gentleman always looks out for the best interests of a lady? Especially a lady on her own.

His interest couldn't possibly have anything to do with an irresistible attraction to the woman.... Nah. Couldn't possibly be that. He immediately shrugged off that ridiculous notion.

"You know what to do, then." Nigel Medford's voice boomed throughout the tiny café as he scraped back his chair and stood. "As a town councilman, I will not tolerate any lawlessness. And those people have not applied for a public assembly permit."

Lawlessness indeed, thought Boone. The old windbag. All he cares about are power and the almighty dollar. Boone almost felt sympathy for the tree huggers in their misguided idealism. Almost.

As Nigel left the café, Boone rose, also. Might as well take an after-lunch stroll around the green. Just to work off the unaccustomed extra food before he headed back to work. Nothing wrong with that. Lots of people did it.

He paid at the cash register, then nonchalantly stepped out onto the sidewalk, scanning the green for any activity. It didn't take long to identify the tree people. Even without their placards. They were the dozen or so individuals wearing primitive crowns of leaves. Crowns of leaves. Dear God. Belle, if she'd joined up with them, was about to be jailed with a bush on her head.

Still unable to identify her, Boone crossed the street to the edge of the green. If she was here, he needed to tell her the police were poised to move in. Maybe that little fact would jolt her to her senses. Then an awful thought struck him. If Alice Rose was willing to get involved in Belle's literacy center, and Cassie was willing to follow her to a controversial school board meeting, might Belle have dragged his mother and his daughter into this, too? The thought made him furious. He hated impulsive decisions and their domino effect.

The sudden unmistakable tinkling of bells made him look off to the side of the group. There, in serious conversation with a leaf-bedecked man, stood Belle. She protected herself from the warm noonday sun with an enormous peach-colored parasol, its design a giant swirling goldfish. Damn. With that parasol and another of her long, floaty dresses and her bare feet, she stuck out like a sore thumb. He almost wished she'd opted for the crown of leaves instead.

"Arabella!" he shouted.

He wanted her to come to him. To separate herself from the crowd. In case the police moved in quickly. If he couldn't get her to leave altogether, perhaps, apart from the tree people, they might look like just another couple out for an after-lunch stroll. Although, as he watched her say goodbye to her companion and half skip through the grass toward him, he ruefully admitted that, apart or not, she looked like a tree hugger. A sensuous, provocative tree hugger.

He hoped he could convince her to leave the green before the police arrived.

Coming to a stop in front of him, she said a little breathlessly, "Boone, I'm so glad you decided to come."

"I didn't." Now that sounded stupid. Why was it he always seemed to come up tongue-tied and inarticulate around this particularly disconcerting woman? He tried again. "I mean, I didn't come to be a part of the protest."

"Then why did you come?" Belle tilted her head in question. The diffused light under the peach parasol made her complexion fairly glow. Shadows danced across her gold-flecked eyes. If he'd found it difficult to speak before, he found it doubly so now. He swore that if he were one to believe in the spirit world, he'd be convinced she was a conjurer. And the magic she specialized in was seduction.

"I came to tell you this group doesn't have a permit," he said with enough gruffness to cover the rebellious attraction he felt. "The police are going to move in. I'd guess the minute anyone starts anything that sounds like a speech."

"Yes, I know."

"You know?" Boone was dumbfounded. If she knew, then why in tarnation was she still hanging around?

"Yes. The man I was just talking to—Gus—is the organizer. He briefed me on the routine."

"The routine?"

"You were quite right, you know," she said with a little cat-who-ate-the-canary smile. "The group's aim is to get themselves arrested. It'll be written up in the *Gazette*. Gus says they couldn't pay for that kind of advertising."

Boone groaned.

"Each time it's happened before," she continued blithely, "the group's membership has increased. Gus likes to encourage registered voters to join. That way any elected official—like Mr. Medford—feels the political pinch."

"You'll feel a pinch," Boone growled, "if you have to spend the night in the Sweet Hope jail."

Belle chuckled. "Gus thinks they won't be able to fit this group in the two town cells. They'll have to make other arrangements, and that'll be an even bigger inconvenience for Mr. Medford and his cohorts."

Reaching out to take her wrist, Boone said, "Come on. Let's leave before we're both part of this craziness."

Despite the fact that he pulled her quite forcefully, Belle didn't budge. "I don't want to go. You may if you want to, but I'm staying."

"For a few trees? Arabella be reasonable."

"For the principle of the thing. And for your information, Boone O'Malley, I am being reasonable."

Oh, no, thought Boone. You're being impulsive and idealistic and maddening and... and...

Suddenly a gust of wind pressed Belle's outfit against her body, perfectly outlining her shapely curves.

Boone sighed. And far too sexy for your own good, he added mentally.

"Come on," he said aloud, tugging at her wrist. "You'll thank me in the morning."

Belle tilted her chin defiantly. "I'm staying. Unhand me, sir."

"You're coming if I have to toss you over my shoulder like a sack of potatoes." He glowered at her and took a step toward her as if to carry out his threat.

"Don't you dare play the caveman with me," she snapped, her eyes blazing. Her look of defiance said that if he was going to convince her to leave, it would have to be with more cerebral means.

He let go her wrist as if it had burned him. Turning his back to her, he kicked at a clod of earth. Damnably stubborn woman. Why didn't he just leave her with these bushy-headed tree huggers? Why did he persist in showing her the folly of her ways when she was determined to have her own way no matter what? Whether that way meant falling flat on her face or not.

He thought of Alice Rose and Cassie and how they'd never let him hear the end of it if Belle got arrested. He sucked in his breath and tried another tack.

"All this for a couple scruffy trees in front of a few billboards?" he asked, turning to face her, trying to keep his voice even. "This is America, you know. Free enterprise and all. What Medford and his company have done is not a major crime in my book." For Pete's sake. Talk about making a mountain out of a molehill. And publicly, no less. Boone began to seethe anew with irritation. Trying to talk to this woman was like trying to talk to a visitor from another planet.

"Oh, no?" Belle retorted. "It's the arrogance of Medford and his ilk. To think they can chop and destroy at will, just to make a few dollars." She trembled with indignation. "I see us all as stewards of this planet. We cannot act without thought as to the consequences of our actions."

Precisely what I was thinking, mused Boone ruefully, as I was trying to head you off. Out loud he said, "Instead of provoking Medford, don't you think it might be more productive if you—as a group—talked to him? Used the good-old-boy system. Took him out to lunch. Made him a proposal that would satisfy your concern for the environment yet would ultimately make him look good. That way he couldn't say no."

Belle narrowed her eyes. "Such as?"

"Such as..." Boone racked his brain for a such-as. He had her attention. He needed to show her things could be worked out cautiously. Without all this public display. It came to him. "Such as, for every tree he tops to clear his billboards, have him donate a sapling. To the town green. Or to a blighted area. Or tell him that your group will transplant the ones he intends to top. Promise him a write-up in the paper. It wouldn't cost a lot on either side. It would just require some patience and some communication. You're so big on communication I'm sure there are other solutions if you just put your heads together."

Belle eyed him thoughtfully.

"This," he added, waving his hand about the green, "isn't about the environment or trees. This is about egos. A power struggle."

Tapping her lip with one finger, Belle mused, "You may be right. We need to talk to Gus about this."

"Well, you can talk to him after we've processed y'all," a burly police officer in a Stetson and aviator glasses said gruffly. "Right now you need to come with me."

Boone recognized Mel Watson. "What the hell's going on here, Mel? How can you start rounding up folks before the speeches have even started?"

"Oh, they started a while back." Mel chuckled. "Problem was, you and the little lady were havin' your own heated debate. Heh, heh. Guess you didn't hear 'em. They've been stopped now. We've got orders to get everyone on the green over to the town council chambers."

"But you don't think *we're* part of the demonstration, do you?" Boone was astounded. He hadn't been in trouble with the law since he and his friends went on a toot senior night in high school and tipped over old man Lindsey's chicken coop.

"Now Boone, my orders are to round up *everyone on the green*. You and the little lady included. If you're lucky, Alice Rose will have you out of the hoosegow in no time. Looks to me like you were just in the wrong place at the wrong time."

Boone looked at Belle. Instead of seeming the least bit upset or intimidated, she looked as if they were embarking on an adventure. "Officer," she asked sweetly, "will the press be allowed in the council chambers?"

"I believe they're already there, ma'am," Mel Watson answered. He then turned to Boone. "Are you comin' along peaceably, my friend—" he grinned "—or do I have to cuff you?"

Boone resisted the urge to growl, more angry at himself than at Mel. Could he really have been so engrossed in his conversation with Belle that he'd failed to notice what was going on around him? If so, things had come to a sorry state. Hell, a night in the slammer with the tree huggers. This was going to be great for business.

Fanning herself with a piece of copy paper she'd found on the floor, Belle sat back in the folding chair in the town council chambers. My, but it was hot in here. She glanced at her watch. Six o'clock. They'd been in this room for hours, and she still hadn't been allowed her phone call.

Others had, but not her or Boone. Things were moving very slowly. This kind of group civil disobedience was new to Sweet Hope. The fact that the jail alone couldn't hold those arrested was testimony to the fly-by-the-seat-of-your-pants nature of the whole proceedings.

None of the group had been mistreated. Mostly, they'd been treated as if they were naughty schoolchildren. It was, as Boone had pointed out, a battle of egos. And here she'd thought it was going to be about trees.

She looked around the room for Boone, who'd sullenly stalked off in search of a drink of water. She couldn't see him. As hot as the room was, that man was hotter still. At her.

She shook her head. The whole arrest procedure was moving so slowly and, for the most part, with such a bizarre air of brittle conviviality between accused and accusers that she almost felt as if she'd been transported to Mayberry.

But, she bet, Mayberry had never been this hot.

April in Georgia. Normally the town council wouldn't need the air-conditioning turned on in chambers. But normally the chambers wouldn't have this many overheated bodies stuffed inside.

Increasing her fanning, Belle could feel a trickle of perspiration run down her neck. That couldn't be so, she thought with a rueful smile. Why, her great-aunt Lizzie had always told her that Southern ladies did *not* perspire. They glowed. If that was the case, she was casting a glow to read by.

"Sheriff!" someone shouted. "Can't you at least open the emergency exits to let in some air? None of us are such desperadoes we'll bolt for freedom."

"Speak for yourself!" someone else shouted amidst scattered laughter.

Belle looked up to see Boone, rumpled and damp, standing before her, a paper cup of water in his outstretched hand, a still-aggrieved expression in his eyes.

"Thank you," she said softly, taking the cup, then sipping the tepid water slowly. "I wish I had a peace offering for you."

She did. She really did. He shouldn't have been there on the green this afternoon. She hadn't had a chance to ask him why he had been.

"So, when it's your turn at the phone," he asked gruffly, "who are you going to call?"

"Well . . ." She hadn't really thought that far ahead. "I suppose I should call Gertie. She lives in the apartment in the building next door. She has a key to my apartment, and she could get in and feed Sebastian."

"You're in jail, and you're worried about the dog?" He didn't attempt to hide his exasperation.

"Of course I'm worried about Sebastian. I did not rescue him from abuse only to throw him into neglect."

Just then a couple of police officers opened the two emergency exits, and the faint stirrings of evening air began to waft into the room. The sound of spring peepers could be heard through the open door. A relaxing, cooling sound if there ever was one.

"Ah," Belle said, patting the seat next to her. "Sit. Please. Things are looking up."

Boone took her hand so unexpectedly she almost spilled the remaining water in the cup. "Come on," he countered. "Let's sit outside. On the stoop."

"But won't someone object?"

"If they do, they'll tell us." When she hesitated, he added, "Weren't you the one hell-bent on flying in the face of authority earlier?" The corners of his mouth twitched. Not a smile exactly. But not unfriendly, either. "Come on before someone else thinks of it."

Rising, she followed him to the exit, then stepped across the threshold into the cool evening air.

Boone sat and patted the stoop next to him. With not a little trepidation, Belle lowered her body next to his.

The stoop was narrow. They couldn't sit side by side without touching. And the feel of his warm, well-muscled bulk beside her, grazing her thigh, her hip, her arm, sent little shivers of pleasure through the rest of her body.

"Cold?" he asked, his voice traveling, husky and sensuous, on the ever-increasing darkness.

"No. Just getting used to the difference in temperature. From inside, you know." She couldn't tell him how his nearness did this to her. Created these shivery ripples of pleasure.

They sat in silence for several minutes. Then Boone sighed and murmured, "Arabella, what am I going to do with you?"

She laughed. "Do with me? Why, whatever do you want to do with me?"

He turned to face her, his eyes burning with an intensity that cut through the duskiness. "Don't ask."

Belle saw the opportunity to ask him why he'd come for her on the green. Maybe he'd just been a hapless passerby. She sensed not, however.

"Boone?" Because his eyes were so intensely focused on her still, she felt compelled to look down at her hands in her lap.

"Yes?"

"Did you come to the green earlier just to get me to leave?"

"Yes."

"Why?" She glanced up at him from under lowered lashes, and found he was gazing skyward.

"What's your favorite thing in the night sky?" he asked. Obviously he couldn't or didn't want to tell her the why of his earlier actions.

Oh, well, she could play along and make chitchat. It sure beat the slow, hot wait inside. "The evening star," she answered. "Venus. It's so intense. So vibrant."

"But its intensity fades as the night deepens and the constellations come into view."

"Ah, you prefer something more constant?" She had the feeling she was going to learn something about Boone

O'Malley with this little astral conversation. "Are you a North Star kind of guy?"

Boone actually chuckled softly. "Give me a little credit for some imagination."

"What, then?" Belle hugged her knees to her chest. "What's your favorite thing in the night sky?"

"Orion." Boone shifted his weight so that he was even closer to her. He turned to look at her, and the nearness of those steady eyes took her breath away.

"Why?" she managed to ask.

"Oh, it started when I was a kid. Did you ever notice how Orion splays himself over the dome of the heavens? No horizon skulker that one. He's big and bold and reaches out across the night. Protective from dusk till dawn."

"Protective?" Now that sounded like an attribute Boone O'Malley would admire. In constellation or man.

"Yeah." He inhaled deeply and, in doing so, brushed against Belle again, sending tiny ripples of pleasure through her. "I told my mama about it when I was young, and she encouraged me. Told me how, as a man, I'd be called upon to be protective. Of those less strong than me. Of those alone. Of those I cared for."

It began to dawn on Belle that he hadn't avoided answering her question as to why he'd been on the green earlier. He was trying to explain his almost innate compulsion to protect. Those less strong than him. Those alone. Those he cared for. She wondered just which category she fit in.

She smiled. "So you thought today you'd protect me from myself?"

"Sort of." With an endearing seriousness he reached out to brush an errant curl back from her face. His fingers, grazing her cheek, electrified her. "You don't seem to care what happens to you," he murmured.

"Oh, I care," Belle replied, her words feeling hot and dry in her throat. "I most certainly care what happens to me." In fact, right now, she most fervently wished Boone would kiss her. Here, under the protective gaze of the constellation Orion. Slowly, so that she could anticipate it. Without a subsequent retreat, as with the quick and passionate kiss in her little entryway.

The world seemed to dissolve away. The crazy reason they were sitting on this stoop in the first place. The differences in their outlooks on life. The very fact that Belle had no intention of getting involved with another reluctant man. All this dissolved and was replaced by a sense of rightness. Of the two of them sitting here. Together. In the growing dark. Under the emerging stars. Together. Barely touching. But linked by some inexplicable attraction. Inexplicable and powerful.

"Well," Boone said brusquely, stiffening. "Alice Rose and Cassie would have had my hide if I'd let anything happen to you."

A little frisson of disappointment ran through Belle. So he'd done it for the women in his family? Yes, that was the kind of man he was. But she'd hoped she herself had provided at least a tiny bit of motivation.

Sighing, she said lightly, "So you and old Orion have always been just naturally protective. Did you ever think your calling was to become a bodyguard? Not a contractor." She, too, could retreat. In small talk.

"I haven't always been a good protector," he muttered. "I'd have made a lousy bodyguard."

"Oh, I don't know. Cassie thinks you're—"

"Overprotective. I know."

He now sounded so grim that a little protective urge stirred in Belle. Reaching out to lay her hand on his arm, she said, "It's tough, letting go."

"What do you know about letting go?" His words were unduly harsh, but his tone wasn't necessarily so. He sounded as if he needed an answer.

"Enough to know it's perhaps the hardest thing in the world to do. And one of the most necessary." She took a deep breath, and because he hadn't shown signs of moving, she left her hand resting lightly on his arm. His warmth and his strength encouraged her to speak. To share with him some of the difficulty of the past year. She'd shared it with no one. That in itself had become a burden.

"The automobile accident changed my life," she began, feeling his muscles tense beneath her hand. "I'd been so cautious before. In how I lived my life. I didn't push. I didn't pursue. I waited quietly and patiently... and consequently life passed me by."

"How can you say that? You were a teacher. You had meaningful employment. Did you have friends?"

"Yes."

"A boyfriend?"

"A fiancé. Porter, my fiancé who could never seem to set a wedding date. For three years he procrastinated."

"Sounds like he was a little altar shy."

"You might say that." Belle was surprised to find that after all this time it still hurt to talk about that time. Maybe because she'd held it in so long.

"So you broke it off?" Boone's voice was gentle and blessedly protective.

"Noooo... Porter broke it off just as soon as I regained consciousness."

"Sounds to me as if you're better off without him."

She thought of the move to Sweet Hope and the happiness she'd found in her hopes and plans, in her new friends and a renewed sense of community. She thought of Boone and how, despite their differences, he kept her on her toes. Provided the spice that had been missing from her predictable past life.

Sighing, she said, "Yes, I think I'm better off without him. But it kind of leaves me with a shaky feeling where relationships are concerned. Now you..." She knew she skated on thin ice here, but she forged ahead, anyway. "You're lucky that you found someone. If only for a while. You know what real love can be. They say those most likely to experience love a second time are those who've had a successful relationship in the past."

Abruptly, Boone stood and shook out his legs. He hooked his thumbs in the pockets of his jeans and stared silently into the night sky.

When at last he spoke, his voice was raw with pain. "I'm not so sure I was any more successful in the end than your reluctant beau. He let you down. I sure as hell let Peg down."

"How can you say that?" Belle rose and stood close beside him. "Alice Rose and Cassie say that you were a wonderful husband."

He turned to face her, his handsome features streaked with anger. At her for bringing up this topic? At himself? "They don't know," he snapped. "They don't know how I took a beautiful, simple, trusting woman and tried to change her. Tried to make her into something she wasn't. Tried to bend her to my way of thinking. And in the end it killed her."

Belle gasped. This was not the man Alice Rose and Cassie talked about. This was not the man she herself had observed. This could not be Boone O'Malley. Cautious and controlled, yes. Stubborn, yes. But manipulative? Destructive? She couldn't believe it.

"But she died in a car wreck," Belle protested.

Boone glared at her. "How do you know that?"

"Cassie told me one afternoon."

His eyes burning, his mouth a hard slash in his face, he growled, "Now, why would she tell you that unless you were pumping her for information?"

Righteous indignation rose in Belle. "I was not *pumping* her for information. For your information, we each have similar family backgrounds. It came out in a normal conversation. The kind new friends have when they're beginning a relationship."

"Well, I'm not so sure I approve of this budding friendship."

"You! *You* don't approve?" Belle was outraged. "Neither Cassie and I, nor Alice Rose and I, for that matter, need your approval for our friendships. In case you'd forgotten, all three of us are adults."

"Cassie thinks she is," he retorted. He appeared to be reining in an anger that threatened to boil over and scald the two of them. "But she still lives at home. She still has an obligation to observe the house rules."

"House rules! My foot! What house rules would forbid a young woman choosing her own friends?"

"House rules that recognize when your daughter might be led down the garden path. Into something that might negatively impact on the rest of her life."

"Speak English, Boone O'Malley. Who's about to lead your daughter down the garden path? And what exactly are these negative situations?"

"You. And your cockamamie schemes."

"Me?" Belle threw up her hands in exasperation.

"Yes, you. You're all she's talked about at home for the past couple days. Haven't you noticed she's begun to follow you around like an adoring puppy?"

"You insult your daughter. She's no puppy." Belle, her hands on her hips, tilted her head and glared at Boone, hoping she could convey with a look the fact that he'd overstepped his bounds as a parent. "Of course we're bound to spend time together. We have mutual interests. Not to mention the barter Alice Rose engineered."

"That damned barter," he muttered, beginning to pace. "Everything was going along smoothly until you three put together that barter. Now my mama's hooked up with a literacy center that'll never fly. My daughter's traipsing around to fire-and-brimstone school board meetings. And I'm spending the night in jail for a protest I don't believe in. If you don't think that's enough to get a body riled up, why, then you, Ms. Sherman, are out of control."

Stepping in front of him so that he had to stop his pacing, Belle grasped his biceps with both her hands. "That's it!" she exclaimed. "That's it! This whole thing is about control. Your loss of control, to be exact."

Boone tried to twist out of her grasp. He was certainly strong enough to overpower her. But she held him with her eyes and her will alone. Held him with the truth of what she said.

"I don't know what you're talking about," he said, his words faintly threatening.

"I think you do."

She kept her voice even so that he'd listen. She moved one hand from his arm to the side of his face where she gently pressed it against the evening-cooled skin of his cheek. She felt him flinch. Her instincts told her to wrap him in an embrace. That, more than words, was what Boone O'Malley needed. While she suspected he'd reject the embrace outright, or misinterpret her motives, he hadn't yet totally rejected her words. He was resisting them as if his life depended upon it, but he hadn't yet wholly rejected them. She hung on to hope, and kept her voice even.

"I think, Boone, that you were a loving husband. I know you're a loving son and father." He recoiled from her touch. "Don't deny it. Just let me have my say."

"As if I could stop you," he muttered.

She smiled. He was listening.

"You just finished telling me that wonderful story about Orion and protecting those you love. There's a fine line between protection and control. Sometimes the only protection we can offer—without manipulating those we love—is love itself. Unconditional love. As with Cassie."

Boone pulled away completely. He didn't turn his back to Belle, but he stood off to the side, not quite looking at her. "You mean," he asked, "I should stand back and let her make mistakes I could help her avoid?"

"They're *her* mistakes. She'll learn from them."

"The learning will be mighty painful."

"Yes."

"What the hell kind of advice is that?" he growled.

"Good advice."

"You know, Ms. Sherman," he said, his eyes hooded and unreadable, "until you arrived in town, the old way the

O'Malley family had of dealing with things seemed to be moving along just fine. How come, now, you've got me second-guessing?''

"I don't think it's me."

"You don't think you're the key element here? You don't think you're the one who's come to town and turned things topsy-turvy?''

"No."

"Well, that's a pretty damned irresponsible attitude. What do you think happened here? Three sane people just up and lost their marbles all at once?''

Belle sighed. "I think your family was on the brink of change. Alice Rose, after years of being wife, mother, widow was ready for a new interest. Cassie has one foot in adolescence, one foot in adulthood. And you…you, Boone O'Malley, have grieved for Peg for six years. It's time, whether I came to town or not, for you to let go of that grief.''

"Damn it all to hell!" Pounding his fist into the palm of his hand with a resounding smack, Boone exploded. "Leave Peg and my marriage out of your two-bit psychoanalyzing. You have no right to dig around in things that don't concern you.''

"Why not?" She would stand her ground. She felt in her bones that if Boone couldn't come to terms with the past, he'd never have a chance at a future. And she wasn't about to stop to analyze right now why she was so desperately concerned with his future. "Did you ever stop and think others—like me—might have a little of Orion in us? Did you ever stop to think you might need a little protecting? A little help dealing with your hurt?''

Glowering at her, Boone snapped, "I'm not some mangy mutt you can rescue from an old drunk. Nor some helpless litter of kittens. Nor some impressionable high schoolers. And although you might see me as some thick country boy, dumb as a stump, I'm no tree, either." He slitted his eyes, lowered his head and took one step forward as if he intended to charge. "I'm not one of your damned causes, Arabella. And I don't intend to be turned into one."

At that moment a police officer stuck her head out the door and said, "Boone, you can make that phone call of yours now."

With a look that said he was infinitely glad of the rescue, he spun around and followed the officer into the council chambers, leaving Belle wondering just whether she did see Boone O'Malley as a cause or a man.

And then she remembered his uncalled-for but still gallant attempt at protecting her on the green. Remembered how, earlier, she'd so urgently wanted him to kiss her under the stars. How, just now, she wanted his past resolved so that he could have a future. Remembering these things, she realized that right from the beginning her interest in him as a cause had been a smoke screen. A smoke screen to hide her true feelings from herself: that right from the start she'd been interested in Boone O'Malley the man.

## Chapter Seven

How did he get himself into these situations?

Boone stared out the windshield of his truck and tried to focus on the road ahead and not Belle seated next to him in the passenger's seat. The past twenty-four hours had been hell, starting with his arrest on the green. At midnight, when Alice Rose had finally sprung him from the imposed company of the tree huggers, he'd vowed to avoid Arabella Sherman. He'd even figured out a plan to have one of his site managers finish up the work on her storefront. He wanted nothing more to do with a woman who always seemed to be at the center of upheaval. A woman who probed his past and his pain until his insides felt like nothing short of a natural disaster. No, sir, it had taken him six years of absolute control to keep his life on an even keel. He certainly wasn't about to let one quirky lady upset it all.

So what in heaven's name was he doing at one o'clock, the afternoon of the very next day, driving Arabella Sherman to the hardware superstore for supplies for Cassie's room?

"Do you suppose Cassie really had forgotten about her exam this afternoon?" Belle asked as if she could read his thoughts.

"That's what she said," Boone replied tersely. That's why, his daughter had said, she couldn't make her date with Belle to pick up the supplies.

"And do you suppose," Belle further mused, "that the paint and wallpaper she *absolutely has to have* are only on sale today—one day only—at this particular hardware store?"

"It's possible." But highly unlikely. More likely was the fact that Cassie had again endeavored to throw Belle and him together.

"I know she wants us to start work on her room tomorrow...."

"You can count me out," Boone warned. "I'm working tomorrow." The lost time this afternoon would be the perfect excuse for him not to be home Saturday when Belle was there. Cassie may have thought she'd worked the perfect script, but he was planning to ad-lib.

"Oh, we don't expect you to help."

Maybe Belle didn't. Against all reason he believed she was innocent in this matchmaking. If he and Belle had been thrown together, the O'Malley women were the key.

"I'm sorry my VW's in the shop. Otherwise I could have done this alone." Belle looked over at him, apology written on her face. He wasn't making this easy on her. He knew his displeasure at ferrying her around this afternoon was obvious. "I called Alice Rose, but she said she had a headache and was just planning to lie down."

Boone harrumphed. If he knew his mother, she was lying down, all right. Lying down with a nice tall glass of sweet tea and a copy of *Southern Bride,* planning Belle's and his wedding. There were no two women who could hatch a plot faster than his daughter and his mother.

"I know how much this redecorating means to Cassie," Belle persisted. "I didn't want to let her down. Or my end of the barter."

For all the grief this barter had caused him, he'd just as soon call it quits right now, and pay an interior decorator to redo the damn room. He said nothing, only glanced down at his watch. It took twenty minutes to get to the hardware store. Only fourteen more to go before he could get out of this too-tight truck cab. Away from Belle. Away from the dizzying array of conflicting emotions she always made him feel.

Like right now.

He'd never been quite so provoked with anyone in his life as he had been with Belle last night. Added to the fact that she'd gotten him thrown in jail, if the circus last night could be called jail, and the fact that she'd probed like a surgeon into the wound that was the memory of Peg, the wound that had never healed—added to all that was her exasperating lack of concern for herself in any given situation. Why, when it had come her turn to make her one phone call, instead of calling someone to come release her, she had indeed called her neighbor to feed the dog. She'd have been up a creek and *still* in jail if Alice Rose hadn't bailed her out along with him.

How could he deal with a woman like that? Short of a case of ulcers. And how could he deal with the feeling that—all this aggravation considered—he still wanted to pull over to the side of the road, drag her into his arms and kiss her senseless. Because that's what he wanted to do. Right now.

He was losing it. Truly losing it. He downshifted in anticipation of a sharp curve in the road, didn't quite get the clutch and shift in sync, and ground the gears. Damn. The horrible, grating sound was just an external indication of his internal state of affairs.

"Sorry," he muttered.

"That's okay," Belle reassured him. "It's the storm coming. Makes us all jumpy. All that oppressive air. And the eerie light. You were right—they've been warning of severe thunderstorms with the possibility of tornadoes all day."

He'd gone and done it again. With his mind all on Belle and the effect she had on him, he'd totally lost any awareness of his surroundings. He reached out to flick on the truck radio, then turned it to a weather station. Better to listen to weather updates than to try to make small talk.

A tornado watch was in effect for their area until late evening. A watch was better than a warning any day. But all that could change in a heartbeat. That was the terrifying thing about tornadoes. One minute you had your classic thunderstorm, the next you were buried in debris. He shuddered at the destruction he'd seen just last month in Cartersville.

"Boone?" Belle's voice gently broke into his thoughts.

"Yes?" He fairly grunted.

"There's been something I've been meaning to ask you. Nothing important. Just out of curiosity."

Those were always the most dangerous questions.

She continued when he didn't object. "The other night—Wednesday—you couldn't work because you had an appointment. Did you make the sale?"

"Sale?"

"Yes. I assumed you couldn't work at the storefront because you were, maybe..." She faltered, giving Boone the impression that she'd started something she now didn't want to finish. "That you were showing prospective buyers one of your houses. Did it go well? Did you make a sale?"

Had he led her to believe he had a business appointment? He thought not. He clearly remembered he'd told her he had another commitment. That could be anything. Even a date. The corner of his mouth twitched involuntarily as he thought of the possibility that Arabella Sherman might be the slightest bit curious about his social life.

"Oh, no," he replied casually. "It wasn't business. Not family, either." He added that last just to see her reaction. Funny, all this time he'd been focused in on how she made him feel. He hadn't thought that he might have stirred feelings in her. The possibility made his pulse race.

He looked over at her. She was looking out the window, but he could see a bright spot of color on her cheek. Why, could it be that the crusading Ms. Sherman thought of him as a man, and not just as a cause? That thought surprised and tickled him. And made him too aware of her discomfort.

"I'd promised to talk to a friend's mother," he explained, relenting. "About taxes."

He caught a faint smile curling the corners of Belle's soft mouth. He heard a little sigh escape her. He felt his heart thump double time as he realized she really had wanted to know if he'd been on a date. She turned to look at him, and there was a curious joy in her eyes.

"Taxes?" she repeated, smiling.

"Yeah, taxes. With all of the subdivisions going up in what used to be farmland, the price of land has gone up. And with it, the taxes. If you don't live in a subdivision, if you're too old to work the land you live on, you get caught in a tax bind. Like my friend's mother. She wanted to talk to me about some of the contacts I have in the legislature. She wanted to know what senior citizens' organizations I knew of. Organizations with clout. She wanted to know about forming a lobbying group. Wanted to know, too, how I managed to work out some tax deductions for Mama and her property. All that sort of thing."

"And she wanted to talk to you and not your friend?"

"Yeah...well...I've had some experience with Mama and other elderly property owners." He didn't want to make a big deal about it. It was just a situation that had evolved out of his concern that the people who'd built Sweet Hope with their sweat and tears would get a fair shake—at least tax-wise—in their old age. If he told Belle of his own behind-the-scenes lobbying efforts, she might think he was some kind of do-gooder. He wasn't. He definitely wasn't one of those.

He cleared his throat with relief as he pulled the truck in to the hardware superstore's parking lot. "We're here," he said. Obviously.

\* \* \*

Having made her purchases, Belle waited patiently for Boone at the store entrance. Once they'd parked, he'd taken off like a shot for departments unknown, with only a muttered explanation about picking up some miscellaneous building supplies.

That might be his excuse, but she knew the real reason was the extreme discomfort he felt at being thrust together with her. Again.

Sitting down on the gallon cans of paint to wait, Belle wondered about the controlled Mr. O'Malley. He was steamed over their arrest yesterday, and Cassie's little ploy today. She knew it. But he'd held his feelings in check remarkably well. Control. She'd hit a nerve last night when she'd told him his biggest fear was losing it. She furrowed her brow as she tried to imagine why. Was he a man whose anger could get the better of him if he let loose? Or was he perhaps, under all that control, a man of passion? Belle smiled at that last thought.

"Done?" Boone's brusque question cut through her thoughts.

He helped her to rise, and his touch, coupled with her thoughts of the past few seconds, made her blood zing. Just what might happen if he unleashed that rigid self-mastery? She was sure he'd never consciously relax his guard in public, but in private... oh, my, the possibilities were endless.

Relieving her of most of her purchases, Boone narrowed his eyes. "That grin says you've been up to mischief. What kind of wallpaper and paint did you and Cassie pick? Aluminum foil and black?" His voice was gruff, but Belle sensed more from habit than genuine feeling. She didn't know what department in the store he'd visited, but his mood seemed to have improved. Slightly.

"Yes!" she exclaimed, her grin widening as she flounced through the automatic doors and into the parking lot. "Just to see the rise we'd get out of you."

With his long strides he quickly caught up with her. "You three—Cassie, Mama and you—you like stirring folks up, don't you?'' Exasperation began to crackle the edges of his voice.

Belle laughed. ''You keep saying that, but, as far as I can see, you're the only one gets upset.''

He stopped dead in his tracks. ''Now, why do you suppose that is?''

At first she thought he was being sarcastic, but the look on his face was so genuinely perplexed that her heart went out to him. ''Perhaps,'' she offered, ''because you see the world in black or white. Either, or. Caution or folly. No shades of gray. No happy medium.''

''And what's wrong with that, I ask you? It sure keeps things simple.''

''That it does . . . except when change comes around. I suspect, Boone O'Malley, you see change as complicating life.''

He looked at her then. Hard. She'd learned to gauge the depth of his emotion by the current color of his eyes. Right now they were a steely gray. He shook his head slowly before speaking. ''Life changes too fast, that's for damn sure. I'm still trying to get used to changes in the past, but the present doesn't even give me breathing room to catch up. Do you know what I'm trying to say?''

''Yes.''

She did. Oh, how she did. As with the Orion story of last night, he was laying a tiny protected part of himself open to her. She might not agree with his way of thinking, but she sure did welcome the opportunity to see into what made Boone O'Malley tick. If he could just find a way to let go of the hurt in the past—the wrenching change that had come with the loss of his wife—Belle felt certain the little quirks of circumstance the present threw in his path wouldn't appear so exasperating.

She'd begun to learn one thing: Boone might be a protector and a preserver, but the main thing he'd determined to protect and preserve was his heart.

Rousing herself from her musings, she saw his back as he made his way ahead of her to the pickup. She inhaled sharply. Even carrying a gallon of paint in each hand and a bag of wallpaper rolls under his arm, he had that long and lanky, loose and sexy way of moving. He might be a man troubled by the hurt in his past, but that did not reduce his raw, physical, masculine magnetism one iota. In fact, the strength he exhibited controlling that hurt merely increased the draw.

Puffing out her cheeks and blowing a recalcitrant curl of hair out of her line of vision, Belle followed Boone the rest of the way to the truck. Did he ever feel attracted to her the way she felt—too often—attracted to him? She sincerely doubted it. And that's what made him a man to shield her heart from. Her next lover was going to *want* her.

Boone slung the supplies into the bed of the truck under a thick protective tarp tied down with bungee cords, then opened and held the passenger door for Belle. "We need to get a move on," he said, scowling. "I don't like the looks of that sky."

So caught up in the dark moods of Mr. O'Malley, Belle hadn't noticed the ominous change in the afternoon. Along the horizon black clouds amassed as if for attack. She could hear thunder in the distance. Her nose told her they were in for a storm. The hairs standing up on the back of her neck told her it was going to be a doozy.

"I hope we get home before it breaks," she said. "Sebastian hates storms."

Boone harrumphed softly. "I'm a dog man from way back, and, unless I miss my guess, old Sebastian recognizes an opportunity for a little added female attention. With his looks, sympathy's the only way he's ever going to get it."

"Really, Boone O'Malley," Belle admonished, smiling and settling back in her seat. "How you do go on."

They hadn't driven more than a couple of miles when the heavens opened up and the rain came down in sheets. Boone flicked the windshield wipers on high and cut on the headlights. He reduced speed until they were barely crawling along the two-lane country road. And Belle still couldn't see more than a few feet ahead of the truck.

Finally Boone said, ''There's nothing to do but pull over and wait it out.''

When at last he'd found a stretch of siding wide enough to accommodate the truck, and had switched off the ignition, the atmosphere in the cab became eerily frozen. It was as if she and Boone were the last two people on earth. Creatures trapped in a gray translucence, like insects in fossilized amber. Even the steady pounding of rain on the roof produced, paradoxically, an absence of sound. So hushed it was, surely Boone could hear the beating of her heart.

Belle felt as if time itself stood still.

Her eyes heavy lidded, her limbs weighted with a strange torpor, she slowly swung her gaze to Boone. He was watching her, the expression on his face more sensuous than inert. Or did she just imagine it? It was possible she had. Despite her body's listlessness, her senses and her imagination ran on overtime. She could smell the leather of Boone's tool belt although it was nowhere to be seen in the cab, could smell the faint residue of motor oil, the fragrance of lumber, the pungent aroma of Georgia clay. She could feel things she wasn't even near to touching. Like the skin on Boone's tanned cheek. Like the silky filaments of his sunbleached hair. Like the soft fibers of his chambray shirt. And she could imagine the unimaginable. Such as Boone wanting her as much as she wanted him this very minute.

What was it in the air today that produced such a strong current of attraction? She closed her eyes and inhaled sharply.

And then, feeling his hand slide over hers resting on the seat between them, she opened her eyes to discover she wasn't imagining his touch. He had indeed covered her hand with his own.

''If you're worried about that dog of yours, don't,'' he said, his words a gravelly counterpoint to the tattoo the rain beat on the roof. ''It may not even be raining on Main Street. You know these isolated storms.''

She smiled a little guiltily. And here she hadn't even been thinking of poor old Sebastian.

He must have mistaken her silence for unease, for he continued to speak, his voice low and reassuring. "When Cassie was little, she hated storms. If I was home when one broke, she'd climb up on my lap and make me sing her favorite song. Over and over and over again. Until the storm passed."

"You sing?" Belle couldn't quite believe it.

Boone chuckled. "Not what you'd call singing. But to a little girl, afraid of a storm, it served."

"What was her favorite song?" Suddenly the image of this big, stiff man protecting his frightened child with a song washed over Belle in a wave of sweet sensation.

"Oh, you know that old folk song. 'Tell me why the stars do shine. Tell me why the ivy twines....'" He spoke the first two lines then faltered into self-conscious silence.

"'Tell me why the sky's so blue. And I will tell you why I love you,'" she finished for him, remembering full well the old reassuring words and tune. "My great-aunt Lizzie used to sing it to me. To comfort me. But not because of storms." Because, motherless, Belle had, at times as a little girl, felt unloved. And not a little lost.

Boone squeezed her hand, ever so gently. "Did it help?"

"What helped most, I think, was knowing someone cared." Like now. The protective manner in which Boone had reached out to her just now moved her in ways she could not put in words. In ways that tilted her insides and made her feel a little off-balance. Made her feel as if magic were afoot.

Suddenly, as abruptly as it had started, the rain stopped.

Boone withdrew his hand, and the magical feeling disappeared.

A tiny, sad frisson running through her chest, Belle turned to look out the windshield at the aftermath of the storm, only to discover that the windows of the truck were completely fogged. She felt color rise to her cheeks as she assured herself she couldn't have been the only one breathing heavily. Rubbing a patch of glass clear with the sleeve of her tunic, she noticed out of the corner of her eye that Boone, starting the ignition and the defroster, looked thoroughly nonplussed, as though he were thinking the same thoughts as she.

"We'll get going as soon as we're clear," he said gruffly.

Belle suppressed a grin and turned to look at the storm-pummeled countryside. They'd pulled over at the side of the road between two newly plowed fields. The land swelled gracefully without a tree or building in sight. Just acres and acres of turned soil awaiting seed. Lucky for them they hadn't parked under any tall but fragile Georgia pines. Falling branches could have done a number on Boone's truck. And Belle knew how a Southern man babied his truck.

"You picked a good spot to pull over," she offered. "Instinct?"

He shook his head as he put the car in gear. "Dumb luck." The scowl he wore was far more intense than his words warranted. Instead of accelerating, he pressed the brake. "Arabella," he said, his voice deadly calm, "we may be staying awhile longer."

She didn't like the tone of his words or the sickish, yellow-green light that had settled ominously over the landscape.

Boone cut the engine and glanced at Belle. He didn't know how much a city woman knew about the weather. Didn't know if she knew that this calm and color was an unmistakable prelude to tornado. Didn't know if she'd ever been caught out in the open and had to make do with refuge. He took a deep breath. He was going to find out.

"Shouldn't we turn on the radio?" Belle asked.

Her voice was calm, but her eyes held worry. Those beautiful eyes. The ones he'd been kind of lost in during their sojourn in the rain. Hell, he'd better not get lost in them now. Right now he'd better damn well keep his thoughts off her eyes and on the seriousness of the present weather situation. He didn't like it one bit. Not the stillness. Not the color of the sky. Not the oppressive feel to the air.

"Honey," he replied slowly, "I don't think a radio's going to do us much good at this point. Just keep your eyes on the horizon . . . and be prepared to get out of the truck real quick."

"I don't like what you're trying to tell me."

"Like it or not, I don't want an argument when I give the word to get out."

Belle's eyes widened. "And go where?"

"Down the road a piece. Away from the truck. In that ditch up yonder."

"In that ditch! What about snakes?"

Boone shook his head. "I know they're right picky about who they share their ditches with, but, if the circumstances warrant, they're going to have to show a little Southern hospitality."

"I wasn't so much worried about *their* feelings," she replied with a rueful smile.

He looked at her outfit. Typical. Some pants and a floaty top in pale shades of green as pretty as a field in spring. Not an outfit that would hold up to lying facedown in a muddy ditch. He sighed. Maybe, with luck, it wouldn't come to that.

"So," she said, tilting her chin bravely, "anything else I ought to know before disaster strikes?"

He had to give her credit. She had pluck.

"Give me your hand," he replied. "I don't want to lose you, Dorothy."

Right now he could see, over her shoulder, a huge black cloud on the horizon. As fast as it was moving, he sure hoped it wouldn't show a tail when it crested the ridge. "Right now I think we ought to get out of the truck. Come on, slide over to my side."

Bless her heart, she didn't argue. Glancing briefly over her shoulder in the direction he'd been looking, she swiftly scooted across the seat. He opened the door and fairly lifted her free and clear.

Her hand tightly clasped in his, they stood for a moment, transfixed by the black mass on the horizon. Then, as if someone had cut on the switch to a high-powered fan, the wind began to swirl about them, kicking up debris from the plowed field, blowing it in their eyes. Boone ducked his head and resisted the urge to take temporary shelter alee of the truck. If this storm played out the way he predicted, he and Belle had a date with the ditch.

"Come on," he urged. "We'd better start walking."

He gave her hand a gentle squeeze, and she began to move at his side.

"You know, Boone O'Malley, if this was a date, I'm not sure how I'd rate it."

"Rate it? You mean you rate your dates?" he shouted against the wind.

"Not usually," she shouted back, her hair frothing about her face, her loose clothing streaming like a banner behind her. "But considering the originality of this outing, I'd have to consider giving it an added notation in my book of memories."

Her last words were blown away. He didn't bother answering. Not just because he felt that she'd never hear his words over the howl of the storm, but because she was so damned cheerful in the midst of this craziness, so infernally bewitching. He didn't want to shout at her that he didn't date. That this wasn't a date. And that he didn't see a date for the two of them anytime in the near future. For those were the only sensible responses to her banter.

The sound cut into his thoughts. That runaway-locomotive sound signifying only one thing. He glanced at the horizon to note with sinking heart that the massive black cloud did sport a tail. A vicious, twisting dragon's tail that lashed from side to side as it stretched to make contact with the earth. He heard the hail on the roof of his truck before he felt it pelt his body. He heard Belle cry out in shock. Clutching her hand more tightly than ever, he began to run. Dear God, he prayed as he ran, help me keep this woman safe.

The roar grew louder. He didn't take the time to see if they were a safe distance from the truck. This stretch of ditch would have to do. He wrapped his arm around Belle's waist and half pulled, half carried her down the steep embankment. At the bottom he thrust her against the side, in the grass, out of the swirling muddy rainwater that coursed down the center of the gully. He threw himself on top of her just as all hell broke loose overhead.

He couldn't tell if it was Belle or the earth trembling. Or both. The roaring threatened to deafen him. Hail slammed into his body, tearing at his exposed skin like stab wounds. He crawled more protectively over Belle, trying to lie pressed flat while cradling her head against his chest, letting his back take the full brunt of the dragon-storm's fury. He must let nothing hurt her.

Intellectually, he knew the twister, no matter how fierce, would pass on in a matter of minutes. But prone in a ditch—exposed—he felt as if they'd already put in hours of damnation.

He remembered the only other time he'd been caught in the open in tornado season. He'd been a boy of ten. Back when his daddy was still alive. Working the fields. Boone the boy had been carrying him a thermos of sweet tea. Watching for snakes and lizards and butterflies, he hadn't even seen the changes in the sky until it was too late. Until he thought he'd be blown away. Then, out of nowhere, his father had tackled him. Had lain across him on the exposed field as he now lay across Belle. Had made him feel—in the midst of hell—protected. Not alone. Dear God, he hoped Belle now felt the same.

Debris mixed with the hail. Deep in the ditch, they were protected from the worst of it, but Boone could hear, amidst the roaring, other sounds. Crashing. Snapping. Popping. The sickening shattering of glass. He shuddered at the fury of the storm, knowing full well the damage a tornado could inflict without even touching down. Touching down…well, he would *not* think of that.

The roaring diminished. Either that or he'd gone deaf. The wounds the hail had inflicted now felt the soothing kiss of rain. Boone raised his head. The rain was falling steadily. Vertically. Without the push of wind. His heart leapt in his chest. The worst of the storm had passed.

He scrambled to a standing position, pulling Belle with him. Her face was ghastly white, her eyes closed. Dear God, in protecting her, had he crushed the living daylights out of her? He shook her shoulders. "Arabella! Arabella! It's over! Open your eyes! Look at me, damn it!"

Slowly she opened her eyes at the same time her body went limp against him. "Auntie Em," she moaned, "are we still in Kansas?"

Boone laughed out loud in sheer relief and wrapped her in his arms. He had never in his life been so overjoyed to hear a smart-mouth reply.

Suddenly he felt her tremble. At first just a tiny shiver, then an incessant shaking growing to great racking heaves. He tried to push her away, to gauge if she'd been hurt, but she clung to him. Twined her arms around his neck, buried her face in his chest and clung to him for dear life. He felt the heat of her body through layers of sodden clothing. Felt her fragility beneath her earlier bravado. Felt her need for him. And his for her.

Murmuring, "It's okay, we're all right, we're safe now," he brushed her rain-soaked hair away from her face, cradled her to him, kissed the top of her head. "It's over. Don't fall apart on me now."

She sniffed. Don't cry, he thought. Please, don't cry. I can't endure tears.

"I...know...it's...just...the...aftershock," she hiccupped into his chest. "I...just...can't...stop...shaking."

Belle felt him against her like a fortress in the wilderness, felt him like a refuge. He was so powerful and so rock steady and so warm. So very, very warm. She couldn't let go. Wouldn't let go.

"There, there, Arabella. There, there." His words fell over her like a protective mantle, the husky way he drew *Arabella* to its full four syllables, sending shivers to compound the shakes.

She snuggled closer to his solidness, only faintly aware that the rain had turned to a fine drizzle. "I guess I didn't fully realize what it was going to be like. Out in the open. At one point I thought we were being run over by a train."

She felt him chuckle softly. Felt him stroke her hair. Hair that must look like the wrath of God. "Like a big old locomotive," he agreed. "And us lying trussed on the tracks."

"Lordy, but that was nothing like sitting in the bathtub, listening to limericks." Belle managed a weak chuckle. "I was scared."

"Me, too," he whispered into her hair. "You know, the part that scared me most was when I could hear crackling and crashing and popping above the sound of the locomotive."

"You know the part that scared me most?" she asked, drawing back slightly so that she could look at him. "The part where the oak tree fell on me."

"The oak tree?" He looked genuinely befuddled.

"Yes." She giggled. "Just after we climbed down that embankment."

Realization dawned in his eyes. "That was me," he said sheepishly, and shrugged his shoulders as if an explanation was actually necessary.

"You knew just what to do," Belle said, unable to keep the awe out of her words. "Have you been through this before? Out in the open, I mean."

"This?" Suddenly he looked unsure of himself. He gazed down at his arms. Arms that still held her protectively close. He looked as if *this* might refer not to the tornado but to the unexpected embrace of a very wet woman in a ditch by the side of the road.

A storm roiled inside Belle. A storm that had nothing to do with the wind and the rain and the hail she'd just endured. A storm of emotions this sometimes difficult, sometimes overprotective, sometimes stubborn, yet sometimes unbearably sweet and gentle man caused inside her.

"This," she whispered, standing on tiptoes and pressing her rain-wet lips to his.

With a groan he dragged his lips off hers, but pulled her into a crushing embrace. "Dear God," he moaned, "I lied to you."

"Lied to me?" His hug left her nearly breathless.

He buried his face in her neck. "I said the scariest part was the sound. But it wasn't. The scariest part was thinking you'd get hurt." He shuddered.

It was her turn to reassure him. Taking his face in both her hands, she gently drew away and looked into his eyes. "I'm fine," she murmured. "Just fine. All because of you. You knew just what to do."

He looked at her. Hard. All over. His gaze swept every soaked inch of her as if to assure himself that she was indeed all in one piece. When he again looked her in the eye, she started at the flicker of hunger she saw welling up from deep within him. Saw it. Caught it. And returned it.

It was when she returned it that he shut down. His deep blue eyes turned steely. His jaw tightened. It was as if she could see the wheels and cogs of self-control move back in place. The moment of wildness and abandon passed. They became two rain-drenched individuals standing beside a lonely country road.

"Come on," Boone said gruffly, taking her hand, helping her to scramble up the rough embankment.

She found it difficult to follow him. Not only because the footing was uncertain. She found it difficult to leave the ditch where, heedless of his own safety, he'd thrown himself over her. Where he'd gently held her until her shaking had stopped. Where he'd admitted his worst fear had been the fact that she might have been hurt. And where he'd looked at her with hunger. Such a hunger.

Whether Boone O'Malley wanted to admit it or not, something had changed between them in that ditch. And

Belle found herself reluctant to return to the way things were before.

But follow him she did. To the siding where they turned to walk back to his truck.

"Oh, Boone!" she cried, spotting the crumpled fender the smashed headlight. "Your beautiful truck!"

Boone's shoulders sagged, but he said nothing. The two of them hurried to inspect the damage. Whatever had slammed into the truck was long since gone. Flung who knows where in the tornado's wrath. Releasing Belle's hand, he knelt on the pavement near the front fender.

"I'm sorry," Belle said softly. "If you hadn't been shanghaied into driving me today this wouldn't have happened."

Boone looked up at her, perplexed.

"The wallpaper run—" Belle's hands flew to her cheeks. "Dear Lord, Cassie's paint and wallpaper!" She raced back to the truck bed, only to find the tarp secure and the contents underneath miraculously untouched and dry.

She looked back at Boone where he knelt on the pavement, a crooked grin playing on his lips.

"What's so funny?" she asked, a mite indignantly.

"You know," he replied slowly, the grin spreading, "the thing I like most about you is the very thing that drives me to distraction."

## Chapter Eight

Belle's curiosity had been piqued. "Just what do you like about me?" she asked, smiling broadly. Well, well. Things *must* have changed in that ditch.

"The same thing that drives me to distraction," Boone repeated. Deadpan. He stood, moved toward the passenger's door of the truck, opened it, then motioned for Belle to get in. "That even in the worst of times you forget about yourself. You're always thinking about others and their concerns. The dog. Me and my truck. Cassie and her wallpaper." He cocked a golden eyebrow. "You're entitled to think about yourself once in a while. In case you'd forgotten, you've just survived a tornado."

"How could I forget?" Touching her matted hair then her mud-stained, sodden clothing, she grinned. "If you were me in my condition, would you want to draw attention to yourself?"

Boone looked down at his own disarray. "Hey, lady, I'm no prize myself." He indicated the open truck door again. "What say we head home to clean up?"

Scanning the windswept and debris-strewn landscape, Belle hesitated. Just a few short minutes ago she'd been scared witless, although she hadn't quite admitted that to Boone. Now she was simply soggy and uncomfortable. But somehow she was unwilling to let go of any of those feelings. Somehow in the midst of the fear and the wet and the discomfort had come a remarkable breakthrough with Boone. He'd protected her. He'd feared for her. And he'd wanted her. If only for a few, quickly retracted seconds.

Now he was telling her there was something he liked about her. Forget that he'd admitted this bit of information as a backhanded compliment. He'd admitted it. So what did all this do to her own vow of staying away from any man who didn't want her—*want* spelled out in Day-Glo block letters? Belle glanced at Boone, whose impatience to get moving began to show. She needn't worry about her resolve. Despite today's breakthrough, the man still harbored enough reluctance to remind her to keep her distance.

Mustering as much dignity as she could in her storm-tossed state, she walked to the door of the truck, then climbed into the passenger's seat. An afternoon like this came along once in a lifetime, but it was over. She turned her thoughts to home and Sebastian.

Boone swung himself behind the wheel, turned on the ignition, then the radio. Reports were coming in of tornado sightings all across northwest Georgia and into South Carolina. Sightings. Not touch-downs.

Belle, glad for a topic of conversation that didn't involve feelings, harrumphed. "You mean what we just went through wasn't the big one?"

Boone chuckled as he eased the truck onto the road. "Just how big did you want it to be?"

"Well, I'm certainly not complaining. I simply think we deserve credit for surviving something really big."

Belle, glancing out the window at the beaten-down grasses and wildflowers at the side of the road, was unprepared for the feel of Boone's hand over hers.

"Hey," he said, an unmistakable tinge of admiration in his words, "I'll give you credit. Whether that monster touched down or not, you were a trouper." He gave her hand a gentle squeeze, then shifted gears. Once he'd shifted, he let his hand rest on the knob.

Belle wished he'd touch her again. She was growing to like his touch. Very much. Perhaps too much.

They settled into a silence that was not uncomfortable. There simply didn't seem to be much more to be said. Belle gazed out the window and noted that, as they came closer and closer to Sweet Hope proper, the landscape showed little evidence of a storm. Maybe Sebastian was home, undisturbed and sound asleep in the dirty clothes basket. Oh, how she longed for his heartfelt welcome, and the peace and quiet of her loft apartment. Not to mention the soothing warmth of a bubble bath.

As they turned the corner onto Main Street, however, thoughts of peace and quiet evaporated as quickly as the morning dew. Parked in front of her storefront was fire engine number one, its hose spilling from its side and winding like a giant serpent into the alley. Fire fighters moved slowly as if wrapping things up. The engine's dispatch radio squawked on and off.

When Boone pulled over and stopped, Belle fairly flew out of the truck. Dear God, let Sebastian and her building be all right. She grabbed the nearest fire fighter. "I'm Belle Sherman, owner of this building. What happened?"

"Just a trash fire in the alley, ma'am. No damage to speak of."

"But how?"

Boone came up and stood beside her.

The fire fighter shook his head. "Eban Smart decided to take his afternoon nap in your alley. It looks like he fell asleep smoking. A cigarette butt. A little spilled alcohol. Some paper from the trash. Next thing you know, we had a fire. Gertie in the apartment next door smelled smoke and called us."

"Smart!" Boone growled. "How do you know it wasn't deliberate?"

"Boone!" The thought chilled Belle to the bone.

"Well, now," the fire fighter replied, "we don't. That's why Sheriff Bratt took Smart into custody. When he sobers up, they'll question him." He turned to Belle. "We're almost through here, ma'am. There's no reason why you can't go in your building."

"Thank you," she said distractedly. "Oh, Boone, Eban Smart could have died in that fire."

"What the devil are you talking about, woman? Eban Smart might very well have intended to burn you to the ground."

Belle felt ineffably weary. "Boone O'Malley, why is it that you are always willing to think the worst of people?"

"Come on, Arabella." He looked fit to explode. "You mean to tell me you can't entertain the possibility that Smart might have started a little grudge fire?"

"Mr. Smart seems to be a troubled man, I'll agree to that," Belle admitted with regret. She didn't regret taking Sebastian away from Eban Smart. She was, however, beginning to think she hadn't gone far enough in her rescue effort. "If you'll excuse me, Boone, I need to get cleaned up so that I can pay a visit to the sheriff."

"To press charges?"

"Let's just say I need to get to the bottom of this."

"I'll wait and go with you."

"No!" No, she most certainly didn't need him hovering. "Thank you for your help today."

"You won't let Smart get off on this one?" He looked worried. But was he worried about her welfare or worried she didn't know how to handle this situation?

"Please. I'll take care of it. Right now I just want to check on Sebastian. And take a bath." She made a shooing motion. "Go. I'll be fine."

He looked as though he didn't believe her, but he did back slowly toward his truck. "I just have to say one thing, Ms. Sherman."

"And what's that, Mr. O'Malley?"

"You sure know how to fill up all twenty-four hours in the day."

Belle picked up her pace, almost jogging toward the O'Malley bungalow on Oak Street. She was late. Again. Cassie had wanted to begin work on her bedroom bright and early, but Belle just couldn't have avoided that business this morning with Sheriff Bratt and Eban Smart. She should have attended to it last night, but exhaustion and sleep had intruded.

Climbing the veranda steps, then pausing before ringing the bell, she hoped Boone did indeed intend to work today. She smiled. She did seem to wear him out. What with the arrest, then the tornado, then the fire at her place. She could see where he might get the impression that she was always at the center of upheaval. But that wasn't the truth about her. Not at all. And someday she'd have to make certain Boone understood.

Someday. But not today. Today she wanted to give Cassie and the Holly Hobbie room her undivided attention. And that's why she hoped Boone was busy elsewhere.

She rang the doorbell and heard Cassie shout, "Come on up!" from deep within the house. Entering, she followed the sound of cheerful, women's chatter up to Cassie's room. She was unprepared for the celebrity welcome.

Cassie and Alice Rose rushed to envelop her in solicitous hugs.

"Why, child," Alice Rose gushed, "you have had some kind of week. First that silly arrest. And then to get caught outside in a tornado..."

"Who told you about that?"

Cassie drew Belle to sit on the bed. "Why, Daddy came home fairly shredded. He didn't want to talk about it, but of course I dragged the story out of him. Then just as I was about to call Grammy with the news, she called me with news of the fire."

"I heard about it on the scanner," Alice Rose explained.

My, my, thought Belle. What a grapevine they have going. It's a wonder they don't already know about my meeting this morning.

"If you have a scanner," she asked Alice Rose, "do you know if the tornado touched down anywhere around Sweet Hope?"

"No, luckily it didn't. There are reports of wind damage, of course. Homer Martin's corncrib blew over, but that thing was on its last legs, anyway. There was a touch-down northeast of us. In Rabun County. Cut a nasty swath, I hear. But we were fortunate. Again."

"But you and Daddy!" Cassie cut in. "What an ordeal! How did you ever manage?"

"Oh," Belle replied a little dreamily, "your father is very resourceful."

Alice Rose patted her hand. "And here Cassie and I had thought you two would have a nice relaxing afternoon. Just getting to know each other."

Cassie stood abruptly, a little guilty flush spreading over her cheeks. "Well, I don't know about you two, but I'm just itching to get to work."

Belle cut a glance at Alice Rose, who seemed to have realized her slip of the tongue. The older woman clapped her hands together and rose as well, saying, "Dearie me, yes. Let's get the rest of this furniture out of the way. Belle, child, grab the end of that vanity. I think we should move that right out of the room and into the spare bedroom."

The two O'Malley women bustled so energetically that there really wasn't an opening for Belle to ask about Alice Rose's little comment. But it did appear, as Boone had feared, that, for whatever reason, these two were bent on matchmaking.

And how did she, Belle, feel about that possibility?

If she was truly honest with herself and let her dreams wander, she had to admit the idea of a relationship with Boone O'Malley had its charms. He was one attractive man. Despite his occasional aloofness, his erstwhile prickliness and his mile-long stubborn streak. Actually, those qualities presented an irresistible challenge, making Belle feel on her toes and *alive* each and every time she locked wits with him. And there was no denying a growing physical attraction between them. Until the ditch yesterday, she'd come to think of that attraction as one-sided, but after the hunger she'd seen in his eyes when the storm had passed...well, *that* had forecast a storm of a different nature.

But then she thought of her ex-fiancé, Porter, and how, ultimately, he hadn't given her his whole heart. How he'd hurt her. And no matter the hunger in Boone's eyes, part of his heart was still locked in sorrow. In the past. And unless he could come to terms with his own hurt, unless he had a whole heart to offer, Belle could see no relationship in the future for him and her.

Tossing her curls, she threw off thoughts of men and threw herself into the work at hand and the camaraderie with the two O'Malley women. The three worked diligently all morning, repainting woodwork. It began to appear that they could have the wallpaper up by suppertime.

As they worked and talked, Belle began to understand why there was such a bond between grandmother and granddaughter. Despite the difference in ages, both struggled with the same problem. As a widow, Alice Rose struggled to be seen as a strong and independent woman in her own right. A woman who needed no "looking after." A woman who was not helpless after her husband's death. And Cassie. Cassie struggled to be taken seriously as an adult. A young woman who, although still living in her father's house, wanted to carve out her own niche in life. Both women expressed their frustrations and their hopes and their dreams freely with Belle. As if she were a kindred spirit.

Belle thought of her great-aunt Lizzie and how she'd always said, "Many hands make light work." How true it was. The morning flew by, until Alice Rose stopped and rubbed a hand across her paint-smudged forehead and exclaimed, "Well, now, girls, I don't know about you, but I could eat a horse."

When she stopped to consider, Belle discovered her own stomach churning with hunger pangs.

"Grammy," Cassie suggested, "why don't you lay out those pimento cheese sandwiches you brought while Belle and I clean up these brushes?"

When Alice Rose had gone, Cassie turned to Belle and said, "I've been dying to get you alone."

"Whatever for?"

"To thank you for keeping Daddy so tied up in knots that he's actually living his own life and not trying to run mine."

Belle stared at the young woman in amazement. "Cassie! I haven't deliberately tried to tie your father up in knots. Some of the recent circumstances were beyond my control."

"I know." Cassie chuckled. "You've had *some* help from Grammy and me."

"You two are incorrigible."

"Why? Because we want Daddy to be happy?"

"Well, if *that's* your goal," Belle protested, "you need to pick a woman other than me to throw at his head. The last thing I bring your father is happiness."

Cassie patted Belle's arm. "Daddy might not realize he's happy—"

"*Arabella!*" Boone's voice roared suddenly, unexpectedly, through the house from below. "*A-ra-bel-la!*"

Glancing at a wide-eyed Cassie, Belle inhaled sharply. Dear Lord, the man did not sound happy.


Boone took the stairs two at a time. This was the last straw. He and that woman were going to have it out once and for all. He was tired of his life being turned upside down. By barters. And arrests. And tornadoes. And fires. And now this. For Pete's sake, he hadn't had a full and uninterrupted day's work since Ms. Arabella Sherman had dropped like a bomb into his life. But it was going to stop. Now.

"Arabella!" he bellowed again as he charged down the second-floor hall to Cassie's doorway. He turned the corner to find Cassie and Belle frozen like two deer in a car's headlights.

Except Boone had never in his life seen a deer dressed in leg-revealing short-shorts and a form-fitting, paint-spattered Georgia Tech T-shirt. But that's how Belle was dressed. For an instant, caught in the reminder that she actually did have a woman's body under all her usual gauzy fabric, Boone froze.

"Daddy!" Cassie finally squeaked. "What are you doing home?"

"You keep on doing what you're doing," he growled, coming back to life and stepping forward to grasp Belle's wrist. "Ms. Sherman and I have a few things to discuss."

"I thought I made it clear on the green," Belle replied icily, shaking her arm loose from his grip. "I do *not* respond well to manhandling. If you wish to discuss something with me, let's do it as two adults."

"Oh, I would, but there only seems to be one adult in this room."

Belle's eyes flashed fire. "And what is that crack supposed to mean?"

Boone threw up his arms in exasperation as Cassie implored, "Would you two take this outside? I don't relish handprints on my new paint job."

"Fine with me." Boone glowered at Belle.

"Fine with me," Belle snapped, brushing by him then out of the room.

As Boone followed her into the hall, he could hear his daughter mutter, "If this is what it means to be an adult, *spare me.*" He had to agree.

He wasn't looking for this fight, but he couldn't let things continue to snowball as they had in the past couple of days. He followed Belle downstairs and out onto the front porch. Her body language alone told him this wasn't going to be easy.

The screen door slammed behind him. "If you don't mind," he muttered, "can we discuss this inside? I don't think the whole of Oak Street needs to hear our conversation.''

Belle spread her arms and indicated her paint-spattered clothes. "If you don't mind, I'd rather stay outside. You didn't give me much chance to clean up.''

The two of them stared at each other like two belligerent kids on a playground, Boone thought ruefully. Finally she blinked and he said, "What the hell do you think you're doing *hiring* Eban Smart to work for you?''

"Not that it's any of your business, but Sheriff Bratt and I decided this morning it just might be something that would work out.''

Boone smacked his forehead with the heel of his hand. "And how did you two come to that conclusion?''

"After the fire—after your doubts about the origin of the fire—I got to thinking that maybe my confrontational stance with Mr. Smart had been the wrong one.''

"Of all the cockamamie confrontations you could have given up, you decide that this one—*this one,* the one you should stand firm on—is one you'll give up. Arrrgh!'' He took a long look at Belle standing firm, her arms crossed over her chest. She was staring back at him with an exaggerated expression of patience as if *she* were waiting for *him* to come to his senses. The woman drove him nuts. "Go on,'' he growled. "I'm just dying to hear the rest of this.''

"So I went over to discuss my situation with Sheriff Bratt.''

"Did you ever think for a minute to press charges?''

"Not for a minute.''

Running his fingers through his hair, Boone shook his head in exasperation. "I didn't think so. *Go on.*''

"I asked Sheriff Bratt to tell me everything he knew about Mr. Smart. Well, he gave me an earful about the man's problems. But he also told me that for a few hours in the morning Mr. Smart is actually sober.''

"And you just thought that for those few hours you could bang the drum and save his soul. Now the picture becomes perfectly clear.''

"Boone O'Malley, I don't know what's gotten into you, but I refuse to believe that you are as heartless as you're acting right now. I am not trying to save Eban Smart's soul. I am trying to give him a couple hours in the morning when he can be productive. When he can see his dog. When the two of us might talk as two individuals who need to iron out our differences."

"The bottom line, Ms. Sherman," Boone replied, narrowing his eyes and lowering his face to where it was inches away from her own, "is that Eban Smart probably swore to get even with you for humiliating him on the green. Now don't get me wrong...." He held up his hand to ward off her objections. "I didn't think you humiliated him. But he thinks you did. And that's all that matters."

"I think Mr. Smart and I can work out our differences."

"I know Smart, and I don't think you can."

Belle inhaled sharply. "Well, I don't really think it's any of your business."

"Damn it, Arabella!" He thumped his fist down—*hard*—on the porch railing. "With Cassie and Alice Rose hanging around your storefront, it sure as hell is my business."

"I'd planned to talk to them about it. They don't need to come in the couple hours Mr. Smart's in *if* it's going to bother *them*. I'll work with him alone. Sheriff Bratt doesn't think it'll be a problem in the mornings. I *am* surrounded by other businesses."

Boone's blood began to boil at her obstinacy. He was finding it difficult to keep his voice down. "Bratt again. Is Sheriff Bratt planning to provide protection?"

"Protection?" Belle's eyes flashed. "Who says I need protection?"

"Let's start with everyone at the Hole-in-the-Wall." Dear God, that had just slipped out. He hadn't meant to use this argument. It was going to end up sounding juvenile, like when you tried to convince your mother with, *All the other kids are doing it*. He grimaced and wished he could suck back those words.

But Belle was on him. "The Hole-in-the-Wall? What does the Hole-in-the-Wall have to do with my hiring Eban Smart?"

Boone crossed his arms over his chest, leaned on the porch post and glowered at the street. He had work to do. He didn't need to be spending the better part of the day straightening out Ms. Arabella Sherman's quirky life. Why had he come so undone with this latest plan of hers? He really didn't know why anything she set out to do raised his blood pressure. But it did. Every time. Never fail.

"Well? What *does* the Hole-in-the-Wall have to do with my hiring Eban Smart?" Clearly, she expected an answer.

He spoke without facing her, his words tightly reined. "I had lunch there. The news about your little visit to the jail had already made the rounds. Nobody thought Smart working for you was a good idea." Although, to his knowledge, nobody in the past few years had tried to deal with Smart as if he might have an ounce of feelings or even dignity left. "Several people wanted to know what *I* was going to do about it."

Silence. There. He'd said it. He'd reached the crux of it. And as much as he hoped she didn't pick up on the implication, he was certain she would. She always seemed able to home in on what made him tick. And what ticked him off.

"Well, well, Mr. O'Malley." Her dangerously soft voice reached out to him. "I begin to see the real problem. The real problem is not that I'll be working with Eban Smart, the real problem is that people in town are beginning to link our two names. Am I seeing the picture clearly? People are concerned for my welfare, and they think you might know what to do. Think you might care enough to help. And that bothers you. That implies some sort of relationship between us."

The softness of her voice began to rasp on his senses. She cut too close to the heart of the matter. He whirled to face her. "I am not your keeper," he growled.

"Ah," she replied, keeping her tone infuriatingly even. "You can't have it both ways. You can't rescue me from a ladder on Main Street, step between Eban Smart and me on the public green, try to prevent my arrest and throw yourself on top of me in a tornado and expect people to think we're strangers.''

''Those were all external circumstances. You could put any two people in our places.''

''Perhaps.'' She smiled her Cheshire-cat grin. ''But how about our discussions? Carried out for all to see. The flyer discussion on your building site. The school board discussion in the front windows of my storefront. *This* discussion—on your front porch. Even if people can't hear our words, they sure as heck can read our body language. And yours always says you're trying to persuade me to come over to the *right way* of thinking. Your way.''

''That doesn't make us a couple.'' Although if anyone had seen the kiss they'd shared in Belle's side entryway, they sure could have come to that conclusion.

''This is a small town, Boone. People have made up wilder tales on less. If it bothers you, ignore it. I certainly don't expect you to protect me, and I think I'm the one that matters. And I certainly don't think of us as a couple.''

Why wasn't he reassured by her words? He didn't want to protect her. She made it impossible for anyone to protect her. So damned self-contained, she didn't want protection. They were in agreement. On something, for once. So why didn't he feel relieved?

''*You* don't, do you?'' Her words cut into his thoughts.

''What?''

''Think of us as a couple.''

''No! Good Lord, no!'' He hoped that settled that discussion. Perhaps they could finish discussing Eban Smart, and he could get out of here. He glanced at his watch. The workday slipped away.

''No, of course not,'' Belle agreed softly. ''Because if you did—you know, see me in that light—you might have to move on with your life. Might have to worry less about Cassie's and Alice Rose's welfare and happiness, and just might have to concern yourself with your own.''

Her words slammed into him. Here he thought their discussion was wrapping up, and she was just catching her second wind. This had gone beyond any reasonable discussion of Eban Smart. This conversation now skidded into dangerous territory. He needed to cut his losses and get back to the safe world of floor plans and lumber. And Spanish-speaking day laborers. As little as he understood their language, he understood Belle's even less.

"I really have to get back to work," he said brusquely, turning to go down the porch steps. "I'll be coming around to the storefront tonight to introduce you to one of my site managers...who'll be finishing your work."

Belle saw red.

Reaching out, she grasped his arm and pulled. "Oh, no, you don't. You don't come in here itching for a fight then turn tail and run when you don't like the drift."

"What the—?" Boone appeared stunned at her reaction. And stunned, he stopped in his tracks.

Where he stood, halfway down the steps, and where she stood, on the porch, the two of them ended up eye-to-eye. She held tightly to his arm.

"You started this crazy conversation, and you're going to finish it," she declared, her normally easygoing hormones starting to rage. The nerve of this guy breezing into her life and trying to make her over. The nerve of him thinking he could dish it out, but didn't need to stick around to take it. Well, she had news for him.

He glowered at her hand on his arm. "It's finished."

"Oh, no, it's not. This whole thing isn't about Eban Smart. This whole thing is about you. About how I make you feel."

"And just how do you think you make me feel, Ms. Sherman?"

"I make you *feel*, Mr. O'Malley. That's the problem as you see it. I make you feel for the first time in six years, and that scares the bejeebers out of you. You don't want me to stop my do-gooder causes. You don't want me to stop making a public spectacle of myself. You don't even want people to stop talking about us...so much as you want me to stop making you feel alive.''

"You're out of line," Boone growled, wrenching his arm from her grasp.

"No, *you* are out of line. Charging in here today on some trumped-up reason—''

"Trumped-up reason!" Boone's voice rose. "Why the hell do you think I came over here today?''

Belle grew very still. She could end this conversation now. She could give up on Boone O'Malley, turn around, go into the house and never give him another moment's thought. He was that exasperating. But way in the back of her mind she heard Alice Rose's voice telling her that there was some hurt that Boone simply had to face. To endure. To work through. That thought made her bold.

"I think," she said resolutely, "I think that it took a while for yesterday to sink in. I think that when it did, and you realized what happened between us in that ditch, you got scared. And when you got scared, you figured the best defense was a good offense, and you came barreling over here to rant and rave and frighten me off. Well, I don't frighten, Mr. O'Malley. So you'd better think of some other way to protect your heart.''

"Protect my heart? From you?" The muscles at the corner of one eye twitched. "Is that what you think I'm doing?''

"I think that's what you're trying to do." Watching Boone's blue eyes change to an ominous shade of gray, Belle almost regretted pushing him. She was scraping the bottom of his soul, and she could only imagine the pain.

He spoke through clenched teeth. "Why would I need to protect my heart from you?''

"Because you want me." Dear God, had she actually said that?

His eyes drilled her with a look that could have been pain...or pure loathing. He said nothing.

Great-aunt Lizzie always said Belle was good at getting her mama's fool in trouble. Remembering that, she forged ahead. "You want me, but I don't think you're a one-night-stand kind of guy, Boone O'Malley. It might almost be better if you were. Might almost be better if we slipped between the sheets and burned off some of this sexual tension that crackles between us every time we're together."

"You don't mean that," Boone growled, taking a menacing step toward her. Hovering so close to her she could smell the need and the denial simmering beneath the surface of him.

"No," she answered breathily. "No. I wouldn't be satisfied with just that." Her admission shocked her. Here, after her vow to *live*, to spread her wings and soar, to sup from every flower, she was still thinking of real romance in terms of commitment and ever-after. What an eye-opener.

"No, I didn't think so. And, begging your pardon," he muttered, his words hard and faintly sarcastic, "aside from physical attraction, we have nothing going for us."

Belle was surprised. "You think not?" Gosh, scratch their surfaces and didn't they both care about people? Care about the welfare and the happiness of others? Belle might have her dream of a literacy center and her ever-present need to care for strays, but Boone looked out for Cassie and Alice Rose and Nat Clayton and that elderly woman with the tax problems. And the whole town of Cartersville. Whatever gave him the idea that they were different?

Boone groaned. "Arabella," he said, drawing her name out like a plea, "I am a man who doesn't want other people poking into my business, my private life. You, on the other hand, draw attention to your every move. For God's sake, you jingle when you walk."

"Of course I jingle when I walk." Exasperation ate at her. This man did not wish to discuss *anything* sensibly. "Any woman who has bells sewn on her underwear is going to jingle when she walks. What does that have to do with the price of tea in China?"

Boone's eyes flew open. "I rest my case."

"Which is," Belle proposed softly, suddenly realizing where his true objections stemmed from, "that I'm not Peg."

A frightening, thunderous look spread across Boone's face. "Damn it!" he exploded. "You think I can't care for you because you're not Peg? That's not it at all." He laughed mirthlessly, almost cruelly. "The truth is that you should be afraid to care for a man who treated Peg the way I did."

Belle inhaled sharply. She'd probed before—gently—into his past. Now on the brink of revelation, she stepped back, reluctant to hear it all.

But he seemed hell-bent on telling her. He stepped forward, grasped her wrist, held her immobile as he spoke. "You know I killed her, don't you?"

"Boone, no!" Denial rose in the back of her throat. She knew the circumstances. Cassie had told her. He hadn't killed Peg deliberately, but he felt as guilty as if he had. Belle twisted her arm but could not loosen his grip.

"Yes." His eyes flared, his gaze burned into her. "She hated that Victorian. Hated the showiness of it. Hated the need I had to be successful. Visibly successful. She vowed she'd never move into that house. But I kept right on with the building. Kept right on pushing her to change her mind. To change her feelings. To change who she was deep down inside."

"Boone, stop. You don't have to tell me this."

"But I do. So that you'll know exactly how different you and I are. One rainy day I'd pressed the workers to finish the roof. I'd come home all excited. Insisted Peg walk through the house, now that you could feel it was becoming a real house. She said no, said Cassie was sick in bed with a cold. I insisted. I wanted her to show some support. Even called Mama to baby-sit. All but forced Peg into the car...."

He stopped. Stopped and dropped Belle's wrist. His breathing came in long, ragged gulps. "If I'd just let her stay home where she wanted to be...if I'd just let her be who she wanted to be..." Belle reached out to touch him, to ease his pain. He drew away. Drew away but didn't release his tortured gaze from hers.

Cassie had said there'd been a car wreck on slick roads. That Boone had made it through. That Peg hadn't. Watching this man before her, Belle knew Boone hadn't made it through. Not at all. No matter his success as a businessman, no matter his attempt to be a loving father and son, his heart was trapped in that car. In the dark and the wet. In the pain. In the past.

"I know what happened," she offered. "Cassie told me." She couldn't bear for him to tell the rest of the story, each word torn from its guilt-shrouded hiding place. Each syllable opening old wounds.

"Then you know you don't want anything to do with a man like me."

She looked at him in confusion. A man like him? A man who hurt. Why would his hurt affect how she might feel about him?

He pinched the bridge of his nose as if trying to ward off a migraine. "A man who'd try to change the one he loved. Who'd push her till he destroyed her."

Belle opened her mouth to contradict, but he placed his whole hand over it.

"Don't try to tell me otherwise," he warned, his eyes glittering feverishly. "You see, all the while you thought I disapproved of you. When in reality, you should disapprove of me. No, disapprove isn't quite strong enough. Ms. Sherman, if I were you right now, I'd run like hell."

In spite of his admission—perhaps because of it—Belle had no intention of running.

## Chapter Nine

Boone hurt all over.

After the encounter with Belle yesterday, he hurt in places long shut off. He hurt in his heart and in his soul. Even his thoughts hurt. Old hurts from the past. New hurts...mostly from longing. That woman sure could scrape open old wounds at the same time she twisted his insides senseless with wondering what it would be like to start anew. With her. And after that encounter on his own front porch, there didn't seem to be a place in town that didn't hold thoughts of her. He couldn't go anywhere—not even his own front porch—without remembering some funny or exasperating or intimate moment he'd shared with her in the past week and a half.

He couldn't go anywhere for release. Except maybe his mama's farm. And that's where he was headed right now.

With a heavy heart.

A dose of Alice Rose's Sunday fried chicken followed by her near-famous banana pudding wouldn't eradicate his pain. But added to the peace and quiet and solitude of the farm, it would come close. He pressed the accelerator even farther to the floor in anticipation. And then immediately slowed.

No sense getting pulled over for speeding. No sense having to say, Well, officer, my foot got a little heavy, trying to outrun the demons of my past. Trying to see if I could stay half a mile ahead of my guilt. Trying to leave in the dust the scary feeling that maybe, for the first time in six years, I've met a woman who's made me feel alive again. A woman as unsuitable for me as I am for her. So, with that in mind, officer, you'd better take me in, lock me up and throw away the key. What say?

Boone shook his head. He'd say he was going crazy. Talking to himself.

And he'd say that Arabella Sherman, if she knew what was good for her, should stay as far away from him as possible. She'd already suffered one relationship in which a man had let her down. She sure didn't need to hook up with him, Boone O'Malley, a man who'd not only let his wife down, but who'd pushed her, who'd tried to change her. And who'd ultimately destroyed her. And had he learned from this terrible lesson? No. Right from the start, he'd set about to tell Ms. Sherman how she should change. How she should conform to his ordered code of the universe.

No, Arabella, despite her quirkiness, was far too gentle a lady to hook up with the likes of him. He'd been blunt with her yesterday. Surely he'd dispelled any lingering thoughts she might have of him as a worthy man. As a protector. As he went about his business in Sweet Hope, he always felt a little like the charlatan wizard in Oz. He wasn't what he appeared. Because of his failure to protect the woman he most loved, he was less than he appeared. And now Arabella knew it.

He hadn't waited around for her censure. He'd condemned himself for the past six years. She couldn't say anything he hadn't already said to himself. And, quite frankly, he didn't want to see that lovely, optimistic expression she most always wore turn to one of disapproval. Or worse. So he'd left her standing on his front porch, hoping to get her out of his mind. For the past twenty-four hours, however, he'd thought of no one and nothing else but her and how she might now regard him.

He pulled off the main road onto the long, winding dirt road that would take him through the tall Georgia pines to Alice Rose's farmhouse, and began to feel the balm of peace that always accompanied his coming home descend upon him.

Fifty acres—fifty of the original two hundred—he'd helped his mother save. It had taken some research and some astute financial planning, but now the best of the original land would remain in the O'Malley family. That was important to Alice Rose and to him and to Cassie. A sense of rootedness. Of continuity. Of belonging. He rolled down the truck window and breathed deeply the scent of the pines and the spring-damp earth. For the first time in twenty-four hours his heart took ease.

The truck lumbered down a slope and across a small bridge. Through the open window Boone could hear the brook splashing over the rocks. Perhaps after dinner, he'd take a walk back down here. The solitude and the restful sound of running water pulled sweet memories from the past. Of Cassie as a little girl catching crayfish in this brook. Of her playing hopscotch on the rounded brook stones. Of her insistence that April wasn't too early to go wading. Boone smiled at thoughts of that simpler time. A time when he knew every minute where his daughter was...and with whom.

His smile faded. How things had changed. When he'd woken up this morning, Cassie had been gone. In her place at the breakfast table, a note saying she'd be with Drew today. Now, who the hell was Drew? And *where* were they going to be today? He shook his head. As Cassie kept reminding him, she was eighteen. For all intents and purposes, an adult. How he hated to be reminded of it.

The truck began to climb, and at the top of the rise the wooded land gave way to pasture. In the distance, in a grove of pecan trees, Boone could see his mama's house. And his beagles lounging in the sun. And a car he didn't recognize.

He suppressed a groan. Although he'd been looking forward to some peace and quiet this afternoon, he knew his mama's propensity for inviting folks for Sunday dinner. You couldn't stop her. Well, he hoped she'd invited some shy and retiring spinster from her quilting circle. If that was the case, he wouldn't be expected to stick around after dinner. He could sneak out for a walk. Down to the brook. Or maybe a ride on old Red. Down to the lake.

Mulling over thoughts of escape, Boone pulled his truck next to the unfamiliar gray sedan. As soon as he stepped foot on the ground, the beagles were all over him. Between the dogs' yips and overjoyed whines, he heard the sound of Alice Rose's voice mixed with male voices coming from the back veranda. He sighed heavily. It looked as if he was going to have to be sociable after all.

Commanding the dogs to stay, he climbed the front steps, then followed the farmhouse's wraparound veranda until he came to the south side—the winter and spring side. He turned the corner to discover Alice Rose entertaining Pastor Matthews and the pastor's son Jacob, a young man several years older than Cassie.

Alice Rose looked up, a welcoming smile on her face. "Why, there you are, Boone, dear. Is Cassie with you?"

It seemed that Jacob was especially attentive.

"No. I'm afraid I don't know where Cassie is today."

"Well, she may be along, anyway. She knows she has a standing invitation to Sunday dinner. I've invited Pastor Matthews and Jacob to join us. Mrs. Matthews is visiting her sister in Albany."

The two men rose to shake hands and exchange pleasantries.

"Oh, Alice Rose," an all-too-familiar voice from deep within the house rang out, "I don't know if that's how you would have set your table, but it's set." The screen door opened. "Belle-style," Arabella said as she stepped through the doorway and onto the veranda, coming to a stop when her gaze caught Boone's.

"I'm sure it will be just lovely, dear," Alice Rose replied, reaching a hand out for Belle. Turning to Boone, his mama said innocently, "Belle's car is still in the shop. I know how I hate to be stranded without a car, so I asked Pastor Matthews if he might bring her on out here for dinner, figuring you could give her a ride back into town."

Boone's spirits sank lower than the belly of a snake. His afternoon of peace and solitude had certainly taken a header. His mama was counting on his good upbringing to keep him from turning around and walking away. He just knew it. And right now, his ingrained Southern manners were all that kept him from doing just that. Alice Rose couldn't help but have overheard Belle's and his heated discussion on his front porch yesterday. She and Cassie sure as heck would have dragged the particulars out of Belle after he'd left. And now...well, there was nothing his mama liked more than getting two people to make up. Unless, of course, it was getting two people to walk down the aisle.

He was stuck.

Leaning against the porch rail, he simply nodded at Belle, who had taken a seat by Alice Rose, and wondered what her unusually subdued expression could mean.

Alice Rose seemed to sense the tension in the air. A little too brightly she said, "We were just discussing how best to advertise the opening of Belle's literacy center."

"And I," Pastor Matthews added, "offered Belle some time when she could speak on my weekly half-hour radio show. But Belle has come up with an even better idea."

"I'm sure she has," Boone replied, trying to keep the edge out of his voice.

"She feels," the pastor continued, "that to be successful, the center must bring home the point that reading problems are not the problems of strangers. She thought if she could get some local people—respected residents of Sweet Hope—to step forward and publicly express learning problems they might have had, tell how they sought help to overcome them, that it might ease some of the stigma.''

Boone's thoughts began to darken. ''And just how would you find people willing to step forward and talk about their difficulties with reading? Short of prying into their school records.''

''Why, Belle won't have to go prying anywhere,'' Alice Rose answered, her chin set firmly as if she expected an argument from Boone. ''I've volunteered to be the guinea pig.''

''Oh, Mama, no.'' Boone didn't like this idea. Not one bit.

''And why not, young man? All my childhood and young adult life I struggled with dyslexia. Nobody knew there was such a thing. Just labeled me slow. It wasn't until I started volunteering when you were in elementary school that I overheard teachers talking about a student and realized the child and I had the same problems. Those teachers got help for that child…and for me. You know the story, but I'm not sure many others do. I think now's the time to tell it when it might do some good.''

Boone said nothing. He wouldn't argue with his mama in front of her company. But he would speak with her in private later. He didn't like this idea, and he didn't like the thought that Belle was behind it. To him it seemed like dredging up old hurts. Public admissions of private problems left him very uneasy.

''Hey, y'all!'' Cassie's cheery voice pierced his gloomy thoughts as his daughter popped her head around the corner. ''Daddy. Belle. Unless you want some pretty weird-looking puppies, you two need to come separate the beagles and Sebastian.''

Boone groaned. The situation was rapidly deteriorating.

Jacob Matthews didn't seem to think so. At the sight of Cassie he fairly flew to his feet, a smitten expression on his face if Boone had ever seen one. ''I'll help,'' he said eagerly.

Cassie waved a hand dismissively. "No, no. My boyfriend's holding Sebastian. Daddy, Belle and I can pen the beagles. Sit and keep Grammy company."

The poor boy sat, but he didn't look as if keeping Alice Rose company had been his intention.

Boone stalked off the veranda and around the side of the house, not waiting for Cassie or Belle. It was bad enough Belle's randy old mutt was messing with his prize beagles, but the thing that really galled him was Cassie's casual little bomb. *My boyfriend,* indeed. Let's get a good look at this kid.

The *kid* stood around front next to the cars. A bored expression on his face, he stooped slightly to hold an antsy Sebastian steady by the collar while the beagles milled restlessly about in an agitated pack. Boyfriend or no, whoever this guy was, he was no kid. He was, unless Boone missed his guess, a man in his late twenties if he was a day. With an attitude a mile long. Now, how the hell did Cassie hook up with him?

Cassie fairly flew around the corner with Belle in her wake. "Drew. Daddy. Belle," she sang out airily as she scooped up a beagle and headed toward the pens in back. She winked at the boyfriend. "Come on, Belle. I'll get you a length of rope so you can tie that stud muffin of yours to a tree."

I'd like to tie that stud muffin of yours to a tree, thought Boone darkly as he whistled to the remaining beagles. As far as he was concerned, the day couldn't get much worse.

Sitting at the dining room table, the remains of a sumptuous Sunday dinner before her, Belle felt sorry for Alice Rose. She swirled the melting ice in her tea glass and thought that the drink she held in her hand had been warmer than the group assembled around the table. And Alice Rose had so wanted things to go well. Had wanted this dinner to foster reconciliation between Boone and Belle. Had wanted them to meet on neutral territory with people who cared for them both. Had wanted them to seek common ground.

That hadn't happened.

Belle gazed around the table at the stiff group. There had been so many undercurrents and hidden eddies throughout dinner someone should have posted a sign warning folks away from treacherous waters. That's exactly what dinner had felt like. Trying to swim in treacherous waters.

Belle felt sorry for Alice Rose, who so wanted people—specifically Boone and Belle—to get on. She felt sorry for poor Jacob Matthews, who obviously adored Cassie, who obviously adored that thick-necked, arrogant lunk Drew. She felt sorry for Pastor Matthews, who seemed to sense something was amiss, but couldn't quite pin that something down enough to rectify the situation. No one more frustrated than a rector who couldn't rectify.

But most of all, her heart went out to Boone, who hurt. Obviously. And who didn't want to be here this afternoon. At all. Because of her, she felt sure.

He'd been brutally honest on his front porch yesterday. And then he hadn't let her respond. Hadn't let her reach out. He'd left her with his admission, his terrible self-imposed guilt, and, now, who knew what he thought she thought of him? Or, perhaps—this thought had been bothering her since yesterday—just perhaps his harsh admission and his abrupt departure had been a deliberate attempt to run her off. If that was the case, she'd be the last person he'd want to see at his mama's Sunday dinner table.

She glanced across the table to discover Boone staring at her. His blue eyes almost black. His mouth set in a harsh line. Oh, my, how she wanted to reach out and touch his face, stroke and soften his features, tell him that she'd heard his admission—the worst thing he knew to throw at her—and that she still loved him.

For love him she did.

That was the most startling admission she could throw at him. Would it startle him as violently as it had startled her when she'd finally admitted it to herself?

She hadn't come to Sweet Hope to fall in love. And loving Boone O'Malley most certainly wasn't the easiest thing she'd ever done. If she'd had a say in the matter she'd much rather have taken on a less difficult enterprise—say, quarrying Stone Mountain with a teaspoon. But right from the start—right from the time he'd caught her as she fell off the ladder in front of the mercantile, right from the time he'd stood in her storefront and resisted working with her, right from the time she'd looked into his eyes and had seen a man who could use a hug—right from then, she'd been drawn to Boone O'Malley and his rebellious heart.

Alice Rose stood. "I think you'll find the chairs more comfortable on the veranda. Cassie has volunteered the young people to do the dishes."

The look of indignation on the boyfriend's face made it obvious, *he* hadn't volunteered, but Jacob Matthews rose as if the thought of working side by side with Cassie would be sheer delight.

Pastor Matthews replied, "Alice Rose, I do thank you for a meal 'fit for a visiting preacher,' but I've promised to call on Carly Ernst this afternoon. She's feeling poorly. Jacob, I could swing by on my way home and pick you up."

"Oh, no," Cassie protested. "Drew and I will be glad to drive Jacob home."

Drew did not at all appear glad.

While the others decided the fate of dishes and rides, Belle looked across the table at Boone once more. He appeared to be rooted to his chair, oblivious to the talk swirling about him, determined, perhaps, to outlast his mama's company. Belle specifically.

Rising from her place, she decided to spare him. "Cassie," she said, "I'll help with those dishes."

"No, no, no!" Alice Rose exclaimed. "You've never seen the whole farm. I'd like Boone to give you the tour... on Red."

In front of company, Boone actually cast his mama a look of exasperation.

Alice Rose smiled sweetly. "In fact, I'd like to speak to you two for a moment in the kitchen. *Privately.*"

Belle felt a little as if she were being summoned to the principal's office, but she followed Alice Rose into the kitchen. She could hear the scrape of Boone's chair on the floor. She could only imagine his irritation.

Once the three of them were in the kitchen, Alice Rose asked, "Are you two going to speak to each other or not?" Her voice was stern, as if addressing two children.

Belle glanced at Boone, who stared at his mama as she continued, "This has gone on long enough. When I walk into the drugstore and hear the men at the soda fountain counter taking bets as to which of you will surrender first…well, then, I know this has gone on too far. You two are developing the reputation as Sweet Hope's Hatfield and McCoy."

Boone opened his mouth as if to protest, but snapped it shut without uttering a word.

"Boone," Alice Rose said, sighing, "take Belle for a ride on Red. Over the property. Talk. I suggest you don't come back until you can be civil, at least."

"Come on," Boone muttered none to civilly to Belle. "There's no arguing with her when she gets a bee in her bonnet." On his way across the kitchen he grabbed an apple from a basket on the counter.

Belle followed him out the door and across the backyard to a barn and fenced-in paddock. Just by the stiff set of his shoulders she could tell he might defer to his mama, but he sure as heck didn't like it.

"Red!" Boone called suddenly.

Belle heard a responding nicker, then from behind the barn appeared an enormous roan horse.

"Red!" Boone called again. The horse whinnied in reply and cantered up to the fence.

"He sure seems glad to see you."

"He won't when he finds out he's in for some exercise. This is one lazy horse." Boone scaled the tall rail fence, then dropped easily to the other side next to the horse. "Well, come on," he said brusquely.

Belle looked down at her clothing, aware for the first time of its unsuitability for outdoor activity. Her full white cotton skirt reached her ankles. The sleeveless cotton tunic reached midthigh. How the heck was she supposed to climb a fence and ride a horse? She sighed.

"You're not really dressed for the occasion," Boone said evenly, feeding pieces of apple to Red. "Perhaps we'd better cancel the tour."

Not on your life, Mr. O'Malley.

Belle smiled sweetly as she undid the lower buttons of her tunic, then tied the loose ends into a knot at her waist. She pulled the back hem of her skirt through her legs, then up to the waistband in front where she securely tucked it in, producing a pair of bloomers that made her feel a little like a wild horsewoman from the steppes of Outer Mongolia. She kicked off her sandals, then clambered to the top of the fence.

From her perch she eyed Boone defiantly. "Let's ride!" she exclaimed as Boone stared back, his mouth slightly agape.

"If you're sure..."

"I'm sure."

Boone maneuvered Red over to Belle. "Then grab his mane and swing yourself astride. I'll hold him steady."

"But how will you get on?"

"Don't worry about me. Just do as I say."

Oh, he'd been wanting her to do as he said ever since he'd met her, she thought with a twist of irony. But she obeyed him this time, and found herself astride a very tall, very warm, very wide mass of rippling muscles. Oh, my.

Practically before she could blink, Boone had swung himself up behind her. He clucked and Red moved toward a gate at one end of the paddock, where Boone leaned down and deftly unhooked the latch.

"You look as if you've done this a time or two before," Belle said.

Boone actually chuckled softly. "Not recently. But as a kid I'd ride from sunup to sundown if I could get out of chores. We had two hundred acres then. A boy's fantasy."

He clucked again to Red, and the horse began to move slowly away from the farmhouse, through a field of waving, blond grasses and shimmering April light. As they moved through the tall grass, hundreds of butterflies rose up on either side. The tallest grass had been bleached throughout the winter, but already Belle could see the new green shoots rising like a velvet undercoat. She could smell damp earth. She could feel sunshine, warm and soft, on her skin.

She could scarcely believe the ride. An experience of erotic sensations. Boone astride behind her pressed tightly against her. His chest against her back. His thighs enveloping her behind. One of his hands rested on his thigh, the other lightly on Belle's waist. Together they rocked rhythmically in the sweet spring sunshine while the aromas of horse and wildflowers mingled to form a heady musk.

Belle half closed her eyes in blissful relaxation. "If I were you," she murmured, "I'd start or end every day with a ride on old Red."

Boone actually chuckled softly. "Ever since I was a boy I have loved this piece of property. I explored it on horseback, hunted and fished on it, and always came here when I needed to be alone. When I had some serious stuff to work out."

Belle twisted a little to glance over her shoulder at Boone's face. "Is that why Alice Rose was so sure you'd come today?"

Boone was silent for so long she didn't believe he was going to answer. She faced forward again, trying to give him some space. Finally, however, he said slowly, as if he were struggling for words, "Arabella..." Dear Lord, how he made her senses tingle when he said her name. "I guess we do need to talk."

"Here? On horseback?"

"Here's as good a place as any. And Red's one of the few souls around who doesn't gossip."

She smiled. "Then what should we talk about?"

"Us."

With an exciting trill, the word cut through her.

"I didn't think you thought there was an *us*."

She felt him sigh. "I sure have been fighting it."

"And have you decided to stop fighting it?" she asked, and then held her breath.

"Arabella, I'm not making excuses for my behavior... I mean... I need to talk to you because I don't recognize the man I've become lately. I don't usually behave the way I have the past couple weeks."

"You didn't answer my question."

"I don't know how to answer." He lowered his mouth to her ear as if what he had to say must be kept secret from the great outdoors. "Yesterday I told you the worst about myself. And today... today, here you are. I don't understand."

Belle turned so that their faces were only a fraction of an inch apart. If she moved, just slightly, she could kiss him. Could try to kiss away his pain. Instead, she murmured, "Boone O'Malley, you're a good man." She saw him wince in protest. "You are. Only a good man would weigh his own part in what observers would call an accident. Only a good man would question his responsibility. Only a good man would worry that he might make the same mistakes in a future relationship."

Sighing, she faced forward to discover they had reached a crest in the landscape. Red seemed to be conducting his own tour. Below them lay a small jewel-like lake. "The problem, as I see it," she continued with hesitation, "is that you've let these good qualities become obsession." She expected him to protest. He didn't. "You've let your feelings of responsibility immobilize you." His silent bulk, unseen but felt behind her, made her bold. "If you let go the pain of losing Peg, it would be, in your estimation, an admission that you hadn't been able to preserve or protect the most important person in your life. And if you couldn't do that, just what kind of a man are you? Am I coming close to the heart of the matter?''

"I think," Boone conceded, his words a rasp of pain, "you've hit the nail on the head."

Staring at the back of Belle's head, listening to her soft words lay open his harshest inner reality, Boone couldn't help but wonder why she was still here.

"You need to give yourself permission to move on," she said, so softly her words were almost inaudible. "You need to give yourself permission to enjoy life and all its little quirks. You need to give yourself permission to love again."

There it was. That word. *Love.* He'd never let himself consciously use that word. Not even mentally. But the feeling creeping through him these past couple days...what was it? He'd tried to chalk it up to lust alone, but it wasn't. Lust couldn't account for the moments of incredible tenderness—such as now. Now while Arabella Sherman reached out to him. Told him she believed he was still a good man. Tried to bring his heart some relief from the six years of pain and guilt and grief.

He lowered his head to her neck. Inhaled her lemony fragrance. Felt the soft tendrils of her hair caress his face. The horse walked on. Rhythmically. Gently thrusting man and woman together. Boone wanted desperately to let himself go. But holding back, he whispered, "Shouldn't love be perfect? Shouldn't you offer someone the best that you have? The best that you are?"

He felt Belle tremble. When she answered, however, her voice was strong. Warm and honey rich. "If we waited for perfection, Boone O'Malley, we'd miss the best life has to offer."

The best life has to offer. A warm April day. A sensuous and loving woman. A feeling of being alive for the first time in too long.

"Arabella?" His voice was foreign to his ears. Ragged. Filled with longing. He brushed his lips against the curve where her neck met her shoulder. Felt the creamy softness of her skin. Felt desire, hot and compelling, deep within the ashes of his heart. Felt arousal quicken his pulse, tug at his loins.

She leaned back against him, her presence real and oh, so tempting. "Yes?"

"I want you."

"I want you, too," she answered silkily.

"Right here. Right now," he insisted, his blood thrumming a primal song throughout his body.

"Right here. Right now," Belle agreed, her voice husky. Willing. More than willing. Yearning. As he yearned.

With pressure from his legs alone, he commanded Red to stop. As soon as the horse complied, Boone slid to the ground, then reached up for Belle. Turning to him with a radiant smile, she ignored the niceties of dismounting. Instead, she flew into his arms. Startled, Red needed no swat on the rump to canter off toward the lake, leaving his master holding an earthbound angel with an unmistakable, devilish glint in her eye.

Strange, he'd never thought of passion wearing a playful grin before. Wasn't passion supposed to be serious stuff? His body, about to explode, felt serious, sure enough. But here was Belle, pressed against him, her arms wrapped around his neck, her warm body trembling softly with desire . . . and an expression on her face that said she expected they were about to have some fun. *Fun.*

Boone laughed aloud, and when Belle looked perplexed, he said, "You do know what I'm proposing here . . . ?"

"I think, Boone O'Malley," she replied, sensuously nibbling the edge of his chin and jawbone, "you're proposing we lie down in the sweet grasses of this field, in the sunshine, under God's blue sky, and make love." She pulled back and smiled an impish smile at him, her eyes sparkling mischievously. "Am I close?"

He groaned as he felt his entire body contract. "Close," he managed to utter before he lowered his mouth to capture the saucy sweetness of hers.

He'd kissed her before, but not like this. Before, it had been an impulse; now it was an admission. Now was better. So much better.

As he felt her soft, warm lips open against his, he felt the searing shackles of his past begin to burst. As he swept his tongue over hers, he felt those shackles swept away in a flood of healing, blissful warmth. He pulled her body closer to his. Felt her mold herself to him. He ran his hands hungrily over her soft curves. Heard her sigh. Deepening the kiss, he could almost taste her desire. For him. The reality intoxicated him.

His head spinning, he released her with a gasp. Felt her hands run slowly over his chest. Heard her chuckle softly, then say, "Oh, my, but you're delicious."

He smiled. He'd never been called delicious.

Looking into her upturned face as fresh as spring itself, he wondered how feelings of tenderness and desire and physical need and forever-after could inhabit his body all at the same time. He reached out to touch her face, almost afraid she would disappear. A mirage.

Closing her eyes, she leaned her cheek into the palm of his hand. Very real. "Yes," she whispered. "Touch me."

He needed no further invitation. He knelt in the sun-warmed grass, pulling her down with him. He pressed her back until they lay with nothing to shield them but the April blue sky and their feelings for each other.

"Touch me," she urged again. Softly. As she ran her hands over his body, creating waves of sensation. Over his chest. Over his hips. Over his thighs. Over his arousal.

He reached for her, reining in his desire to plunder. Reining in his need to possess, he reached out to touch her. Tenderly. The gentle swell of her breast. The soft skin of her belly exposed under the knotted tunic. The creaminess of her inner thigh where her skirt had ridden far up her leg. The contrast between his gentle exploration and the driving hunger deep within him knotted his body, drove his thoughts to distraction. That and her bewitching half sigh, half purr of encouragement.

Bending to kiss the path his fingers had traced, he felt her fingers thread his hair. Heard her murmur, "Oh, Boone...."

The sound of his name on her lips snapped his reserve. The hunger in his loins growled and would not be stilled. The primal desire to possess, to make her his, overcame all reason. "Arabella," he moaned. "I need you now."

"Yes," she urged breathily, reaching for the snap and zipper of his jeans. "Yes."

Roughly he pressed aside the fabric of her skirt. In one motion he pulled the silky panties down her legs, only half conscious of the tiny, silver tinkle of bells. He rose above her, saw the desire he felt reflected in her eyes.

"Give me your mouth," he growled.

She wrapped her arms around his neck, pulled herself up to meet him halfway, kissing him with a hunger that matched his own as he entered her. Entered her and felt her hot moistness claim him, possess him, as he had sought to possess her.

He was beyond holding back. He thrust and felt her responding thrust. He drew his mouth away from hers but felt the flick of her tongue on his lips, drawing him back. Back inside her. He captured her mouth again as he thrust deep within her. Again and again and again. Until his body pulsed and his thoughts were obliterated. All thoughts except for Belle. Belle who enveloped him. Belle who consumed him. Belle who possessed him.

Near the brink, he wanted to keep his eyes open, to watch her face transposed with sweet desire. But the overwhelming physical sensation that washed over him constricted every muscle in his body, forced his eyes closed, muted his cry as he thrust one last time before the universe broke apart.

He heard her cry. Felt her legs wrap around him, drawing him deep, deep within her. Smelled her sweetness as he collapsed half on, half off her tender body. Saw her luscious, sated smile as he tried in desperation to open heavy-lidded eyes. Succumbed to her gentleness as she soothed the twitching muscles of his back and shoulders. She kissed the top of his head where he lay on her soft breast. The simple gesture undid him.

What had just happened?

He'd let go.

He'd let go the past and had accepted the best life had to offer.

## Chapter Ten

In the midst of the sun-drenched field Belle lay in Boone's arms and gazed dreamily at the cloudless blue sky. Her mind felt in harmony with this glorious April day. Her body still thrummed with Boone's touch. Her heart, for the first time in a year, felt full to overflowing. Nothing had ever felt so right as giving herself to this man.

She sighed a sigh of blissful contentment.

And then she felt his body tense.

"Dear God!" he exclaimed, sitting upright, pulling Belle with him.

"What is it?"

The dark expression on his face as he turned to her did not bode well. "I forgot—totally forgot—about protection."

Reaching out to him, Belle softly assured him, "I'm on the Pill...if it's pregnancy you were worried about."

Boone's scowl increased. "I *was*." Was he now implying that her use of the Pill made her promiscuous?

"I never got off it after Porter broke up with me," she said in explanation. "Maybe, at first, I subconsciously thought he might come back. Later, it was habit." She took Boone's big hand in her small one. "I haven't been with a man in a year's time, if that's what you're worried about."

"No. Arabella, no. I have no right to ask you—"

"You have *every* right," she interrupted. "As do I...."

His eyes widened as if her forthrightness surprised him. "You don't have to worry on that account," he replied, then shook his head ruefully. "I guess we should have sorted all this out beforehand."

"I guess," she agreed softly. They hadn't been the most mature of lovers in that regard. Passion and the moment had won out over reason. "Are you sorry...that we...?"

"Dear Lord, no!" Boone exclaimed, wrapping his arms around her and drawing her close. He chuckled, the sound rumbling through his chest. To Belle, there could have been no sweeter sound. "Lady, for what we just shared, I'd walk through hell and back. Scary, huh? And we wonder why teenagers can't just say no."

"Why, Mr. O'Malley, I do believe you have just performed one impetuous act!"

"Let's say I did let go some." He kissed the top of her head. "You think there's any danger of it becoming a habit?"

She drew away from him, a fairly outrageous idea bubbling up from within. "Shall we give it a test?"

"What did you have in mind?" he murmured, lowering his mouth to hers.

She dodged the kiss, and tried not to be influenced by his subsequent crestfallen look. "Not that! At least, not now. I had something a little more daring in mind."

"Oh, damn, Arabella. I don't like the sound of this." He rolled his eyes, then flopped back onto the grass, his arms spread-eagle.

He looked so big and strong lying there. Rumpled and sexy. For a moment Belle considered his idea more inviting than hers. But there'd be plenty of time for his idea later. Maybe the rest of their lives if she got lucky. But how many perfect April afternoons were there? How many absolutely perfect opportunities for...

"Skinny-dipping!" she shouted gleefully as she hopped to her feet and began to disrobe. "Last one in's a rotten egg!"

Boone groaned, rolled on his side and tried to grab the hem of her skirt. "You are out of your mind, woman. That lake is spring fed. Freezing cold. Full of snapping turtles. Come back here and make love to me."

"Not until you've gone underwater. Once." Belle danced around him, just out of reach. "And then we'll warm each other up."

"Snapping turtles..." he warned.

"Oh, pooh. Snapping turtles. I know my biology. They're still hibernating."

"That's because they're a lot smarter than you," he muttered, abruptly rising to his feet. He lunged at her as she skipped beyond his grasp. "That water is damned cold!"

"Chicken!" she shouted as she streaked, now naked, through the waist-high grasses, toward a pebbly beach thirty yards or so from their trysting place.

*"A-ra-bel-la!"* he bellowed. Oh, how she loved the ways he used her name.

She turned to taunt him again, only to discover him bearing down upon her, frantically shedding his clothing as he sprinted through the grass. She shrieked, her adrenaline beginning to pump full force, and fairly flew the remaining distance to the tiny beach, praying the momentum of the chase would propel Boone into the water, as well. She had no intention of being a lonely-only icicle. Not even the pebbles under her bare feet slowed her as she plunged headlong into the spring-frigid lake.

Sakes alive, but the water was *freezing*. She dived, only to resurface seconds later, pushing off from the bottom, exploding into sunlight like a Titan rocket launched from the ocean's floor. With a scream of exhilaration that she could only hope Alice Rose and the visiting preacher couldn't hear, she floundered in the shallows in a desperate attempt to regain the beach and the warmth of her clothing.

With a roar Boone surfaced behind her, reached out, grasped her arm, pulled her under a second, heart-stopping time.

When she again surfaced he pulled her up against him hard. So hard she could feel the intense heat of his body despite the frigid water. Could feel the slippery ripple of his muscles along her nakedness. "Say *uncle,*" he growled, his eyes dancing with merriment. "This was your crazy idea, and I want to hear you say *uncle.*"

Belle opened her mouth to speak, but her teeth chattered so violently she could only make a halfhearted attempt at a proper surrender.

"Good enough." With a full-throated laugh, Boone scooped her up and carried her to the shore. He didn't stop to put her down on the beach; instead, he strode through the grass toward the spot where they'd made love. "Some idea you had, Ms. Sherman. Well, I tried it and can't say as I thought it was so great. Now I think we'll try *my* idea."

Her teeth still chattering, Belle could only nod her assent.

Gently Boone lowered her onto her full cotton skirt that lay on the grass where she'd discarded it. "Don't go anywhere," he admonished with a mock scowl. "I'll be right back."

Oooh, she wasn't going anywhere. The sun-warmed fabric of her skirt beneath her shivering body felt wonderful. She half closed her eyes and nestled into its comfort.

Seconds later Boone returned with the clothing he'd discarded on his run to the lake. Kneeling, chambray shirt in hand, he began to dry her cold and wet limbs, muttering all the while. "So this is what you consider a test of my spontaneity. You are *crazy,* woman. And I'm certifiable for following you. What if anyone had seen us? Hmm? What then, Ms. Spontaneity?"

The rubbing he was giving her was beginning to take effect. Warmth crept into her numbed body. She stretched under his ministrations. "You liked it, didn't you?" she purred. His grumbling didn't fool her one bit.

"You'd have liked it if my mama had decided to show Pastor Matthews the lake, now, wouldn't you? Or Cassie. Suppose she'd brought old muscle-headed Drew down for a look-see. They'd have received an eyeful."

Oh, they'd have received an eyeful, Belle mused as Boone finished drying her, then stood, gloriously naked, to dry himself with the now damp shirt. How gorgeous he looked, drops of water spilling from his tousled blond hair, sun glinting off his hard, slick muscles, his scowl only accentuating his handsome features.

She reached up for the shirt. "Come down here beside me, and let me do that."

Boone stood stock-still, his blue eyes wide. A smile slowly twitched one corner of his mouth.

"You sound like a fussy old schoolmarm," Belle teased. "Come down here so that I can see for myself that you aren't."

With a look of dawning desire, Boone lowered himself until he was stretched, reclining, alongside Belle.

"Just what did you have in mind?" he asked, his voice husky.

"Well . . ." Belle took the shirt and began to rub it lightly along Boone's body. "You did say you wanted to try *your* idea. . . ."

Boone reached out to touch the end of her nose with his index finger. "Sweetheart," he growled, "after that dip in the lake, I might not be able to do anything about my idea for several years."

A peep out of the corner of her eye told Belle he was lying.

"Well, then, we'll just have to concentrate on getting you dry." And what fun that was turning out to be. Running the shirt and her hands over his big, strong body. Over his broad chest. Over his well-muscled arms. Over his washboard-hard stomach. Feeling his skin turn warm under her touch. She found herself warming to the task.

And found that Boone was responding just as she had to his ministrations. He half closed his eyes. He stretched. She could almost hear him purr.

She loved the power she exerted over this man. She loved the freedom to reach out and touch him. To tease him. To look at him without having to veil her interest. She loved drawing out the seldom-seen side of him. The passionate side.

She bent and kissed the skin right over his heart. She heard him groan as he rolled over and pinned her shoulders to the ground. She saw the flash of longing in his eyes. Knew that they were making love. Again. Her body tingled in anticipation.

Bending over her, he took a nipple into his mouth, branding her with a searing, wet O. How could it be that just moments ago she froze when now she burned? With his hands—touching, caressing, exploring—he left molten streaks on her skin. With his mouth, his tongue, his teeth, he claimed her, driving her wild with an overload of sensations. She felt complete. She yearned for more. She felt at peace. Her insides warred in tumult. She felt all woman, and yet she fused with him, became part of him.

She loved and felt loved in return.

Embracing him, murmuring his name, she drew him into her. Drew him in to claim him as completely as he had claimed her. And when she did, it was as if she were the only woman on earth and he the only man. It was as if he were her first lover. Each kiss, each caress, each movement together felt that new.

A tiny part of her felt greedy. Their lovemaking thus far had been the lovemaking of two starving people. Impetuous. Rough. Demanding. As if they both were making up for long years of emotional famine. Consuming, partaking in a frenzied feast of desire. A banquet for the senses.

"Look at me, Arabella," Boone groaned, grasping her hands. Threading his fingers through her own, he pinned her arms by her head. "Look at me."

Palm to palm, locked in each other's gaze, they moved together in a rhythm that would drive them to the final chaos.

Belle felt the escalation in every fiber of her body, felt each hair tingle, felt her heart sing, felt her soul soar. Felt the driving, nameless need. Before she closed her eyes and surrendered to the final free-fall, she took in the sight of Boone above her. Took in the sight of this man lost in her. Etched the memory of him thus on her heart. On who she now was—forevermore changed by him. By him, only him. Boone.

Crying out his name, she arced through the dazzling fireworks to plummet breathlessly into the void. Floating, tumbling weightlessly in the senseless deep, she heard his cry as if from a distance. Knew he, too, fell with her into this sweet oblivion.

It seemed as if she remained forever senseless, boneless, drained, before she felt strong arms around her. Felt Boone pull her into his warm, protective embrace. Heard him croon her name. Breathed the wonderful musk of love-making. Settled once again to earth.

"Magic," she heard him say.

She turned in his arms to where she could see his face. "Magic?"

He chuckled and stroked her cheek with a finger. "You've been waving it all over town. Bewitching everyone." He kissed the tip of her nose. "I tried to hide from it. But some must have fallen on me, anyway."

She smiled at his admission. Come to think of it, he did look bewitched. "Are you sorry?" she asked softly.

His eyes smiled before his mouth did. "I wouldn't describe my present state of mind as sorry. No, not by a long shot."

"Then I'd say we've done exactly what your mother sent us out here to do."

Boone cocked one eyebrow. "Well, now, I don't think she had this in mind. *Exactly.*"

Belle laughed out loud and reveled in the way the afternoon air absorbed the sound of her voice.

Raising himself on one elbow, Boone ran a finger over Belle's thigh, her hip, her waist, sending delightful shivers throughout her body. "Arabella?" he asked softly.

"Yes?"

"Where are your tattoos?"

"Tattoos?"

"Fess up, Arabella. I know I'm not crazy." He flashed her a grin to toast her toes. "You had a rose tattoo on your ankle, and one here...." He bent and kissed the swell of her breast. "And now you don't. What gives?"

She felt the mischief rise in her. So Boone O'Malley had noticed a little more than was quite proper. The thought tickled her. "Those tattoos," she began, a giggle surfacing, "were temporary."

"Temporary?" Poor Boone looked confounded.

"Oh, I flirted with the idea of getting a permanent one, but couldn't decide where I'd put it. So I bought several press-ons and experimented. I decided finally I'm not the tattoo type. What do you think?"

"I think," Boone replied, groaning and pinching the bridge of his nose in obvious disbelief, "that I will never, ever be able to predict what you'll do next."

A cloud passed over the sun, temporarily chilling their trysting spot. Boone looked skyward.

"And as much as I hate to," he said, "I think we'd better get going. I'd say it's about four-thirty." He craned his neck and scanned the landscape. "And I'd say our ride has headed back to the barn."

Belle sat up. "What will Alice Rose think if she spots Red coming home without us?"

"The worst." He nuzzled her neck quickly before rising and extending a hand to help her stand. "Absolutely the worst."

They shook out their damp and rumpled clothes and slipped into them. There really was no denying the fact that they hadn't spent all afternoon on horseback. Belle glanced ruefully at her badly disheveled tunic and skirt, then ran her fingers through her hair, combing out assorted grasses.

"Oh, my," she murmured. "Whatever are we going to tell your mama?"

Boone laughed as he pulled her into his arms. "Is this the woman who doesn't give a hoot for appearances? It's a little late to be worrying about what my mama's going to think."

"Yes, but I'll feel very foolish, acting as if nothing is amiss."

"Well, then," Boone replied, holding her at arm's length and grinning from ear to ear, "let's tell her a bald-faced lie!"

"Boone O'Malley!"

"Yes! Let's do! Let's tell her Red threw us into the lake."

"And what will she think then?"

Boone picked Belle up and swung her in a circle. "She'll think we're lying through our teeth, but she won't say so."

"And what's that supposed to solve?"

He stopped and lowered her gently to the ground. "It'll make *us* feel better, thinking she swallowed it." His eyes fairly danced with mischief.

Belle thumped him on the chest. "Such nonsense! What has gotten into you?"

"This," he growled playfully as he lowered his mouth to hers in a kiss of such exquisite tenderness that Belle forgot about her rumpled clothing, forgot about what Alice Rose might think. Thought only of how good—how right—it felt wrapped in the arms of this big and complex man.

He released her only to wrap one arm around her shoulders. "Come on. We'll start back. If your feet get tired, I'll give you a piggyback."

Belle stopped short and pinched herself.

"And what's that for?" Boone asked with an expression that said he knew without asking.

"I need to see if I'm dreaming. Skinny-dipping. Alfresco lovemaking. And piggybacking. All in the same afternoon.

Either I'm dreaming or you're not really Boone O'Malley."

"Outside this field of dreams, I'll deny everything." Boone held up his hands and shook his head, husks of field grasses flying in all directions. "This just might be a Boone O'Malley only you can see."

Belle wrapped her arm firmly around his waist and began walking again. Slowly. "Well, then, we'll just have to make regular trips back here."

"Promise?"

"Promise."

They walked in silence, arms wrapped about the other until Boone said, "Arabella, what did you think of Cassie's boyfriend?"

"Drew?" Belle stalled. She didn't want to be disloyal to Cassie, but she didn't want to be dishonest with Boone.

"Yeah, Drew. You know, the guy with the attitude at the dinner table today."

Belle inhaled sharply. "He did seem a bit taken with himself."

Boone harrumphed. "Not only that. Didn't he seem old for Cassie?"

"I don't know about that . . ." she demurred.

"He can't be in school with her. Where did she meet the guy?"

"She told us at the table—" Belle gave his waist a squeeze "—when you were a million miles away. She said he runs a custom paint shop. For cars. Said he was taking a business course. A girlfriend introduced them."

"Well, I sure would like to get my hands on that girlfriend."

"As if that would do any good."

"You have a better suggestion?"

Belle stopped and looked up into his face, a face now clouded with worry. "You could talk to me about your concerns. Share the load. It's amazing how that helps."

Squinting against the late-afternoon sun, Boone gazed intently at the horizon. When he spoke, his voice was gruff, sealed off. "I'm not used to sharing thoughts like this. I haven't done it in a long, long while. I'm afraid I'm no good at it anymore."

The tone of their afternoon was changing. The magic was slipping away with the brightness of the day. The shadows had already begun to lengthen.

Belle reached out to touch Boone's chest. Laid the palm of her hand softly on his heart. "It's not that you're no good at it. It's just that you're rusty. Rusty's easily remedied."

He sighed and looked at her. "Arabella Sherman, do you know what people in town say about you?"

Her eyes widened involuntarily. "No. What?"

The color of his eyes had changed to the softest blue. "They say, 'You can*not* inflict discouragement upon her.'"

"Well, now," she replied, patting his chest gently before she laced her fingers through his and resumed walking, "There's a lesson in that somewhere."

"I expect there is, Ms. Sherman. I expect there is."

Out of the corner of her eye Belle could see that Boone's face had relaxed into an expression of peacefulness.

Boone looked down at the woman walking languorously beside him, her hand clasped in his. The descending afternoon sun bathed the field and everything in it in a soft gold. A gold that lent a precious quality to Belle's features. She was precious. To him. He'd suspected as much recently, but he'd tried to hide that dawning realization from himself. This afternoon he'd let go and admitted it. In actions.

This afternoon. What an incredible roller-coaster ride of emotions it had turned into. At the beginning of the day, as disgruntled as he'd been, who would have thought that by the end of the day he'd have found his heart's ease? And in between he would have fussed and fumed and worried and laughed . . . and hungered . . . and loved.

All because of this woman. Arabella. The thought of her name alone brought a smile to his lips.

"A penny for your thoughts," he heard her say.

"Oh," he replied, glancing over to her lovely face bathed in sundown and anticipation, "you'd need a whole Swiss bank account to gain access to these thoughts." He squeezed her hand and kept on walking.

She didn't press the issue, but merely continued to walk at his side, kicking her bare feet out in front of her, humming a sensuous little tune.

That was one of the surprising things about her: the ability she had of stepping back and allowing a body breathing room. Oh, she could question and pursue and persist and probe to distraction. But she could also—uncannily—be still at just the right moment and allow a man his thoughts.

He liked that about her. A lot.

Just earlier she'd encouraged him to open up, to share his worries about Cassie with her. He'd said he wasn't any good at that sort of thing. What he hadn't said was that every time he did voice a concern, every time Belle listened, every time he shared the burden with her, it did help. It didn't necessarily solve anything, but it made him feel somehow better. Just sharing the load. With her.

He should tell her. She wouldn't gloat. Wouldn't say, I told you so. That's another thing he liked about this woman: she always operated out of a sense of caring, never out of a sense of one-upsmanship.

He chuckled to himself. Why, he was accumulating quite a list of things he liked about this woman.

"That's it, Boone O'Malley," Belle declared, turning to stand in his path. "I may not have a Swiss bank account, but I sure as heck would like to know what's causing all this grinning and all this chuckling."

Boone looked into her upturned face and felt bewitched by her soft brown eyes and her sensuous full lips. Bewitched. That was a feeling he was growing to like, too. He reached out to touch the creamy smooth skin of her cheek, felt hunger and desire leap within him.

"I was just thinking," he replied, his voice husky to his own ears, "of the things I like about you."

"Oh, yes." She cocked one eyebrow mischievously. "The same things that drive you to distraction."

He laughed. Surprisingly, that was something else he had grown accustomed to since Belle's arrival: the sound of his own laughter. It was an amazingly satisfying sound, one few people, himself included, had heard much in the past six years.

"Actually," he murmured, kissing the tip of her nose, "there are things I like about you that are free of any downside."

"Do tell."

Mmm. She said *do tell* with a purr that reminded him of their lovemaking.

Lord, what lovemaking. Fast and furious. Demanding. Hungry and passionate. He'd forgotten he had such feelings inside him. Had forgotten what a woman could do to a man's body and soul. And not just any woman. Arabella. Belle.

It was not just loneliness and abstinence that had made this coming together earthshaking. Heaven knew that in the past six years attractive women had made themselves available to him. And several times, out of desperate physical need, he'd succumbed. But never—*never*—had those experiences come close to this afternoon. This afternoon had been *love*making. Plain and simple. It had engaged his body and his mind and his heart. And all because he'd been making love with Arabella Sherman.

The power of the experience shook him to his very core.

And then an equally powerful thought struck him. Feeling the way he now did about Belle, how was he going to keep himself from acting crazy in love in public? Their lovemaking this afternoon didn't change the fact that he still had an eighteen-year-old daughter. A still impressionable daughter who needed a mature example. A sensitive daughter who loved the memory of her mother.

A shadowy twinge of guilt passed over Boone's heart.

He took a deep breath, then said, "Arabella?"

"Yes?" She stopped walking and turned that heart-stopping, angelic smile upon him.

He reached out and slipped his fingers through her dark cap of tousled curls. She responded by twining her arms around his waist, by leaning her head against his chest, by sighing contentedly. As if he were the most wonderful man on the face of the earth. At that moment he felt like a jerk.

"About this afternoon . . ." he began.

She chuckled. "Scared you, didn't it?"

Jolted by her insight, he held her at arm's length. Held her and gazed into eyes so gold-flecked brown and deep—and understanding—that he couldn't muster any upset. He felt his lips curl in a half smile. "So you think I was scared?"

"If you're smart, you were." Her grin broadened.

Then it struck him. "Were you? Are you . . . ?"

"Yes. Was. Am. Will be."

"But you're Arabella Sherman."

She laughed out loud, her infectious, bell-like laugh. "And *what* does that have to do with anything?"

Running his hand through his hair in exasperation, Boone searched for the right words. "It's just that nothing seems to faze you. Getting an unusual business venture off the ground. Eban Smart. Jail time. Tornadoes. You name it."

Belle's expression turned serious. "Never knowing my mother. A car wreck that nearly took my life. A fiancé who decides the hospital's the best place to dump me."

Feeling her sudden pain, Boone reached out to touch her, to bring her back into the circle of warmth and happiness and magic that she'd created this afternoon. "I didn't mean to dredge up old hurts."

"You didn't." She shrugged. "They're always there. Beneath the brightness, the merriment, the Holly Golightly whom everybody sees." Her eyes pooled with unshed tears. Now, what the devil had he said or done to bring those on? He felt like a double jerk for worrying earlier about himself. "Scratch beneath the surface of anyone's life," she continued softly, "and you'll find the unexpected."

"What are you saying, Arabella?" He wanted to pull her into his arms, but her stance said she didn't wished to be held.

"I'm just telling you not to worry. As beautiful as this afternoon was, you needn't worry that I'll make any claims on you."

"I wasn't—"

She raised her hand to stop him. "Be honest, Boone. We're both commitment shy, in our own ways. You because I'm not the reserved, ladylike woman you require. And me...well, to be honest, I really don't want to get hurt again."

Why was his heart hammering in the back of his throat? Hadn't he just moments ago been worrying that she'd now expect to carry on a relationship? Hadn't he secretly wished for some detachment until he could deal with his concerns over Cassie and the memory of Peg? Why now, when she voiced hesitation, did his heart leap with jealous little yelps?

"Why are you commitment shy?" he asked, not sure that he wanted to hear the answer.

"Because of my mother. Because of Porter."

"I don't understand. What does one have to do with the other?"

"They were two people I loved deeply. They both left."

"But your mother couldn't . . ."

She attempted a wan smile. "Don't ever try to talk logic to the heart. The heart doesn't think. Doesn't reason. It *feels*. My mother couldn't help her leaving. Porter could. My heart wept equally at both departures." She looked up at him, her lashes glistening with tears. "I couldn't bear your leaving, Boone. And you would. Because you see us as so thoroughly unsuited. The very things you like about me drive you to distraction. It's better that we live from day to day. Without promises. Without commitment. That's the only way either of us could survive."

Speechless, he pulled her into an embrace. Not a passionate embrace. A protective embrace. He'd never even speculated that she could harbor such reservations. He'd been so caught up in his own. But now that she'd voiced hers, he wanted to shake her, to convince her of her faulty logic, to tell her how much he loved her and how that love could overcome all obstacles.

But now his words would ring hollow. The time to have said all that would have been *before* Belle told him of her fears. Right from the start, he should never have held back the truth of his growing feelings. Not from Belle. And not from himself. Instead, he'd been prickly and picky. Had tried to make her over just as he'd tried to make Peg over. And Belle now had every right to be leery of a relationship with him.

That didn't soothe his own heart, however. He'd experienced heaven this afternoon, only to have it snatched from his possession.

He stroked her shoulders. Kissed the top of her head. Murmured, "What now, Arabella? What now?" Dear Lord, please, don't let her push him away completely.

She did pull back from him, but when she did, the look of pain was gone from her face. In its place was a sweet serenity. "How good are you at flying by the seat of your pants?"

He had to laugh, she asked so innocently. So sincerely. "What do you mean?"

"Well...can we manage something light? Can we enjoy the moment and not worry about the future?"

"You're talking about friendship?" Somehow—now—a platonic relationship didn't appeal to Boone. And somehow he'd always felt Arabella Sherman would have to be an all-or-nothing proposition.

She cocked one eyebrow and tilted her head. Her eyes fairly danced. "I was thinking more along the lines of lighthearted lovers. We are adults, you know. We're both free."

Free. Not exactly.

Sure, on the surface he was. But those unseen chains of responsibility—of accountability—weighed him down. How could he carry on a no-strings-attached sexual relationship at the same time he was trying to instill in his daughter the idea that relationships required maturity and commitment? How could he have even the most lighthearted of relationships with Belle without trying to get her to see reason—his reason—at every turn? He'd destroyed Peg, trying to make her over. Belle didn't deserve that.

As he hesitated, Belle said softly, "Well...maybe not." She threaded her fingers through his again and began to walk slowly. "What we shared this afternoon was joy and beauty. But joy and beauty are ephemeral. Not necessarily workable. And I understand, Boone O'Malley, that you like your life to be rock solid and very workable." She looked up at him, her gaze totally devoid of recrimination. "I understand that you don't see *us* as workable. I understand. I really do."

The kicker was, Boone thought, she did understand. Her understanding, combined with his intransigence, made him feel miserable.

Preparing for bed, checking locks, dousing lights, Belle padded around her apartment, Sebastian at her heels. What a day. With thoughts of Boone whirling through her head, she could bet that she'd get no sleep tonight.

For a while, for a glorious short while after their lovemaking, it had seemed as if Boone was about to break free from the pain of his past. From the self-imposed worries and constraints of the present. To break free and allow himself to explore an unfolding relationship.

Oh, how she'd wanted that. Not just because of the new physical development. She'd seen their lovemaking as an admission on both their parts that they were willing to take the risks inherent in pursuing the growing attraction between them. For there was attraction. No denying that. A powerful chemistry despite the differences in their outlooks on life.

And how different—really—were their outlooks? Sure, there were surface differences in the way they dealt with life. But the things they both held most dear—good friends, a mate, family, home and hearth, a sense of place—these things dovetailed perfectly. If only Boone could see it.

But it certainly hadn't appeared as if Boone could see it. Not on their silent walk back to Alice Rose's farmhouse. Not in the subdued ride home in Boone's truck. Not in the quiet goodbyes at the door of her storefront. No, it certainly didn't appear as if he'd settle for a make-it-up-as-you-go-along kind of love affair.

And that, sadly, left Belle with nothing. For she was convinced, as he was, that, surface differences getting in the way, the two of them weren't headed for anything permanent.

Sebastian woofed, jolting Belle out of her musings. Someone was ringing the doorbell.

"Who is it?" she called out.

"Boone."

Of all the... What had gotten into the man?

Opening the door, she inhaled sharply at the sexy sight of him leaning on her doorjamb, a what-the-hell-am-I-doing-here expression on his face.

She said nothing. After their parting this afternoon, there wasn't much to say.

He raked her with his gaze. "What do you have in that refrigerator of yours for breakfast?"

"Breakfast? But I thought we'd agreed this afternoon—"

"Don't ever try to talk logic to the heart," he growled softly as he stepped into the room and swept her into a mind-drenching kiss.

## Chapter Eleven

Oblivious to the lunchtime crowd, Boone sat by the window in the Hole-in-the-Wall café and waited for Belle. For the past month—ever since he'd thrown caution to the wind and landed on her doorstep late that night—they'd been nearly inseparable.

She felt like an addiction to him. The more he experienced her, the more he wanted her. Needed her. He'd given in to the compulsion, and to hell with what folks might think. But a small—almost minuscule—part of him worried that no good could come of acting like a lovestruck fool.

"You waitin' for Belle, sugah?" Edna the waitress stood next to the table, one hand on her hip, the other clutching a coffeepot.

"Yeah." Everyone in town now thought of Belle and him as a twosome. After a while wouldn't everyone expect them to make a more mature commitment? More mature than the present unstructured, free-love kind of liaison they now shared. What was wrong with him? Wasn't this just the kind of relationship most men salivated over? Good company. Clean fun. Great sex. No strings. Why did a niggling little voice in the back of his head keep reminding him that this was not Boone O'Malley's kind of relationship? Why couldn't he just relax and enjoy?

Because he wanted more. But, because of his responsibility to Cassie and because of the persistent memories of his past failure with Peg, he was still hesitant to commit to more.

"Well, she may be late." Edna's voice cut through Boone's thoughts. "She and Eban are putting the finishing touches on the signs for her grand opening." Edna poured him a cup of coffee. "Who'd of thought old Eban Smart could have stayed sober enough to work every morning, let alone keep his hand steady enough to paint signs?" She winked before turning to tend to her other customers. "That woman of yours is a miracle worker."

A miracle worker. You could call her that. Or you could call her a foolhardy risk taker. After a month of virtually living with Boone, she still did exactly as she pleased. Still drove him straight up the wall with her concern for others and her total disregard for her own safety.

Take Eban Smart. Please.

Sheriff Bratt and Belle had worked out conditions for Smart to be released from jail after the suspicious fire in the alley behind Belle's storefront. Those conditions were that, for Belle not to press charges, Smart would perform "community service" every morning—the few hours he was miraculously sober—with Belle as she readied her literacy center.

Everyone, Boone among them, had said she was crazy to take in a man who wished her ill. Belle ignored the lot of them. Everyone thought that once she had him working she'd try to reform Smart, or, at the very least, try to clean him up. She hadn't. Instead, she worked with him every morning and treated him just the same way she treated everyone else in Sweet Hope. With kindness. With respect. With a gentle consideration. She didn't try to clean up his amazingly ragged and ripe personal appearance. She didn't lecture him on the evils of drink. She didn't try to talk him into joining any programs. She simply treated him as a human being. In a month's time he still looked like something that had crawled out from under a rock. He still got drunk in the afternoon. But if you looked closely, as Boone had done, you could see that a change had indeed occurred. The gray meanness had begun to seep out of Eban Smart, replaced for a few hours each morning by a spark of life. Boone had noticed, and so, it seemed, had Sebastian. The dog no longer cowered when the man entered the storefront.

A miracle worker. That's what the residents of Sweet Hope called Belle, and, secretly, Boone had to agree. She sure had wrought a miracle in his life. What with her optimism and her laughter and her sensuality. He felt like a new man with his old zest for life. A man living a little dangerously. On the edge. Not quite doing what was expected of him. A man who dined royally at life's banquet, but who always remained hungry. Deliciously, devilishly hungry.

He felt arms slide sensuously around his neck from behind, felt hot breath on his cheek, heard a sultry voice whisper, "Hey, sailor, looking for some fun?" Belle's voice. Liquid. Soft. Sexy as hell. Pulling on his innermost desires. Turning his insides upside down.

As he turned to clasp her hand and pull her into the seat opposite him, he could see, out of the corner of his eye, the café patrons smirking knowingly. To hell with them. They should all have it so good.

Belle lowered herself into her seat. Actually, she floated. She had on that filmy lavender outfit. His favorite. The one she'd been wearing when he'd caught her falling from the ladder, aeons ago. She smiled at him. An angel's smile. But in place of a halo she wore a crown of daisies. He started at the sight of it.

No matter how long he knew her, she still had the power to discombobulate him. He looked at the flowers and cocked an eyebrow in question.

Her soft, bell-like laugh wrapping its music around him, she reached up to touch the earthly halo. "Do you like them? Eban brought me a bouquet this morning. I didn't ask, but I'm sure the flower beds on the green are short a couple dozen blossoms. I put some in water. Some into a crown. Eban seemed pleased. He actually blushed."

"He should, the old coot."

Belle reached a hand across the table and stroked his. "Why, Boone O'Malley, I do believe you're jealous."

Boone harrumphed, but squeezed her hand affectionately. "Actually, I don't want to talk about Smart." He might as well cut to the chase. "I want to talk about Cassie."

Belle sobered as if she knew what was coming. Hell, had he been so caught up in his pursuit of Belle that he was the last one in town to notice a change in his daughter?

"What about Cassie?" she asked softly.

"I went out to visit Mama this morning. She's the one who brought it up. For the past few weeks she's been worried about Cassie's mood. Says she's acting too subdued. Withdrawn. Damn, I just thought she was caught up in finals. Have you noticed anything odd?"

"Yes...." Belle frowned. "Cassie still comes around the storefront to help... but always when another volunteer is around. We never seem to be alone anymore."

"Is that odd?"

"At first I didn't think so. But then I began to think of how eager she'd seemed when we first met. Eager to share her thoughts and experiences and hopes. How she seemed to want to hear mine. To obtain another woman's perspective. Now... it's almost as if she wants to be with me... at the same time she wants to avoid me." Belle looked him in the eye. "And, yes, she seems very subdued. I thought maybe she was having boyfriend trouble."

"I don't know about that." Boone felt a hot, uncomfortable flush come to his cheeks. "I've been so caught up in my own...life...that I haven't paid much attention to hers." He rubbed his chin. "Some father, huh?"

Belle smiled and squeezed his hand. "Don't beat yourself up. You're a terrific father. Cassie is eighteen, in case you'd forgotten. Almost a woman."

"It's the *almost* that scares the heck out of me."

As Edna the waitress approached, the two lapsed into silence and scanned the menus. They ordered quickly. Belle seemed as eager to get back to their conversation as he was.

When Edna had gone, Belle leaned forward, her brow furrowed, her voice worried, and asked, "Do you think Cassie is upset about you seeing me?"

"No! Not at all." Whatever Boone had or hadn't noticed about his daughter, he'd noticed how, right from the beginning, she seemed to love Belle. As did Alice Rose. No, Cassie would be pleased that Belle and he were a couple. That is, if she was pleased about anything these days. From what his mama had said, she wasn't. "No, I think it's something in her own life."

Belle, her face pinched in thought, fingered the salt-shaker on the table. "When you've seen her, has she been alone?"

"No...." Odd bits and pieces of seemingly inconsequential memory bubbled to the surface of his thoughts. "Although I haven't seen her with Drew...and, odd, I haven't seen her with any of her girlfriends. Only with Jacob Matthews."

"Jacob Matthews? The pastor's son? The one who seemed smitten with her at your mama's dinner a month ago?"

"One and the same. Although the few times I saw them together he didn't look smitten. Now that I think of it, he looked deadly serious. Worried, even."

"Do you think Cassie's worried about Jacob Matthews for some reason?"

A dark and awful feeling began to creep over Boone. "No...I think Jacob Matthews was worried about her." He looked across the table at Belle and saw, mirrored in her face, the concern he now felt. "What do you think is the matter?"

Belle attempted a smile. "Maybe nothing. The only way to find out for certain is to talk to Cassie."

Boone glowered at the hot open-faced sandwich Edna placed in front of him. Suddenly he didn't feel hungry. He shook his head. "Cassie always brought her problems to me. Why wouldn't she this time?"

"As I said, she may not have a problem."

"Or it may be that she does...and I haven't been around. I haven't been there for her."

With Boone's words, Belle felt an almost palpable drop in temperature at the table. She reached across the table to squeeze his hand again, but he withdrew his own hands quickly, grasping his knife and fork. She noticed he didn't touch his food, but his hands were conveniently occupied.

And for the first time in a month she saw his eyes go from a deep and clear blue to a steely, unreadable gray.

Oh, Boone, she thought, don't draw away. Don't blame Cassie's problems of the moment on your happiness.

But as she silently, fervently prayed, he seemed to distance himself. To withdraw from her in hard determination.

Softly she declared, "You *have* been there for her. Just as you always have."

He rose abruptly from the table. "I need to find her."

"Of course you do. Call me later."

He simply scowled, dug deep in his pocket, then threw a twenty on the table. "That should cover lunch," he muttered as he turned and left the café.

Belle gazed out the window after him and tried to convince herself he was simply worried about his only daughter. Tried to focus on that and not on the horrible possibility that he somehow blamed his new relationship with Belle on this current upset—if upset there was—in Cassie's life.

No longer hungry, she stared at her salad. Should she stay here and pretend to eat, or go back to tackle the seemingly endless tasks necessary before the literacy center's grand opening next week?

Oh, Boone.

She loved that man so.

But over the past month she'd almost held her breath as he'd worked side by side with her to ready the storefront, as he'd bitten his tongue when he'd obviously thought some idea she'd tried to implement had been off-the-wall, as he'd more often than not relaxed and laughed, as they'd gone out in public together as a couple. And as they'd made love. Passionately. As two people who feared their world might end at any time.

That's why Belle held her breath. Because as eager and loving as Boone had been, she had the impression that here was a man who felt he didn't deserve this wild happiness. Whether because of his normally reserved nature or out of a sense of responsibility to his eighteen-year-old daughter—or his wife—Belle couldn't say for sure. But it was obvious that Boone held back a part of himself. For safety's sake, perhaps. His own safety.

Pushing the salad greens around the plate with her fork, she sighed. How she longed to tell him that she loved him. How she longed to hear he loved her. But they'd never spoken those words. Had never come close. She sighed again.

"Sweetheart, you and Boone have a spat?" Edna stood over the table, a concerned look on her face. "'Cause if you did, I'm gonna have a word with that boy."

Belle forced a smile. "Now, why would you do that, Edna?"

"Because *you* are the best thing to happen to him in six years, and he'd better not mess up this chance at happiness." She bent and murmured, "Honey, didn't your mama teach you not to play with your food?" She chuckled as she whisked away the salad plate. "I'm gonna take away these nasty greens and bring you a slice of coconut creme pie. On the house. That'll fix your mood. Uh-huh, uh-huh."

Belle had to smile then. Effortlessly. Edna was one of the reasons she loved Sweet Hope. One of countless reasons she felt so at home here. One of the reasons she'd hate to ever have to leave. Now, why was she thinking of leaving?

Was it because she'd painted herself into a corner with Boone O'Malley? Falling for him, carrying on for a month, she'd found her emotions tightly, inextricably wound with Boone and his family. If their relationship should ever end...well, it was like the saying in the old movies: this town wasn't big enough for the two of them.

This new life of hers, this second chance, was not working out the way Belle had anticipated. She'd anticipated the freedom to soar. And if love happened to cross her path, she'd anticipated a lover who would pursue her wholeheartedly. Not a man who always seemed to hold on to a few misgivings. Today when he'd left the table Boone had seemed to have more than a few misgivings. And Belle felt sure that they didn't all center on Cassie.

What had she done? Hadn't her fresh start, her move, her dream of a literacy center been enough? Why did she have to become embroiled with another reluctant man?

Edna returned to the table with a carry-out container. "I boxed the pie for you, sugah. Thought maybe you'd like to curl up in front of the soaps at home and eat it." She handed Belle the container and smiled comfortingly. "Now, don't you go worrying about Boone O'Malley. As men go, he's got more sense than most. He'll come around. You'll see."

Belle put on a brave face, took the container with the comfort food, then stepped out into the hot noon sunshine. Why did she feel so gloomy on this bright, late-spring day? Why did she have this feeling of impending doom? Boone had merely said he must talk with Cassie....

But the way he'd said it. The way he'd looked at Belle, his regard cold and somehow accusing, had made her shiver deep inside her and pray Cassie was only going through a case of freshman finals nerves.

She turned toward her storefront. She had much to do if she was going to be ready for her grand opening next week. She hoped several volunteers would stop in this afternoon. She hoped Alice Rose would make an appearance. She had the feeling she was going to need the comfort of people around her.

Boone didn't have far to search for Cassie. He started at home on the off chance she had a break from classes and was studying for finals. He found her sitting at the kitchen table, wrapped in an old robe, cradling a cup of hot tea, gazing out the window. Ashen faced.

"Oh, baby," he murmured as he slid into a seat across from her. "Do you want to talk?"

She turned red-rimmed eyes on him. Eyes with large dark smudges encircling them. Eyes that told of grief or illness. Had she been this way for the past several weeks, as Alice Rose had said? How could he have been so blind?

He reached across the table and took her small hand in his. "Talk to me," he implored her.

"About what, Daddy?" she asked softly, turning her gaze away from him, toward the window again. "About what?"

"About you, sweetheart, of course. What's wrong?"

Her lower lip quivered. "Nothing . . . nothing and everything."

Boone squeezed her hand as his heart felt about to burst with shared pain for his daughter. "Let's talk about the everything, then. Is it school?" He fervently hoped it was something at school. Something that a new term would take care of. He never thought he'd find himself praying for a failing grade, but a failing grade wouldn't be the end of the world.

"No," she barely whispered.

"Boyfriend trouble?"

She didn't answer.

Boone's heart sank when he began to tally the myriad scenarios boyfriend trouble could encompass. "Tell me," he urged softly. "Cassie, you know you can tell me anything. I love you, honey. Let me help you sort this out. Whatever it is. No matter how awful it looks to you right now, sharing it helps. It does."

He caught himself with his words. Now, who had taught him that?

Belle. The woman in whom he'd lost himself this past month. Had so lost himself, in fact, that he hadn't seen his daughter's pain. Well, that could change. Would change. Right now. Now Cassie had his undivided attention.

"Cassie, please...."

When she finally turned to look at him, he could see the tears glistening in her eyes. Could see a look of pain. And desperation. A trapped look. A look he'd prayed never to see on a child of his. It took everything in his power to remain in his seat. To affect an air of calm. So that his daughter would feel safe with him. Would tell him her heart's sorrow. If and when she did, he prayed he could make it right.

"Daddy!" she sobbed, lowering her forehead to the table. "I'm pregnant."

Boone sucked air. Felt the bottom drop out of his stomach. "Cassie! Are you sure?"

"Positive," she muttered, her voice the soul of desolation. "I saw a doctor in Atlanta yesterday."

"But the condoms you carried..."

Cassie laughed bitterly. "Condoms aren't foolproof," she declared.

Dear Lord, he'd feared this. Had feared it and had hoped against hope this wouldn't be the cause of her distress. He rose slowly and moved to where she sat, slumped over and sobbing. Put his big hands on her tiny, trembling shoulders and said the only thing that came to mind. "I love you, baby. I love you."

"That's not enough this time, Daddy," she sobbed, throwing her arms over her head. "That's simply not enough."

His world began to spin. This wasn't the first time that love alone had simply not been enough. It hadn't been enough to save Peg. And now it wouldn't be enough to spare his daughter the momentous and painful decisions that lay before her.

Gently but firmly he pulled her out of her chair. Pulled her to his chest. Cradled and rocked her as he had when she'd been just a baby. Crooned her name. Racked his brain for a way out of this quagmire. Tried to think of the right thing to do. The right thing for Cassie. And the baby. And the young man involved.

He clenched his teeth at the thought of the man involved. Pushed down the violent urge to seek him out. To pummel him senseless. "Cassie...the father?"

Cassie pushed away from him. "I will *not* talk about the father," she insisted bitterly, her body tensing, her tears drying on a face that was now a cold, hard mask.

"But you have to. We're going to have to make a lot of decisions."

Cassie whirled out of Boone's grasp, turned her back on him, crossed her arms tightly over her chest. "Well, we'll just have to make them without *him*," she hissed.

Dear God, he prayed, give me the wisdom to pick the right words to get me safely through this minefield. Don't let me misstep and drive her away. She needs me. Give me the sense to say the right things. Those things that will keep her talking. That will let her open up to me.

"If it's Drew—" he began.

"I told you I don't want to talk about the father."

"But, Cassie, honey, he has responsibilities...and rights."

She turned to level a chilling gaze at him. A gaze filled with an animal-like fear. "Let's get this clear—the father, whoever he may be, will be interested in neither his responsibilities nor his rights."

An awful thought slammed into Boone. "Do you know who the father is?" He held his breath, waiting for an answer he didn't want to hear.

Cassie lowered her gaze to the floor. Her shoulders slumped so, she looked half her age. A mere child. "You've got to believe me, Daddy," she whispered. "No matter what it looks like, I haven't been sleeping around."

"I didn't mean to accuse you." Damnation. He was making a royal mess of this. He stepped to her side and took her in his arms again. She crumpled against him, but didn't cry this time.

He almost wished she would cry. It would seem more natural somehow. Unlike this unearthly silence. This pall of abject defeat.

He massaged her back and shoulders. Kissed the top of her head. Took a deep breath and tried again. "Sweetheart ... what does Jacob Matthews have to do with all this?"

Cassie stiffened in his arms. "Jacob has been there for me."

Like a high-voltage surge, Boone felt the unfinished accusation: Jacob had been there for her as he—Boone—had not.

In silence he hugged his daughter to him. And just where had he been? Chasing after Belle. Crazy with hormones and desire and hunger for the pleasure of her company. Blind to his responsibilities. His responsibility to behave maturely. As an example to his only daughter.

He smoothed the hair back from Cassie's face. "How far along are you, sweetheart?"

Cassie sniffled. "Only a few weeks."

Only a few weeks. Just as he'd cut loose. Just as he'd started leaving his truck parked—at all hours—in front of Belle's. Hell, he might just as well have placed a full-page ad in the *Gazette* telling Cassie to pull out all stops because her old man had. He sure was a fine example of a father.

He seethed inwardly at himself. He was going to be a grandfather...and the first time he'd made love with Belle, he hadn't even thought of protection. Luckily she'd been on the Pill. But the Pill wasn't perfect, either. What if she were to get pregnant? That would make him a grandfather *and* a new father at the same time. Now, wouldn't that just be grist for the mill for the patrons of the Hole-in-the-Wall and the old checker players in the back of the drugstore?

He groaned aloud and immediately wished he hadn't as Cassie pulled away and looked up at him in concern. Her eyes welled with tears again. "I don't have to have it, you know," she barely whispered.

"Cassie, honey, no," he implored, his heart aching with the dilemma she faced. "That's the choice of last resort. We have other options open to us. We need to think things through. Carefully. We have time. We needn't make any rash decisions." He pulled her tight against him again. She clung pitifully. "Darlin', just know you're not alone."

Cassie began to sob. "How am I going to face Grammy?"

"With me by your side, Cassie-of-mine. With me by your side."

Through her sobs Cassie murmured, "You used to call me 'Cassie-of-mine' when I was a little girl. Do you remember?"

Remember? It seemed like yesterday. Could his baby be having a baby? Dear Lord, it wasn't as if there wasn't enough love in the O'Malley family to embrace a new member. Oh, there was love aplenty to go around. It was just that Cassie was so young. So much in her life would be interrupted. Postponed. Canceled, even, because of a baby. Alice Rose and he could only do so much. The rest was up to Cassie. For the rest of her life, if that was the choice she made.

"Oh, Cassie-of-mine," he crooned, "I remember every little detail about my girl. I remember her kite always flew the highest of all the other kids. I remember her mud pies were always the tenderest. I remember she always cried the loudest at the Fourth of July fireworks noise.'' He felt Cassie rub a hand across her eyes. Heard her snuffle. ''And I remember thinking this girl of mine could be or do anything she set her mind to.''

''Oh, Daddy, I've failed you.''

No, Boone thought, I've failed you. But all that's going to change.

Taking Cassie's small, tear-stained face in his large hands, he replied, ''No, sweetheart, you haven't failed me. But now you're going to have to take all that strength I know you have inside you and put it to the test. You're going to have to be strong to make some tough decisions. I'll be with you every step of the way—as will your grammy. But the decisions will be yours.''

Tears once again threatened to spill over her lashes. Her lower lip trembled. ''Is this what being an adult is all about? Decisions that seem too tough to make?''

'''Fraid so, honey.'' He kissed her on the forehead. ''You go get into a shower. When you're all cleaned up, we'll go see your grammy.''

Cassie looked as if that was the last place she wanted to go.

''Don't look as if the world's about to end.'' He forced a smile. ''Three adult, intelligent, good-looking O'Malleys can surely figure out what to do about one itty-bitty baby. Now, scoot.''

Turning to go, she stopped. ''What about Belle?''

Hell. He'd just told Cassie that being an adult was all about making too-tough decisions. This was one decision he sure wasn't looking forward to making.

He sighed. ''One step at a time, Cassie-of-mine. Let's talk to your grandmother first.''

As Cassie turned to shower and dress, Boone crossed his arms and gazed out the window. What was he going to do about his relationship with Belle?

Belle.

Standing in his kitchen, he could conjure up the sight of her. The feel of her. The taste, the smell, the sound of her. It was as if this lovely, free-spirited woman now resided inside him. Was a part of him. The part he'd never dared unleash. She was funny and sexy and gentle and sexy and quirky...and sexy. Sexy as hell in her one-of-a-kind way. But her total disregard for what others might think still drove him up the wall.

For the past month he'd abandoned his usual reserve and caution in the pursuit of a woman so different from him that he could foresee no permanent relationship. So different that he could only live from minute to minute. Minutes filled with pleasure and gratification. Pleasure and gratification that isolated him from the world moving around him. Isolated him to the point where he didn't even recognize that his own daughter was in trouble.

He hadn't seen Cassie's distress. That was reprehensible enough, but the trouble itself...could it be laid at his feet, as well? Had she chosen to run fast and free because she saw her father doing just that?

Irresponsible. That's what he'd been. He thought of Peg and how saddened she'd be that, having sworn to safeguard their daughter, he'd let her down instead.

Peg.

Because of Peg, he'd tried not to change Belle. Instead, *he'd* changed...and not for the better. He'd let his hunger for Belle become so...so public. Not only had he failed to protect Cassie, he'd failed to preserve his own dignity.

He slammed his fist into the palm of his hand. Damn. The worst was yet to come. When word got out of Cassie's situation—and word *would* get out—he was going to have his hands full shielding her honor. This past month he'd taken the chuckles and the little jokes concerning his capitulation to Belle, but he would not tolerate a word breathed against Cassie. Not a word. Not even in jest.

Dear God, what kind of a man was he? All his adult life, folks in Sweet Hope had turned to him for advice. For help.

They'd seen him as a strong man who could reckon all sides of an issue, who could stop trouble before it happened. Hah! He hadn't seen the danger signs that led up to Peg's death. Hadn't seen the danger signs that led up to Cassie's pregnancy. Hadn't prevented either. Two strikes against him. Before that third strike and inevitable out, he sure as hell was going to devote himself to protecting his daughter's name . . . and the welfare of his grandchild.

As much as the part of him that had tasted freedom hated to do it, Boone knew full well what he had to do. As soon as he and Cassie had visited Alice Rose, he needed to talk to Belle.

Glancing at her watch, Belle paced her loft apartment. Eight o'clock in the evening. And no sign of Boone.

Sebastian lay on a small rug, nervously following his mistress with his eyes, occasionally emitting a pitiful moan.

"I know, Sebbie," Belle said, pushing her hair off her forehead in an irritated gesture. "I'm driving *me* crazy, too."

Crazy. That's what all this worry was. Boone had gone to find Cassie. In the Hole-in-the-Wall this afternoon he'd become so very concerned that he had to talk to his daughter, of course. And then, having taken time out for lunch with Belle and additional time out for a father-daughter chat, he'd thrown himself into his work. Yes, that was it. No need for all this crazy worry. Worry over the fact that there hadn't been a word from him in over seven hours.

In the past month they'd been in almost constant contact. Phone calls. Unexpected visits. Walks on the green. Notes. Flowers. Work on the storefront. Breakfasts, lunches, dinners. And nights drenched in lovemaking. Well, nights mostly, but a fair share of mornings, afternoons and evenings. Belle sighed at the thought of their lovemaking. If Mr. Boone O'Malley still held back a tiny portion of his inner self, he held nothing back of his body. His body was hers and hers alone. She sighed again, more deeply, as she imagined his body in intimate detail.

She blushed and stopped pacing. "Oh, Sebbie, it's not as if this is just a physical relationship. Oh, no. There's so much more to it than that. But, to tell you the truth, I'm afraid to admit the full scope of my emotions."

As if understanding perfectly, Sebastian rose, waddled to Belle's side, then licked her hand that hung limply at her side.

She ruffled his shaggy head. "I love him so much. But this glorious physical relationship is all I'm ever going to get, I'm afraid. A part of Boone is locked tightly away. A part he withholds from me. If I'd been smart—which I obviously wasn't—I'd never have become involved with another reluctant man."

Sebastian whined softly, and Belle sank to the floor next to him. She buried her face in his neck, drawing strength from his dog's unconditional love. She had her new life. She had new friends, Alice Rose and Cassie chief among them. A new hometown she felt was truly home. And a literacy center, a dream, that would become reality next week. So what if she had to guard her heart? Guard it from wishing to join—permanently—with the off-limits heart of Boone O'Malley.

The doorbell rang, jolting her out of her musings. She rose reluctantly. It couldn't be Boone. He had his own key. But Boone was the only person she wanted to see right now.

She opened the door to find him, feet planted, arms crossed. His body language was so severe her heart constricted. But his facial expression was so fraught with pain she actually took a step backward as if someone had hit her. He made no move to come in.

"Did you forget your key?" she asked. An inane question. She had no desire for any real answer. In her heart of hearts she only wished to stave off the inevitable.

"No. Somehow I didn't feel comfortable using it."

Dear God, what had happened in the past seven hours to exact this change in the man she loved? "C-come in," she managed to stammer.

"I can say what I have to say right here." His regard hooded, his normally expressive eyes were flat, gray, telling her nothing.

"What is it?" She knew. She knew and didn't want to know. Already her heart flinched in pain. Already the tears clawed at the back of her eyes. But more awful than knowing what was coming, was knowing that there was nothing she could do to avert the impending calamity. And not knowing the why of it.

"Arabella . . ." The way he said her name. Not the caress of the past month, but a brutal shove. "I think we should stop seeing each other."

## Chapter Twelve

Belle reached her hand out toward the wall. Suddenly her legs alone wouldn't hold her upright. She felt her forehead constrict as if in the grip of a monster migraine. She looked at Boone, who seemed immune to her distress.

"What do you mean, you don't think we should see each other anymore?" Her voice sounded hollow to her own ears. Unreal. As unreal as the words Boone had spoken. "Boone, what has happened to us since lunch?"

"It's what's happened to Cassie. She's pregnant."

Still reeling from the first blow, Belle didn't see the second one coming. She felt the pain as if the punch were physical.

"Pregnant? *Pregnant?*" She plopped into the little wicker side chair next to the door. "But she was always so proud of being prepared."

Boone snorted. "Prepared or not, she's now pregnant. And I think you and I have to shoulder our responsibility in this matter."

"You and I? *Our* responsibility?" As much of this conversation as Belle understood, Boone could be speaking Martian.

Boone suddenly looked uncomfortable. "*My* responsibility...to be fair," he amended.

Standing slowly, Belle motioned Boone into the apartment. "You said you didn't want to stay, but I need to know what's going on here. Come in, please. Right now I'm terribly confused. What does Cassie being pregnant have to do with us? Are you planning to leave town?"

He shook his head abruptly.

"Then what?"

After a moment's hesitation Boone entered the room, shutting the door deliberately behind him. He showed no indication, however, of moving from his spot near an easy exit.

Panic grew in Belle as she became more and more aware of the cold aura that surrounded him. He was angry, yes, but his anger wasn't wholly directed at Cassie's pregnancy. That was evident. It chilled her to think his anger was, for some reason, directed at her.

"Boone, please, talk to me. Is Cassie all right?" No wonder, as Alice Rose had said, the young woman had appeared withdrawn and preoccupied the past few weeks.

His words came out rat-a-tat rapid and hard. "She's fine. At least, as fine as circumstances allow."

"Is she planning to keep the baby?"

"As of now, she's planning to go through with the pregnancy." He spoke through clenched teeth as if the very words pained him. "She hasn't decided whether she'll give the baby up for adoption after it's born."

"Of course, she and the father will have to—"

"The father's out of the picture," Boone interrupted. "Cassie refuses to name him."

"*Refuses?*" Oh, dear, there was more to this than met the eye. It was difficult enough to go through a situation like this, but to attempt it alone...

"Refuses," Boone repeated, his mouth an unyielding slash across his face. His mouth may have been hard, but his eyes held pain... and something else. Guilt? Or blame? "It seems she's confided only in Jacob Matthews. If I hadn't confronted her this afternoon, I'm not sure she would have told me until she was so big I could see for myself."

"Oh, Boone...." Belle stepped forward to comfort him, but the warning look he leveled at her froze her in her tracks. Instead of wrapping him in her embrace as she longed to do, she simply asked, "Does Alice Rose know?"

"She does now. I just came from there. Cassie's with her now."

Belle thought of the Sweet Hope grapevine and the three proud O'Malleys. How difficult this would be for them. "What will you do? All of you?"

It seemed impossible that Boone could turn stiffer than he already was, but he did. "Arabella," he began, and Belle did *not* care for the harsh sound of her name on his tongue this particular time, "you've been a part of my life—my family's life—for the past month or so. For that reason I owe you an explanation of what's already happened. But since you won't be a part of my life in the future, I ask you not to worry what will happen to any of the O'Malleys."

He could have spoken no crueler words. Belle stepped back, a hand over her heart, trying to still the awful thudding in her chest.

"B-but why?" she stammered. "Why, if you're not leaving town, can't I help? Cassie will need all the love and support she can get. You will need all the love and support you can get. I don't understand why you're pushing me away."

His eyes flaring, Boone suddenly came to life. "Why? *Why?* I'll tell you why we can't see each other any more. We can't see each other because I feel—deep down in the heart of me—that our relationship, our free and easy affair, contributed to Cassie's own sexual experimentation."

Belle gasped. "You can't think that. Cassie's a young adult. Determined to act as she wants. To live as she feels is right for herself. If anything, she lives in a fairly self-centered universe, as others her own age tend to do. I don't really think she's overly influenced by your behavior or mine."

Lowering his face near hers, he snapped, "That's where you and I disagree. I believe, whether consciously or subconsciously, Cassie saw our relationship as tacit approval of free love. Uncommitted relationships. Experimentation. Whatever you choose to call it. I believe, as her father, I should have been far more concerned with the example I set for my daughter than with the pleasure I derived from you."

Now Belle was angry. Clenching her fists at her sides, she rose on tiptoe to speak her words directly in Boone's face, so there would be no mistaking the message. "Boone O'Malley, you are trying to make our relationship into something shameful, and I won't have it. There was nothing wrong with what we shared." She'd almost said *with the love we shared,* but it was evident now that any love had been one-sided. She turned slightly away from him so that he wouldn't see the tears that threatened to spill from her eyes. "There was nothing *wrong,*" she repeated softly.

It seemed that Boone struggled to believe his own rhetoric, for his next words were a little softer, although halting and raspy, as if he had difficulty uttering them. "Maybe not…if we were both free of responsibilities. But, damn it, Arabella, I had a responsibility not only to Cassie but to Peg, as well."

"Peg?" Belle turned to face him once more and saw his face bathed in grief.

"I…failed Peg once. I owe it to her memory to raise our daughter right. By failing Cassie, I've failed Peg . . . again."

Dear Lord, with the weight he took upon his shoulders, would she ever get through to him? Would he ever allow himself to heal? To accept life in all its shades of gray, all its ups and downs, all its strengths and weaknesses? He was his harshest critic.

Reaching out and grasping his arm, she wouldn't let him pull away. "Boone O'Malley, you listen to me. You have been a wonderful father. That's all that matters here. You have done your job. Cassie is an adult now. She doesn't need you to run her life or wear a hair shirt for your perceived shortcomings. All she needs from you is love. Unconditional love. You cannot, simply cannot, take on responsibility for the whole world. Neither for those who are dead nor for those who are yet to be born. You can only love and support and let others make their own decisions. Make their own mistakes. Take responsibility for their own actions." She gently squeezed his arm. "You cannot preserve and protect the entire world."

He glowered at her hand on his arm until she removed it. "I can damn well try to make sure my corner of it is clean."

Tightness constricted Belle's chest. She wasn't getting through to him. "Are you suggesting," she asked, fearing the answer, "that our relationship was unclean?"

"Arabella . . ." Her name was a pain-filled plea. "From the beginning, our relationship has been . . . inappropriate, to say the least. It couldn't have lasted."

"Why not?" Strange, but she couldn't force her voice above a whisper. And even the whisper hurt her. "What is so *inappropriate* about two people who take pleasure in being together? The world holds such hardship, such discord, any oasis of pleasure should be cherished."

"You know what I mean."

"Yes, I'm afraid I do. You see the world in terms of black and white. I don't. Because of Peg's untimely death, you've endured the pain of loss by cloaking yourself in the status quo, by wrapping yourself so tightly in what you call responsibilities that you've choked off a future. While I . . . I, having stared death in the face, have chosen to live. Living—especially living in a world where, more often than not, choices come in gray, not black and white—scares the hell out of you."

Belle's voice had risen as had the passion in her. She couldn't believe she'd spoken so bluntly to him. But these were words he needed to hear. Hadn't even Alice Rose said at one time that Boone needed to work through the river of pain? Needed to ford it in order to get to the safety of the far shore.

If Belle was going to lose him, she wasn't going to do it without a fight.

Boone stared at Belle. Her words had felt like an icy slap across his face. It was the truth in them that stung. Yes, he was uncomfortable living in a world where choices came in shades of gray. Where emotions were never clear. Never pure. Like now. How could he feel such pain at the predicament his daughter had gotten into and, at the same moment, such intense desire to take his lover in his arms, to kiss her, to tell her he didn't want to make this awful decision to part?

But part they must.

"Arabella," he implored, "don't make this any harder than it is."

Planting her hands on her hips, she became the definition of indignation. "And what am I supposed to do? Roll over without a fight and let you walk out of my life? You mean more to me than that."

Her words tore at him. *He meant something to her.* What a warm feeling that knowledge should engender. Instead, he felt cold, knowing he must hurt her.

"Cassie needs me now. Sweet Hope isn't going to be easy to face. My grandchild, if he's not going to have a daddy, will need me. Arabella, you don't seem to understand. I'm going to be a granddaddy. I owe it to my family to behave with the dignity of one."

Belle screwed up her face. "And being seen with me would be undignified, right?"

He sighed, trying to picture Belle as a grandmother. Did grandmothers waltz around town with toenails painted bright red? Did grandmothers sew silver bells on their underwear? Did grandmothers experiment with rose tattoos? Did grandmothers make love in fields of spring flowers and fire a man up so he could barely think straight? Not the grandmothers he was acquainted with.

"Let's just say," he replied slowly, "that my time and energy will be focused elsewhere from now on. It wouldn't be fair to you—"

"Hold on a second, Boone O'Malley. I can spot a smoke screen a mile away. If you're going to break up with me, at least have the gumption to give me the real reasons. You wouldn't have time for me... hah! You don't want to make time for me. You don't want me around Cassie. You think I'm a bad influence."

Boone backpedaled. "Not a bad influence. But unorthodox." He watched Belle's deep brown eyes turn smoky. Smoldering. He was playing with fire, but he didn't know how to stop. "I think Cassie needs stability right now. She needs to focus. On her health. On the baby."

"And I'm not a good example of the ability to focus?" She did it again. She stood on tiptoe and stared right into his face, holding him with her challenging regard as steadfastly as any physical constraints.

To free himself, he blinked and looked away. "Arabella, you are a wonderful woman..."

*"But?"* The staccato of her voice drew his gaze back to her face. She wasn't going to let him off easily. Not until they'd explored every reason, possibility or concern to a conclusion that convinced her, if not satisfied her.

"But you juggle a million projects. A million dreams. You throw things—like your literacy center—together like a tossed salad without a thought to the compatibility of the ingredients. You collect abandoned animals and cast-off humans with nary a thought to your own safety. You let town gossip roll off your back like water off a duck. You're always trying to fix things with no regard to prioritizing. Do you know what people call it when you buzz through town on one of your latest projects?"

"I'm sure you intend to enlighten me," she replied, her caustic tone not lost on Boone.

"They call it 'Sherman's Second Coming.' And I don't have to tell you what Southern folks thought of the first Sherman."

"Oh, for pity's sake, Boone O'Malley! If you spent half the time you spend listening to gossip trying to develop a sense of humor, you'd be far more content."

"I am content. Or *was,* until you turned my life upside down. Made me feel like a wild man. Bewitched me. Made me forget about everything except you. Made me blind to my responsibilities."

Belle crossed her arms securely over her chest and began a staccato toe tapping. "Little ole me did all that? Why, I must be some dangerous woman. I wonder where the five-foot-four-inch, former kindergarten teacher went."

Boone groaned. *"A-ra-bel-la!* Maybe you see the life you lead as having some kind of focus. Who am I to say? Maybe the greater truth is that I can't stay focused when I'm around you. And right now, for Cassie, I need to stay focused. Good God, the first time we made love, I forgot about protection. *Forgot!* Because I was so wrapped up in you. If the scales had tipped a little differently, I could be standing here on the brink of becoming a granddaddy *and* a daddy."

She glared at him, her foot still tapping a mile a minute.

He'd told her the truth. He had a responsibility to Cassie. And how could he fulfill that responsibility if his head was full of Belle? If his heart was full of that magic that made the whole world pale beside her. If his body hungered for hers. Like now, damn it. In the middle of this crisis he wanted her. Really *wanted* her. He saw that never-say-die, upturned face and wanted to kiss the lids shut over those blazing eyes. Wanted to reach out and with his fingers tame those dark curls that fairly flew about her head. Wanted to caress her until the angry blush in her cheeks turned to passion's fire. Wanted to hold her, to tell her that she made him feel—*feel*—as he'd never felt before.

And because of all this, he had to give her up. To keep his sanity, he needed now to function in black and white, and Belle represented all the confusing colors of the rainbow.

"Cassie needs me," he said finally. Softly.

There was a fleeting moment wherein, if Belle had said, *I need you, too,* the belief in his own arguments might have wavered. And that uncertainty might have nudged him to ask her forgiveness. Or even if she'd thrown out the challenge, *You need me,* he might have admitted he did. Might have asked her to stay by his side. To help him through this difficult time.

But there was none of that. In her own way, Belle was as proud as he. She'd stopped her toe tapping. Had unfolded her arms, which now hung limp at her sides. The look of anger on her face had turned to one of sorrow. He knew just from looking at her that she would let him go.

"I care too much for Cassie," she said softly. "I won't try to compete with her. But, Boone..."

He inhaled sharply. Somehow, he got the feeling he wasn't going to like what he was about to hear.

"Cassie's a strong young woman. You may discover she doesn't need you in quite the way you envision. And when you find yourself with a lot of emotional time on your hands, I may not be free."

Oh, he knew what she was saying. She was saying that this was it. Stay or leave. He couldn't expect her to wait while he sorted through his life. She had a life of her own to lead.

She was lovely. And the fact that she was so strong, so proud, that she wouldn't beg if this was what he truly wanted—all that added to her loveliness. He couldn't help but think his tried-and-true method of dealing with the world was somehow failing him now. Couldn't help but think he was making a terrible decision no matter how black-and-white logical it seemed.

In the past month she'd shown him something rare. Had offered him something precious. Herself. No strings attached. And without strings, the two of them had soared above the ordinary. Unfettered. But now ... now he felt the tethers of responsibility coiling about him, binding him to the stasis of everyday life. To his duty to protect and preserve. With Belle he'd found the bright but fleeting evening star. Venus. Now the constancy of Orion beckoned. Reminded him of who he was. What he needed to do.

"I'm sorry," he said, gazing at her one last time, with an intensity to memorize her every contour. "I wish I didn't feel my behavior was in some way responsible for Cassie's predicament, but I do. And now she needs me to behave like a proper father and grandfather. I plan to give it my best shot."

"Without me." Although she didn't pose it as a question, it was clear she expected an answer.

He took a deep breath. Two little words. Perhaps the two most difficult words he would ever have to utter. "Without you," he admitted at last, and felt bereft.

He wanted to remember much about Arabella Sherman, but not the terrible, sad look on her face when she realized, finally, that he would go. Unfortunately, he feared, that image of her would be the one to crowd out all others for a long, long time.

There was no more to say. He bent swiftly and kissed her cheek. Felt the wetness of her tears. "Goodbye," he said, turning abruptly toward the door. He had to get out of this room. Had to get a grip. Get away from the hurt in her eyes. Remind himself that what he'd done was right: he'd chosen responsibility over desire.

As if frozen, Belle watched him go. Watched him walk out of her life without a backward glance.

He was a man who felt that responsibility to others and his own needs were mutually exclusive. She couldn't fight that. That was part of who Boone O'Malley was. Until he made room in his life for his own dreams and desires, she was powerless.

Powerless and empty. Why, oh, why hadn't she followed her instincts and steered clear of the complex and reluctant

Mr. O'Malley? Porter had taught her the result of a relationship with a reluctant man. What was her great-aunt's expression? Once burned, shame on you. Twice burned, shame on me. A cliché it might be, but truer words were never spoken. Belle had known, right from the beginning, that there was a part of Boone he wouldn't give her. A part he kept hostage. A part he used to keep himself on the safe and narrow.

This past month had been heaven. She'd seen it as a joyous, passionate awakening for both of them. Boone had let loose and become a funny, attentive, sensitive beau in public, and a wild, adventurous lover in private. She shivered with lost pleasure as she recalled their moments of intimate exploration. She could hardly believe that they would share that world no more.

She felt a wet muzzle in her hand, heard a plaintive whine. Looking down, she discovered Sebastian gazing up at her with an expression of misery that, she felt sure, matched her own.

She scratched behind his ear. "What am I going to do, old boy?" she asked, thoroughly miserable. "What am I going to do?"

News—at least the scent of news—traveled fast.

The next morning, having dragged herself out of bed and down to the storefront to work on the final preparations for next week's grand opening, Belle found herself besieged by "volunteers." Oh, Sweet Hope didn't know the particulars yet, only that Boone O'Malley looked like a tornado brewing. That much residents could tell from his glowering, solo appearance for breakfast at the Hole-in-the-Wall. They hoped Belle could fill in the details.

She wouldn't. No amount of hints or prodding or unfinished sentences could get her to discuss Mr. O'Malley. Of his own making, he was history. As much pain as that brought her, she had a literacy center to ready.

Surprisingly, help came in the form of Eban Smart. Capitalizing on his naturally antisocial nature, the man literally stepped between Belle and her questioners. No matter their curiosity, the townspeople were not eager to get too close to the rough-around-the-edges Mr. Smart. One by one the "volunteers" found excuses to leave until Belle and Eban were the only ones remaining in the storefront.

Belle stopped her inventory of the new shipment of coffees. "Thank you."

Eban shrugged. "No need for thanks. I know what hurtin's like. Know it don't help when folks wanna poke around in your insides."

Smiling ruefully, Belle asked, "Does it show that I'm hurting?"

"Like you put up one of Nigel Medford's billboards."

"That bad?"

"That bad," Eban agreed soberly.

"Well, Mr. Smart, I have a grand project to get off the ground by next week. I can't afford to give vent to my low moments. I'll rally. Then folks will have nothing to buzz about where I'm concerned."

"Oh, you'll do fine, Miss Belle. You'll do fine. But folks won't stop buzzin' so long as Boone O'Malley rages about town like a hound who's met up with the wrong end of a porkypine. He's fit to be tied, Miss Belle, that he is. And, Lord knows, folks ain't gonna get no information offa him. So's they'll be comin' round pesterin' you to get the story."

"Me?"

"You're his woman, ain't you? Or were...."

Belle looked into the ravaged face of Eban Smart and saw not mere curiosity but true compassion.

"I *was*, Mr. Smart," she admitted. "*Was* being the operative word."

Eban turned to a stack of used books he'd been shelving. "Well, you hold yourself together, and I'll take care of the nosy."

Belle smiled. Amazing how knights in shining armor turned up in the most unlikely disguises.

"But remember one thing," Eban added, looking Belle straight in the eye with a gaze that was free and clear of any alcoholic haze or befuddlement. "The good Lord only gives out a few big chances in life. A few *really* big chances. Don't be foolish like me and let one slip through your fingers."

He turned and set to shelving with a stolid determination that brooked no response.

Belle blinked. If Boone was one of those few big chances, how was she ever going to convince him that loving her was not incompatible with loving Cassie—or even with the memory of Peg? Or not incompatible with his code of honor. His sense of responsibility. She certainly couldn't convince him if she didn't see him. And it was now unlikely she'd see him for any meaningful period of time. With his work at the storefront completed and with her work on Cassie's room finished, there was no reason she and Boone would run into each other for more than a fleeting second around town.

Normally, she might have called Alice Rose. But, poor woman, she had more pressing thoughts on her mind right now than Belle's lack of access to Boone.

Cassie.

For a brief moment Belle felt the slightest twinge of guilt. Here she'd been caught up in her own dilemma, while Cassie faced decisions of earthshaking proportions. Boone was right. Cassie did need him. But Cassie needed her, too. Needed her friendship. Needed her older-woman support and encouragement. Needed to know that, in a town that would whisper and titter, Cassie could count on at least one person who'd refuse to pass judgment.

For, Belle feared, as much as Boone loved Cassie, he was judgmental. Harshly so. On himself and on others. He would help with every fiber in his body, but that help might be costly to both father and daughter.

They both needed her, Belle mentally declared. If only as a buffer. There was no denying it. She needed to be vigilant. Needed to seize the most opportune moment to convince Boone of that.

Returning to her inventory, she barely heard the bells on the front door as it opened to let in, she hoped, a legitimate volunteer. She didn't look up. She'd trained her volunteers so well that they could often slip in for no more than fifteen minutes to accomplish a task before returning to their usual day's routine. They were all used to finding Belle often engrossed in her own project. Silence as they worked was neither uncommon nor uncomfortable.

If the "volunteer" was a mere curiosity seeker, she counted on Eban Smart to take matters in hand.

"Belle." A soft, shaky voice at her elbow startled her.

She turned to see Cassie looking vulnerable and much younger than her eighteen years.

"Can we talk?" Cassie asked before Belle could even utter a proper greeting.

"Why, certainly." Belle took the younger woman's arm and steered her to the soundproofed classroom in the back. As they walked through the storefront, Belle noted that Eban Smart didn't even glance up from his task of shelving books. Funny how real consideration, too, showed up in the most unlikely places.

Closing the door to the classroom behind them, Belle asked gently, "Now, what is it you want to talk about?"

"Daddy's already told you about my pregnancy, hasn't he?"

Belle nodded silently.

Cassie's eyes filled with tears. "I feel like such a coward, not telling you two sooner."

Reaching out to draw Cassie into an embrace, Belle gently scolded, "Now, Cassie O'Malley, you stop beating yourself up over that." She smoothed Cassie's long blond hair. "You had a powerful weight on your mind. Decisions piled upon decisions. No one is going to fault you for feeling overwhelmed. For not sending out engraved announcements the moment you knew.''

Cassie sniffled and pulled back, but Belle could see her smiling wanly through her tears.

"Belle Sherman, does anything ever get you down?"

Belle could think of one thing. A six-foot-something mountain of prickly reluctance. "Nothing," she lied.

"Then for the next nine months," Cassie replied, taking a seat at the long central table, "I'd better keep you around. As an object lesson."

Belle slid into a seat next to Cassie. "I'd rather you kept me around as your friend."

Cassie laid a hand over Belle's. "Done."

Looking closely at Cassie, Belle thought the young woman appeared drained of her former zest. Dark circles under her eyes highlighted the unnatural pallor of her skin. She seemed smaller somehow. Less sure of herself. More childlike. The shock of the pregnancy had certainly taken its toll.

"If you ever feel the need to talk," Belle urged gently, "I'm here."

A strange look came into Cassie's eyes, not unlike the closed-off cast that would occasionally fall over Boone. "Thanks. But I'm not ready to get into details."

Cassie's brusqueness tweaked something elemental in Belle. Unless she missed her guess, there was more—much more—to Cassie's distress than coping with pregnancy. It wouldn't serve, at the moment, to press, however.

"Okay." Belle spread her hands on the table before her. "Unless you say otherwise, it will be business as usual between us."

Cassie let out a long breath and looked at Belle with marked relief. "I'd like that. I wondered if you'd still want me to work at the center."

"Just try to get out of volunteering." Belle reached out to give Cassie a quick hug.

"I did finish the initial literacy training in Atlanta." A sense of pride tinged Cassie's voice. A hint of the old Cassie. "Right before finals."

In a motherly gesture, Belle brushed a lock of hair from the young woman's forehead. "It's amazing the load you've been carrying. I'm proud of you."

Cassie harrumphed. "I don't feel very proud of myself." Her voice faltered. "I've let a lot of people down." Tears began to pool in her eyes.

"Cassie, Cassie," Belle crooned, stroking her hair, "what's done is done. What you must do now, each day, is wake up and tell yourself you're going to handle life today the best way you can. Everyone makes mistakes. But the foolish don't learn from them. The wise, however—of whom I'm sure you're one—start each new day over as if they'd been given a clean slate."

Cassie leaned into Belle's shoulder. Her weight was featherlight. Insubstantial. "I wish it was that easy," she sighed.

"It is. I'll remind you if you forget." She patted Cassie's shoulder. "Now, what about finals? Are they over?"

"I have one more. This afternoon. Jacob Matthews is going to drive me."

Belle smiled. "This Jacob Matthews seems to be a good friend."

"Oh, you don't know the half of it." Cassie sat up and dabbed at her eyes. "After my final he's driving me to the hospital to sign up for prenatal classes. He's offered to be my coach and birthing partner."

Belle wondered if Boone knew this bit of information, and, if he did, how he felt about being excluded. She merely said, "That's a generous offer, Cassie."

Cassie bristled. "He's not the father. He's just a friend."

Reaching to touch Cassie's hand, Belle said gently, "I wasn't implying anything. I'm just glad you have such a good friend."

Cassie turned to look out the room's only window. She clenched her jaw, the muscle twitching crazily. When she spoke, she didn't look at Belle. "Yeah, well, it's funny how something like this lets you see who your real friends are."

"I hope you think I'm a real friend," Belle suggested softly.

Cassie swung her gaze to Belle's. "I do. I think of you as more than a friend. You're the best thing that's happened to the O'Malley family in a long, long time."

The young woman's words startled Belle. Obviously, Boone hadn't told his daughter of his decision not to see Belle again. Considering all Cassie had to face at the moment, it wouldn't be wise to broach that subject now. Belle held her tongue.

A knock on the classroom door startled both women.

"Yes?" Belle called out.

"It's Boone."

Belle's heart lurched at the sound of Boone's gruff voice, as Cassie rose and said, "I'd better be going." Rising reluctantly, Belle opened the door.

Boone glowered first at her, then at his daughter. "Cassie! What are you doing here?"

There was none of the usual exuberance in Cassie's face as she greeted her father. "Belle and I needed to get a few things straight," she said, her voice distant, chilly even. "But I need to get going now. I have my last exam this afternoon."

As Cassie brushed by Boone without her customary farewell kiss, Belle saw the hurt in the man's eyes. Things were obviously not going well between father and daughter.

After Cassie had gone, an uncomfortable silence settled over the classroom. Finally Belle asked, "What brings you here?"

Boone reached into his jeans pocket and withdrew a key. Handing it to her, he replied, "The key to your apartment. I forgot to return it last night."

Belle's heart sank. Had she really thought for the most fleeting of moments that Boone had come to make up? Although she might not have believed it, she'd most fervently prayed for just that.

She took the key and said, just for something to say, "Cassie stopped by because she wanted to tell me...about her situation...herself."

Boone shook his head. "I can't imagine how she'll do on that final this afternoon."

"She'll do just fine. She's a strong young woman. And Jacob Matthews is driving her. For moral support, I think."

"Jacob Matthews?"

"Yes. He's going to drive her to the hospital afterward to sign up for prenatal classes. He's volunteered to be her coach. Her birthing partner."

*"Jacob Matthews?"* Clearly he hadn't been told this.

"Yes," Belle replied softly, resisting the urge to reach out and touch him. "She says Jacob has been a good friend to her."

"No." Boone's voice came out strangled and raw. "Jacob Matthews is a good excuse to push me out of the picture."

"Don't believe that for a moment. It's hard for Cassie to face you now, let alone ask your help. She feels she's let you down. Terribly. Give her time. And space. And lots of love."

His gaze was icy. "That's easy for you to say. You have no children. You couldn't possibly know the pain."

As the echo of his words sliced through Belle, Boone turned abruptly and left the classroom. She could hear the heels of his boots echoing off the hardwood floor in the main room, each thud a blow to her heart.

How dare he say she couldn't possibly know the pain? She knew the pain of separation from a loved one. Parent, lover or child. Pain was pain. If his pain could possibly be worse than hers, she prayed never to feel it.

With a sinking heart she realized at last how wide the gulf was between them. She couldn't cross it if he was unwilling to meet her halfway. She would drown in unfulfilled longing for him. Better to stay safely on the shore. Wrap herself in her work and her friends and those, such as Eban Smart, who needed her.

As much as she loved him, Boone O'Malley didn't need or love her. Enough.

## Chapter Thirteen

A tired-looking Alice Rose gazed sadly at Belle. "Will it help, dear, if I invite you two out to Sunday dinner? It seemed to do the trick last time."

Belle stopped in her setup of the café tables. Shaking her head ruefully, she said, "It's going to take more than that this time."

"Has he come around this past week to check if you need any last-minute work on this place?"

Didn't she wish. "Not a chance. He finished his original bargain some time back. Recently he'd been helping me because...well...we were..." Belle shrugged with the pain of remembering.

"I know, dear heart." Alice Rose reached out to rub Belle's back comfortingly. "Maybe he'll show up for the grand opening tomorrow."

Although Belle said nothing, she doubted very strongly that Boone O'Malley would consciously put himself in her path. Ever again.

She inhaled sharply and tilted her chin a little higher. She would not cry. She'd shed her tears—copiously—in private. Right now she had a grand opening to attend to. The old mercantile was renovated, spotless and ready. She'd ordered special open house refreshments. The coffee bar had been stocked with exotic blends. She and Eban Smart had organized the used-book section so that it looked like an inviting home library. Manuel Navarro had agreed to head up the English-as-a-second-language component of the literacy center. A subdued Cassie and her faithful shadow, Jacob Matthews, had organized the volunteers to act as guides and hosts. And now Alice Rose was helping her put the finishing touches on the café tables.

Everything was ready.

So why wasn't she ecstatic?

Why did she feel so empty and alone despite the outpouring of community support she'd received?

Belle harrumphed softly, and Alice Rose looked up from straightening a checkered tablecloth. "Belle Sherman," the older woman scolded softly, "I forbid you to despair. It's not all over between you and that pigheaded son of mine, just you wait and see."

"I wish I could be as certain as you," Belle replied, catching sight of a suspiciously mischievous glint in Alice Rose's eye.

Bells jingled as the front door opened. Belle stared at Boone's unmistakable shape silhouetted against the late-afternoon sun. If there had been any doubt that she'd missed him, it dissolved in a flash at the sight of him. Dissolved as her heart lost that empty feeling and leapt with joy.

The thunderous look on his face told her, however, that his heart did not, at the moment, leap with joy. Narrowing his eyes, he glowered right through her to his mother beyond. "Mama," he growled, "would you have any idea where my best wrench set might be? The one that stays in my truck?"

Belle turned to Alice Rose, who looked the model of innocence.

Waving her hand airily, Alice Rose replied, "Why, son, you must have left it somewhere."

"I never *leave it* anywhere."

"Oh, pooh. You're entitled to forget once in a while. You've had a lot on your mind lately."

"I don't forget my tools."

"Then maybe you left it here . . . when you were helping Belle."

Belle wanted to assure Boone that he hadn't left it in her storefront. "We would surely have found it as we readied—"

Alice Rose cut her a warning glance. Now what was going on? Sweetly, the older woman suggested, "Perhaps you left it in Belle's apartment."

"Mama!"

"I don't think so," Belle sputtered.

Alice Rose looked sternly at Belle. "I've seen your apartment, Belle Sherman. Can you honestly say that that wrench set is not amid all your clutter?"

Belle felt herself flush. With the preparations for the grand opening, her apartment had become unusually messy. Chaotic, even. "I haven't actually seen it, and I don't remember Boone using it up there. But I couldn't say no for certain. I mean . . ."

"Well, then, the two of you run along to look for it. I'll hold down the fort here." Alice Rose put her hands on her hips and waited as if for two youngsters to obey her order.

"Mama, if this is one of your schemes . . ."

"Don't use that tone of voice on me, Boone O'Malley." Alice Rose pulled herself up to her full height and skewered her son with a warning look. "Now, if you want to find that precious wrench set of yours, I suggest you follow Belle up to her apartment to look for it. I actually think I remember seeing it when I went up there for some masking tape."

Boone and Belle exchanged uneasy glances.

"Come on," Boone finally said. "We'll never hear the end of it till we do as she suggests."

Belle would have liked him to show a little more enthusiasm. Or a little less hostility. But, nonetheless, she led the way out the storefront and around to the side entrance of her walk-up. As she did, she felt his eyes boring into the back of her as certainly as if she were facing him. Sure, she'd prayed for an opportunity to pull him aside and try to reason with him. Here Alice Rose, bless her meddling heart, had provided one. Was it too picky to despair that it wasn't what one could describe as an optimum opportunity?

Sighing, she climbed the stairs and pushed through the apartment doorway.

"You don't keep it locked?" Boone asked irritably.

"Not in the past week. Too many things we've needed to cart between here and downstairs. Too many volunteers to be passing around my key."

Boone cocked an eyebrow and opened his mouth to speak. But then he must have thought better of it, for he clamped his mouth shut and merely scowled.

Scowled at the mess before them.

Sebastian lumbered toward them through a mountain of boxes and packing material, stopping only long enough to slurp from a Chinese take-out box on a coffee table littered with computer printouts.

For the first time, Belle saw the apartment through another's eyes. Like Spanish moss, cast-off clothing lay draped over nearly unrecognizable lumps of furniture. The profusion of drooping houseplants throughout the loft showed clearly it had been a long time since waterings. Hey, she'd been busy. But she did realize how awful this must look to an everything-in-its-place kind of guy.

Belle shrugged defensively. "Getting ready for the grand opening, I've sort of let the housekeeping slip."

Boone looked unimpressed with her excuse. "Let's start looking. If my mama says she *thinks she saw* my wrench set

up here, you can bet we'll find it right where she planted it."
He began gingerly to push aside boxes.

"Why, Boone O'Malley, whatever are you implying?"

Boone didn't stop in his tentative search. Didn't look at
Belle. "I'm not *implying* anything. I *know* Alice Rose set
this whole thing up." He dropped to the floor on all fours
to look under the sofa, only to have Sebastian lick his face
in anticipation of some sort of game. He groaned. "A-ra-
bel-la! Can you not put this hound out? He's caused enough
problems already."

Belle moved protectively to Sebastian's side. "What
problems?"

Turning to a sitting position, Boone threw his arms in
obvious frustration over his bent knees. "My prize beagle's
pregnant. I'll bet you ten to one it's the result of Sebastian's visit a month ago."

Belle blushed, but bent to scratch behind the dog's ears.
"Well, I wouldn't have brought Sebbie with me that day had
I known you were going to throw temptation in his path."
Silently she thought, Dear Lord, ease up on Boone some.
He can't handle all this fecundity.

As Boone harrumphed and got back to the business—or
at least the appearance—of looking for his wrench set, Belle
led the dog to the kitchen area where she filled his dog dish
with fresh food. That and his usual nap after meals should
keep him out of the way for a while.

She returned to find Boone muttering to himself.

"Is that why you're so prickly today?" she asked.

Boone swung around to stare hard at her.

"Your beagle," Belle prompted. "Are you angry because she's pregnant with my mongrel's puppies?" Or are
you still mad at me because I was equally unable to keep
Cassie protected? she added mentally.

Taking a deep breath, Boone replied, "Arabella, it's been
a hard week. Cassie's news. Breaking up with you. Trying
to shield Cassie from the news of our breakup...."

Belle couldn't believe her ears. "Cassie doesn't know we're no longer seeing each other?" It had been a week. She could understand Boone wanting to spare his daughter more bad news, but... "Surely if you haven't told her, she's heard it through the Sweet Hope grapevine."

"In self-defense, Cassie's closed her ears to the Sweet Hope grapevine. And I... well, I was waiting for an opportune time."

Oh, aren't we all, thought Belle, looking for that opportune time.

Dusting himself off, Boone rose and began to move about the loft, cautiously picking up debris in his search for the missing wrench set. He so obviously wanted to find those tools and get the heck out of there. But until he did find them, Belle had his attention. Sort of.

She folded her hands before her, took a deep breath, then took the plunge. "About our breakup. Do you really think it's such a good idea? Pardon my saying so, but you look... as if you've been through the wringer."

Throwing his hands in the air in exasperation, Boone turned to face her, his blue eyes clouded with emotion. "And why the hell shouldn't I look as if I've been through the wringer?" he growled. "I have a pregnant, unmarried eighteen-year-old daughter who barely speaks to me, a mother who plays juvenile games trying to throw me in your path, a town that wants to know at every turn how Miss Belle is, and a prize beagle that's about to deliver pups that'll probably look like they came from another planet. All that and I'm trying to maintain my dignity and run a legitimate contracting business. Not very successfully at the moment, I might add." He glared at her in frustration. "I guess I have a right to look as if I've been through the wringer."

Belle took a step toward him. "I could help," she offered softly.

Taking a step backward, Boone raised his hands in self-defense. "Lady, you exacerbate the situation."

"Oh, Boone," she said, sighing, "I've tried to give you space."

Pain was clearly visible on his face. Straining his handsome features. But beyond the pain was something else struggling to remain beneath the surface.

Longing. Hunger. Passion, even.

It flickered in his eyes and quivered in his tensed muscles. And gave Belle immeasurable hope.

"I've tried to leave you alone to sort things out," she almost whispered.

In a startling instant he crossed the room and roughly grasped her arms. In a voice filled with barely controlled emotion, he rasped, "To sort things out, huh? How the hell am I supposed to sort things out when all I can think about is you?" He shook her.

"*Me?*"

"Yes, you. And this . . ." He lowered his mouth to hers, claiming her with his kiss. Possessing her. Devouring her. Firing all those desires she'd tried for a week to suppress.

With a little moan, she leaned against him, letting the wave of passion carry her on its crest. Oh, how she'd missed this man. As if a part of her had been stolen away. She raised her arms to twine them about his neck, but, as abruptly as he'd kissed her, he grasped her wrists and held her at arm's length.

Through heavy-lidded eyes she saw his look of exasperation. She felt sadness seep into her heart where only seconds ago passion and hope had bloomed. He'd kissed her, yes. But he hadn't succumbed to the kiss. Hadn't let go of propriety. Of responsibility to his rigid, self-imposed code. Hadn't let himself love her.

"I can't be near you, Arabella," he murmured, his breathing ragged, his dark regard that of a man torn. "It's bad enough the thought of you torments me—awake or asleep. I can't be near you. Not and survive."

Belle gasped at the ferocity of his words.

"I want you too much for my own damn good," Boone hissed through clenched teeth.

Dropping her wrists as if they burned him, he strode stiffly to the door, then muttered, without looking back, "Have Alice Rose tell you where the wrench set is. Then have her return it to me. She owes me that much."

He left, slamming the door so hard a stack of books fell off the wicker side chair near the doorway and thundered to the floor with too much noise for paper and pasteboard. Amid the bent bindings and fluttering pages lay the wrench set.

Boone heard the crash even as he thundered down the stairs. The noise was nothing compared to the pounding of the blood in his ears.

Dear God, he thought he could handle seeing Belle again. But a week away had only whetted his appetite for her. Increased his longing. Intensified his torment. He still firmly believed he'd done the right thing in breaking things off. His daughter and his future grandchild needed him now. Needed him to be focused and dignified. He couldn't be either if he were to be bewitched, bothered and bewildered by Arabella Sherman.

Roughly, he pushed through the doorway into the hot, late afternoon. Hell, who was he kidding? Was he focused now, apart from her? He bumped into a flower box fixed at knee level under the plate-glass window of the storefront. Hobbling across the sidewalk, rubbing the painful bruise, he cursed loudly and kicked a lamppost, only to hear the cackle of Homer Martin, who happened by.

Was he dignified? With another muttered curse, he opened the door to his truck parked at the curb and heaved himself into the cab. Quickly, he turned the key in the ignition and started the engine. Then, without a rational thought, he turned the key again, only to hear the high-pitched, grinding scream of an ignition in protest. Passersby on the sidewalk winced. He slammed the truck into gear and accelerated, leaving the parking space with a little chirp of rubber.

Damn. He was declaring this day officially over. He'd head on home, throw a couple steaks on the grill, break out the beer. Maybe Cassie could be convinced to make a salad. Maybe they could settle down in the kitchen like old times. Just the two of them. He sighed deeply. Make that three.

He pulled around the corner onto Oak Street and spotted Cassie's car in the driveway. Cassie herself sat in a rocking chair on the front veranda. For a change her shadow, Jacob Matthews, wasn't with her. Maybe things could be almost like old times tonight. Just maybe.

And then he thought of Belle. Thought of the feel of her lips under his. Thought of the warmth of her body pressed against him. Thought of her willingness to be kissed. To be loved. Thought of how complicated it would be to love her. How he couldn't and still maintain control. Of his life. Of his world. Of his heart.

No, things could never be like old times again. Certainly not after Arabella Sherman.

He parked his truck behind Cassie's car and got out, a reflex grin stealing across his face at the sight of his daughter waiting for him. It didn't take long, however, to determine that Cassie was not as happy to see him.

She rose from the rocker. Crossing her arms over her chest, she scowled down at him from her height on the veranda. "Can we talk?" she asked tersely.

"Of course." Boone bounded up the front steps, worry creeping into his thoughts. "Are you okay? The baby?"

"*We're* fine," she snapped. "It's *you* I'm not sure of."

"Me?"

"Yes, you. I do believe you've gone round the bend." Her eyes flashing, Cassie reminded Boone of Alice Rose at her mother-hen best. "Why in heaven's name," she asked icily, "have you broken up with Belle?"

Boone plunked his hands on his hips and looked at his daughter, regret beginning to nibble at his conscience.

"Where did you hear this?" he asked, trying to keep his emotions under control.

"For goodness' sake, Daddy," she cried in exasperation, "I'm pregnant, not deaf. How long did you think it would take before I heard it through the Sweet Hope gossip mill?"

"I meant to tell you." He knew that sounded lame, but he couldn't think of anything else to say. She had him.

Cassie unfolded her arms and began to pace the wide veranda. "I don't know what I'm madder at you for—dumping Belle or treating me like a child. Again."

Boone reached out to Cassie as she approached him in her pacing, but she turned quickly and moved away from him toward the far edge of the veranda where she leaned on the railing and looked sadly out over the neighborhood.

"Oh, Cassie," he breathed softly, "I don't mean to treat you like a child. I love you."

At the sound of his words, Cassie turned toward him, her eyes brimming with tears. "But, Daddy, your kind of love is suffocating me... in fact, it's suffocating you."

"Me?" Boone shifted uncomfortably, not liking the turn of conversation.

"Why did you break up with Belle? The truth."

"Because you and the baby were going to need me. It wouldn't be fair to Belle. I wouldn't be able to give her the attention she deserves."

She skewered him with a piercing O'Malley stare. "Maybe I need you *and* Belle."

He didn't want to get further into this. He really didn't. But for the life of him he could see no escape. "Right now, Cassie," he began, uncertain of his next words, "you need stability in your life. A sense of rootedness. Of calm and focus. Traditional values...."

"Are you preaching to me?"

"I'm trying not to. I'm trying to give you a sense of how I think things should be."

Cassie narrowed her eyes. "And you think Belle should be out of the picture."

For the life of him Boone couldn't explain to his daughter how Belle made him feel like a reckless kid. How, when he was around her, he didn't give a fig for public opinion. Or his reputation. Or his role as a responsible father and future grandfather. How when he was with her he just wanted to love and laugh and live. Just how dignified would that sound if he voiced it? But without understanding this underlying truth, Cassie wouldn't understand how he had to put Belle aside.

Instead of telling her the truth, he said, "It just didn't work out between Belle and me. We were two too-different people."

"Meaning, she isn't Mama." Cassie said these words so softly Boone almost missed them. But he didn't. And the sound of them slammed into him as if she'd shouted.

Helplessly, Boone ran his fingers through his hair. "Cassie...I loved your mama like life itself, but I'm not so stuck in my ways that I don't realize you can love again. And differently. But Belle isn't exactly my idea of...an ideal woman. At least, not my ideal woman."

"Meaning?"

Damn. She had no intention of letting him off the hook.

"Meaning...she's unpredictable. And quirky. And highly visible. She doesn't give two hoots about what people think or say of her. She adopts stray animals and people with no regard for her personal safety. And she bites off more of life than I think she can chew."

"And you love her."

Boone was stunned. Now, when the devil did his baby become a mind reader?

"And even though you broke up with her because you thought it was the *right* thing to do, you miss her, don't you?"

Like a missing piece of his very soul.

"Tell me I'm wrong," Cassie persisted.

"I'll tell you something." Struggling emotionally to maintain the high ground, Boone felt the heat rise to his face. "I'll tell you that Arabella Sherman is *not* what this family needs right now. What you need."

Cassie walked over to him. Stood with her hands clenched at her sides, blinking back tears. "I'll tell you what I don't need now. I don't need a preacher. I don't need a judgmental schoolmarm. I don't even need a mother hen. All of which you've tried to be. And I sure as hell don't need a jailer."

Stunned yet again, Boone asked, "Is that how you see me? A jailer?" Dear God, he loved her. All he ever wanted was for her to be safe and happy.

Closing her eyes for a brief moment and sighing deeply, she said softly, "Daddy, if the truth be known, the jailer part applies to you. How you treat yourself. Your heart."

Reaching out for her hand, he murmured, "I don't understand." But he did. He did and he had all along.

Cassie squeezed his one hand, then reached out for the other. "You've got to let me live my life if only so that you can live yours. You can't lock us both up to keep us safe."

"But where does that leave us? What do you need from me? Nothing?" The thought made him feel empty inside.

She smiled up at him. "I'll always need your love."

"Oh, baby." He clasped her to him. "You'll always have that. You and that grandbaby of mine you're carrying."

Cassie pulled away enough to look up into his face again. "About that grandbaby...do you know what she or he will need?"

"You'd better tell me."

"Baby O'Malley's not going to need a joyless family that's caught up in doing what appears right. She or he is going to need lots of love and laughter. Spontaneity and creativity. And all the sparkle life has to offer. Now, I can't think of a better role model for that than Belle."

Belle had said he might discover that Cassie's emotional needs were not what he'd anticipated. She'd been right on the mark. "You're saying that Arabella Sherman is exactly what this family needs right now?"

Cassie's smile broadened. "What other kid would have a grammy whose underwear jingles?"

In spite of himself, Boone chuckled. "I can't think of a one."

"And the little one's granddaddy... I can't think of anyone more than Belle that *he* needs right now."

Boone stepped away, afraid of the truth in her words. He'd botched it with Arabella and botched it badly. How could he repair the damage? The hurt. She'd warned him that when he discovered himself with emotional time on his hands, she might not be free.

"Cassie, honey, I wouldn't know where to start."

Laying a hand gently on his arm, she replied, "She'd love to see you at her grand opening tomorrow. That would be a start."

Maybe. Just maybe... if he could get up the courage to admit that the rigid, rather sanctimonious Boone O'Malley code might not be right for everyone. It might not even be exactly right for its creator.

Boone stood on the sidewalk in the May afternoon sunshine and stared through the plate-glass window of Belle's storefront at the crowd gathered within. And what a crowd it was.

It seemed that all of Sweet Hope had turned out—whether from enthusiasm or just down-home curiosity, he couldn't tell. But they'd turned out in force. By the look of it, some must have temporarily closed their own businesses to be here. There was Edna from the Hole-in-the-Wall, daintily nibbling pastry and nodding as Nigel Medford held forth. On his own importance, Boone could guess. There was old rich-as-Croesus Simon Mayfield thumbing through a stack of used paperback books. With his penchant for a bargain, no wonder the man still had his first nickel. And there was Amanda Best of the *Gazette,* holding her tape recorder microphone out to Alice Rose. He had a feeling his mama's struggle with dyslexia was going to be breakfast reading material for a whole town. Despite his own dislike of the spotlight, he was proud that Alice Rose had the courage to step forward and tell her story. He must let her know exactly how proud he was.

He heard knuckles rap on the window and looked down to see Homer Martin—Mr. If-it-ain't-beer-it-ain't-fit-to-drink Martin—looking up from a tiny café table, his upper lip a mustache of foam from the cappuccino in front of him. Boone nodded and chuckled. Cappuccino and Homer Martin. Who'd have thought it?

He felt a hand at his elbow, then turned to find his old friend Ray Clark staring at him. "You look like a little lost kid outside a candy shop," Ray said. "Come on in."

"Yes, come on in," Sheriff Bratt echoed behind him. "You know, Boone, how we're always talking in Rotary Club about positive ways to promote Sweet Hope? Well, someone should have told us years ago about Arabella Sherman. She's a one-woman chamber of commerce." The sheriff clapped Boone on the shoulder, then pushed through the crowded entryway, leaving Boone and Ray alone on the sidewalk.

Boone looked at his best friend and took a deep breath. "I need to make up with Arabella."

Ray chuckled. "Hell, that's not news. The whole of Sweet Hope knows that. Tell me something I don't know."

"I think this is going to be one of the hardest things I've ever done."

"Nah," Ray contradicted. "Things are hard when you've gotta do 'em, knowing you'll get no reward in the end. Now, making up with Miss Belle and knowing the reward..."

The thought of making up with Belle pumped blood into every extremity in Boone's body.

"Oh, but Ray, I can't live without her, and I can't—"

"Live without her," Ray finished with a wink. "There she is, pal. What's it going to be?"

Boone stared through the window in the direction Ray had nodded, then inhaled sharply. Yes, there she was.

Wearing the same floaty lavender outfit she'd worn when she'd fallen off that damned ladder the first time he'd laid eyes on her. Sakes alive, but she was beautiful. Healing balm to his tired eyes. But would she even want to talk to him?

As if reading his mind, Ray gave him a shove and said, "You won't know until you approach her. Go on, man. Do something for yourself for once."

Do something for himself for once. Slowly Boone put one foot in front of the other until he'd passed through the storefront doorway into the noisy crowd. He might as well do something for himself. Everyone else in his family had made it clear they didn't want him running their lives. Cassie had out-and-out told him she and the baby needed nothing but love and support from him. Alice Rose had made it crystal clear from the minute she'd become a widow that she didn't want to be coddled as an old helpless woman. And Peg... dear Lord, Peg would be ashamed of the way he'd shriveled up and died these past six years. In her own quiet way, Peg had been a great believer in love.

Love.

At the moment Boone thought the word, Belle turned and looked at him, drenching him in her sweet regard.

It was as if the world fell away. The room became a blur except for his smiling Belle, a lavender helium balloon on a long ribbon tied to her Little Mermaid watch. All sound melted away except for the thudding of his heart. Thudding in uncertainty and anticipation. How would she treat his sudden appearance? After the rough way he'd treated her. Hell, she was smiling. That had to be a good sign.

Belle's heart flip-flopped. He'd come! She truly hadn't believed he would, but he had. And here he stood, not looking prickly or angry or exasperated. He looked... despite his size, he looked like a boy consumed with shyness. Consumed with shyness but wanting desperately to say his piece.

Oblivious to the party around her, she made her way toward him, sweet sensations skittering up and down her spine. Could he have come to start fresh, or had he come to maintain appearances? No, the warmth in his clear blue eyes said nothing of maintaining appearances. Her heart skipped with hope.

She reached his side, saw him run his fingers self-consciously through his blond hair, heard him murmur, "Arabella." A shiver of pleasure passed over her. Lord, Lord, what this man could do with four syllables.

"I'm glad you came," was all she could find to say. Words couldn't capture the feelings in her heart.

"Are you?" he asked, as if he'd seriously doubted a welcome.

"I am," she replied, beaming. She reached for his hand he didn't draw away. "I couldn't have done all this without your help."

One corner of his mouth turned up in a half smile. "Oh, I think Arabella Sherman would have found a way."

"But it wouldn't have been half as rewarding." Or half as sexy. Or half as painful ultimately. Belle sighed.

Boone looked down at his moccasins, then slowly up at her. "I don't think I ever told you...it was rewarding for me, too." His voice was soft and husky and tinged with longing.

"Was it, now?" she asked, unable to keep a playful tone out of her words. She caught his cool blue gaze and held it.

He took her other hand in his. "Arabella..." he began, then faltered as the balloon attached to her wrist floated into their line of vision.

"Yes?"

He blew at the lavender orb. "Could we set this thing free?"

She laughed softly. "And then what?"

"Could we talk?"

Her heart fluttered at the hope his words held out. Slipping her hands out of his big, callused grasp, she slipped the knot that tethered the balloon and released it to bob on the ceiling with others like it. Funny, but that setting free seemed like the perfect symbolism. A sign. A good omen. She smiled and looked back at Boone.

His intense regard implied he was trying to memorize her. It caught her off guard. Rendered her temporarily speechless.

"What do you want to talk about?" she managed to ask at last.

"Us."

Us. What a lovely word. So filled with promise and future.

She waited. He was going to have to do this. She'd said her piece before. He knew how she felt. If anything was going to happen this afternoon, Boone O'Malley was going to have to overcome his reluctance and make it happen.

The waiting seemed endless. She began to become dimly aware of the swirl of the party around them.

"Do you want to go somewhere quiet?" she asked.

"No. I don't care who hears."

Now, *that* was new.

"I made a fool of myself," he said slowly. Deliberately.

"Letting yourself care for me?" It hurt her to even ask.

He reached out and took one of her hands in both his. His grip was warm and protective. His gaze was even warmer. "No. Letting you go."

"What about Cassie?"

"You were right about Cassie. She and the baby need me to love her. Nothing else."

"What about Peg?"

"You were right about her, too." He looked deep into her eyes as if what he was about to say was so important she must believe him. "If I let go the pain of losing Peg, it would be an admission that I hadn't been able to protect and preserve the most important person in my life. I thought that if I hadn't been able to do that, just what kind of a man was I? I used my guilt to hold on to the past. I used the past to protect me from the present."

Belle looked at him questioningly.

"I never wanted to feel that pain again. But this time—with you—it was worse than being unable to prevent a horrible loss. I actually caused it."

"And did you feel lost?" Belle asked softly. "Without me?"

Boone shook his head and smiled a rueful smile. "Lost? Let me tell you that last week I tried to get my sense of decorum back. But did that old decorum bring me any warmth or laughter or joy? Not one whit. Life might have been more dignified, but it sure was dead. You, Arabella Sherman, with your off-kilter way of doing things, have brought me to life. And for that I love you right down to the bells on your underwear."

"Oh, Boone." Belle sighed and leaned against him. "Does that mean you're not going to worry about what folks think of our relationship?"

His eyes twinkling, Boone shook his head and chuckled. "Oh, no. I'm real worried about what folks might think about our relationship... and for that reason, I think you ought to make an honest man of me."

Her toes began to tingle. "What are you telling me?"

"I'm *asking* if you would marry me."

Throwing her arms about his neck, she breathed, "Yes. Oh, yes, yes, yes," before she captured his mouth in a kiss.

Oh, and did he ever return her kiss. With joy. And passion. And abandon. In front of the assembled folk of Sweet Hope. Pressed against him, she could actually feel his reluctant rebel heart burst its chains and beat wild and free against her own.

She pulled away from him and murmured, "I love you, Boone O'Malley. I have ever since the day you swept me off my feet."

Suddenly Belle realized she'd uttered the words to dead silence. Not the silence that had come from the two of them wrapped up in each other in a crowded room. But dead real silence. The kind that came when a crowd riveted its attention on one spot. Looking about, she saw every face in the room trained in utter amazement on Boone and herself.

Oh, Lord, how was Boone going to handle this?

With a quick kiss to her nose and a grin that could melt a glacier, Boone spoke up in a voice that was loud and true and filled with joy.

"Folks," he said, his embrace of her tightening, "Belle and I have a public announcement to make. Miss Arabella Sherman is about to become the new bride in town!"

# Epilogue

Alone for a few unexpected moments in Alice Rose's spare bedroom, Belle glanced in the mirror at herself dressed all in white. Dreamily straightening the garland of flowers in her hair, she glided to the window to gaze on the lawn below. A lawn edged with June flowers and sprinkled with arriving guests.

In a few short minutes she and Boone would be joined as husband and wife.

A quiet knock on the door brought her attention back into the room.

"Yes?"

The door opened and Boone stepped into the room, looking like every woman's fantasy.

"Boone O'Malley," she declared, covering her bodice with mock horror, "you are not allowed to see the bride before the ceremony. Whatever will people think?"

"They'll think," Boone growled sensuously, covering the distance between them in two long strides, "that the groom can't wait to marry his bride." He took her in his arms and enveloped her in his strength and his warmth. Lowering his face to her neck, he purred, "Do I get a preview of the wedding kiss?"

"Most certainly not!" She rapped him on his shoulder and slipped out of his grasp. Her heart beat a fluttery tattoo in her chest. "Now say whatever it is you have to say and be gone."

"Like . . . I love you, Arabella Sherman-soon-to-become-O'Malley?"

Belle tilted her head and looked at his handsome, smiling face. "Arabella O'Malley. It's a mouthful, but it has a heavenly ring to it. I must say it sits well on the ear."

Boone cocked an eyebrow. "How does Cassie Matthews sit on your ear?"

"No! Did Jacob propose?"

"This morning." Boone grinned.

"And did Cassie accept?"

"She hasn't yet. She told Jacob she needed time to think."

Eagerly, Belle crossed to Boone and laid her hands on his arms. "And how do you feel about all this?"

Boone shook his head. "I'll tell you one thing. I'm a man who recognizes a person crazy in love, and that boy loves my daughter. For sure."

"So are you going to try to influence Cassie one way or another?"

"Arabella, you wound me." And he did make a show of looking adorably wounded. "Do I look like the meddling kind?"

Belle stood on tiptoe and kissed his smooth cheek. "You've come a long way, Boone O'Malley, and I love you for it."

"We both have come a long way," he replied, a hint of mischief in his voice. He looked down at her feet. "You're wearing shoes today."

"Oh, pooh," she replied saucily. "If Alice Rose's lawn is as soft as it appears from up here, I may just kick them off halfway down the aisle." She fluttered a flirtatious glance in his direction. "Especially if there's a really good but impatient kisser waiting for me at the other end."

"Lady," he growled, pulling her hard up against him, "let me show you my samples." He lowered his mouth to hers and kissed her with such soul-drenching passion that she knew those shoes were going to be an encumbrance.

Lordy, lordy, could life hold any greater sweet hope?

\* \* \* \* \*

*Will Cassie be the newest bride in town? Or will she leave her groom-to-be WAITING AT THE ALTAR? Look for another SWEET HOPE WEDDING to take place next month— only in Silhouette Special Edition!*

**FORTUNE'S Children™**

In July, get to know the Fortune family....

Next month, don't miss the start of Fortune's Children, a fabulous new twelve-book series from Silhouette Books.

**Meet the Fortunes—a family whose legacy is greater than riches. Because where there's a will...there's a wedding!**

When Kate Fortune's plane crashes in the jungle, her family believes that she's dead. And when her will is read, they discover that Kate's plans for their lives are more interesting than they'd ever suspected.

Look for the first book, *Hired Husband*, by *New York Times* bestselling author **Rebecca Brandewyne**. PLUS, a stunning, perforated bookmark is affixed to *Hired Husband* (and selected other titles in the series), providing a convenient checklist for all twelve titles!

**FREE**
Keepsake
Bookmark

Launching in July wherever books are sold.

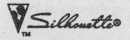
*Silhouette®*

## "As the father of six adopted children,

I'm not your typical bachelor. But I may not stay one for long, now that I've met the woman of my dreams—Kristen Fielding. I can only hope she'll grow to love my kids as much as I do. Then I'll make her Mrs. Fernando Ibarra—and when she's the mother of my child, she'll say these words to me..."

## HAPPY FATHER'S DAY
### by
### Barbara Faith
### (SE #1033)

In June, Silhouette Special Edition brings you

**Sometimes bringing up baby can bring surprises...
and showers of love.**

TMB696

**Harlequin® Historical**

Don't miss your opportunity to read a very
special historical romance from three-time
RITA Award winner

# Cheryl Reavis

# The Bartered Bride

Keep an eye out for this unforgettable story.
Coming this June from Harlequin Historicals!

BIGB96-4

This July, watch for the delivery of...

An exciting new miniseries that appears in a different Silhouette series each month. It's about love, marriage—and Daddy's unexpected need for a baby carriage!

Daddy Knows Last unites five of your favorite authors as they weave five connected stories about baby fever in New Hope, Texas.

- **THE BABY NOTION** by Dixie Browning (SD#1011, 7/96)

- **BABY IN A BASKET** by Helen R. Myers (SR#1169, 8/96)

- **MARRIED...WITH TWINS!** by Jennifer Mikels (SSE#1054, 9/96)

- **HOW TO HOOK A HUSBAND (AND A BABY)** by Carolyn Zane (YT#29, 10/96)

- **DISCOVERED: DADDY** by Marilyn Pappano (IM#746, 11/96)

Daddy Knows Last arrives in July...only from

## My three sons...

Single dad (and one-time lady-killer): Craig Haynes
Nanny (two parts sweetness, one part sin): Jill Bradford

Pint-size redheaded nanny Jill Bradford proved a wizard
with Craig Haynes's three rambunctious boys. Could
a houseful of Hayneses ambush her wary heart...and
make her a mother and wife?

Find out in

## PART-TIME WIFE
### (SE #1027)
### by Susan Mallery

Don't miss **THAT SPECIAL WOMAN!** every other
month from some of your favorite authors and
Silhouette Special Edition!